to capture a heart

She never believed in love. Until she met him.

zoe aviya harris

[pen + paper]

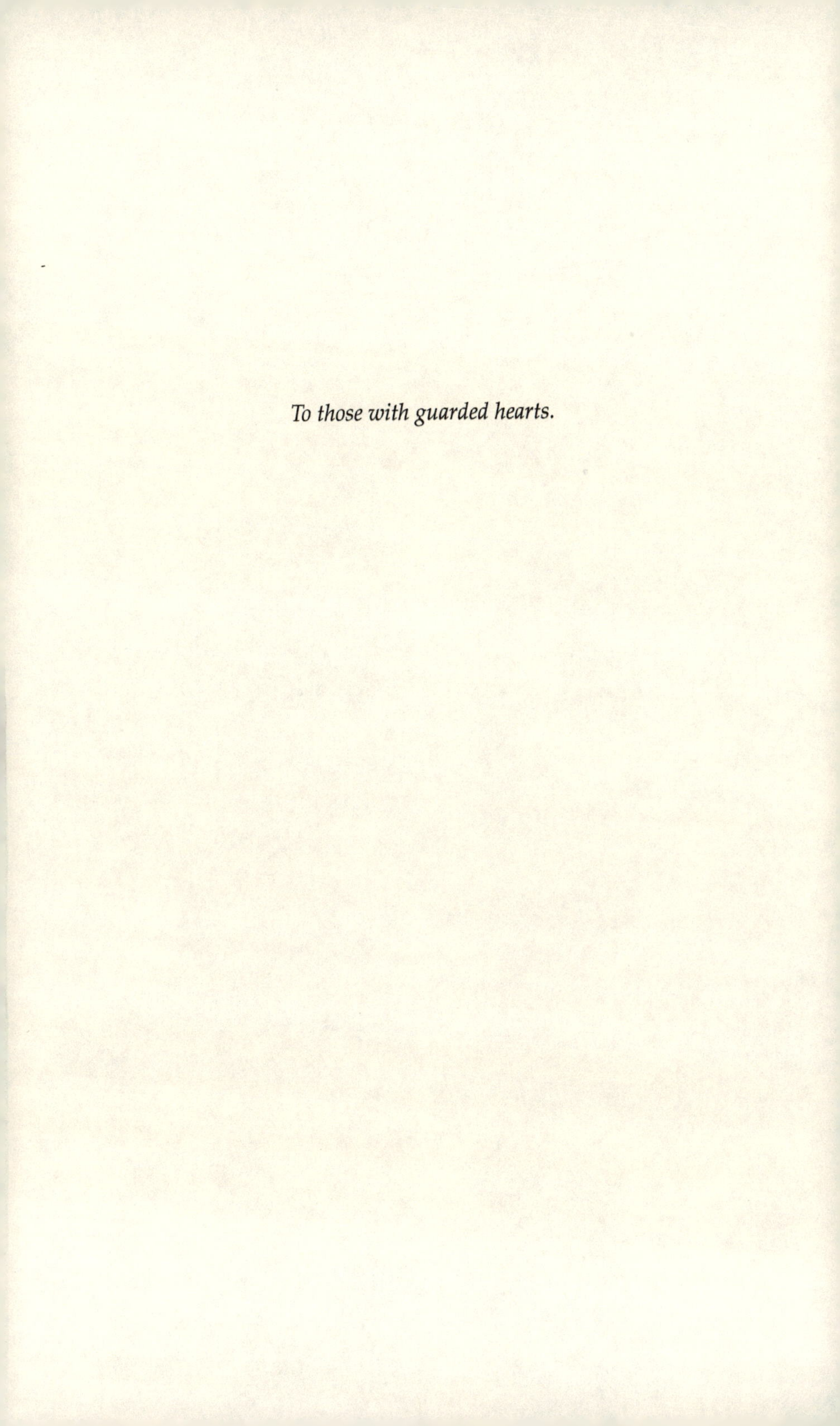

To those with guarded hearts.

I used to think love simply did not exist. One look into your eyes is all I needed to know about the depths and bounds of love.
     Miami Lewis

playlist

The following music is specific to Essence and Aaron's dynamic throughout this book.

<u>*Listen on:*</u>

Spotify: https://spti.fi/ub5O1Qc
YouTube: http://tinyurl.com/2zudekrb

<u>*or*</u>

Continue reading for the list of songs.

1. Love Again by Alex Isley ft. Jack Dine
    2. All For You by Amaria ft. DESTIN CONRAD
    3. Nothing Even Matters by SiR
    4. I WANT YOU BUT YOU'LL NEVER KNOW by Rory ft. DRAM & Alex Isley
    5. These Four Walls by Khamari
    6. I Just Want You by JAEL ft. Alex Isley
    7. I Think That I Love You by Zyah Belle ft. ROMderful

8. ...Exclusively by Tiana Major9
9. Electric by Aliana Baraz ft. Khalid
10. it's you by Rayana Jay

note to the reader

I would like to start off my clarifying that the following content is written throughout this book:

Stress and Anxiety
Substance Abuse
Physical, Emotional, and Psychological Abuse
Sexual Abuse/Harassment

I want to let you know that this book discusses certain topics that may trigger negative memories or thoughts.
Thank you for your understanding.

Zoe Aviya Harris

essence

. . .

"THE SPARKLIER, THE BETTER."

Turning my gaze away from the mirror, I peer at my phone screen, which holds the view of my best friend, Yasmyn, from FaceTime.

"Plus, it shows a bit of skin," she continues, and I can't help but smile as I take one more glimpse.

Yasmyn's my best friend and has been for years. We met in Algebra One our freshman year, becoming inseparable. Ever since then, she has been my hype man, my girl date, my ride-or-die, even my girlfriend for times I desire. I rely on her at any time—and she relies on me just as much.

"Ooh! Wear those black sparkle ribbon shoes!" Yasmyn proclaims, and I smirk.

"I swear that'd be a look right there," she acknowledges.

"Yeah," I utter, and reaching for the tag, I check the price.

$145.

If I had been shopping for a dress about 5 years ago, this would've been my last option.

But this isn't 2017, and I'm not the broke college student I'd been once before, meaning this is my top choice and the best option.

"At what time are you planning to head out tonight?" Yasmyn questions, and I shrug as I struggle to unzip the back of the dress.

"Around ten or something. Why?"

A knock from the door behind me interrupts our conversation, and I stare at the camera before walking over to open it. As I do so, my hand leads between the frame and the door itself as I speak to identify who stands outside of the fitting room.

"Who is it?" I sputter, and the smile that had once been on my face fades away within seconds as I spot my manager, Christopher Evans, who gives a fake smile in response.

"Hey," I declare. Before opening the door, I glance toward the phone, a silent signal to him I'm on a call.

It's one of the many rules Chris had made just seconds before offering the business deal to me. Letting him know when he's recorded or listened to, and he's big on that.

As Chris walks through the frame, he looks around the room before looking back at me. His gaze travels over my body, making me feel uneasy instead of flattered.

"Is this what you're wearing tonight?" He asks, tone rough. I lick my lips and I nod, watching as his eyes bounce between the phone and I.

"Zaara's going with you tonight, right?" Yasmyn says, a hidden attempt to lighten up the mood. With the thought of making her feel at ease, I toss on a smile and nod.

"Yeah, she invited Journey and Imani, too," I respond, and Yasmyn reciprocates with a dull smile.

Christopher's menacing presence returns to the room.

"Did you have any plans to have an extra dress to slip into?" He exhorts, and once again, I stand silently.

I can't help but get frustrated by my silence, and how often it happens. How much he'll say things and hover, or how overpowering he tries to be.

A single gaze into his eyes reveals the resentment he struggles to conceal. Uncomfortably, I walk toward my phone and grab it, and my eyes nervously dabble between the screen and Chris, unsure of his upcoming actions.

"Hey, Yas, I'll call you back, okay?" I say, my voice quivering.

Silently, I wait for her reply, hoping she wasn't aware of it as well.

"Okay. Send me pics before you leave. Love you, Essie."

Within seconds of the call's hang-up, Chris's hands quickly find their way around my wrist, tightening with each sound I make.

His eyes burn with anger, and dropping my phone, I fumble to loosen his grasp.

"Chris, I can change. It's just an option I was looking at—"

Suddenly, his grip's gone.

I watch as it slowly bruises, glancing down at my skin.

The sound of the door's hinges creaking reaches my ears as I glance up, and Christopher's silhouette comes to a halt in the doorway as he speaks.

"Pick something else. You're not wearing that fucking dress."

❥ ❥ ❥ ❥

Jazz music plays through the speakers as I walk in, and the small coffee shop's door shuts slowly behind me.

While making her way towards the counter, a young woman with twists takes her place behind the register. She smiles, causing dimples on the side of her face to appear. I smile back before looking up at the menu, and the woman speaks.

"Welcome to The Caffeine Fix. How may I help you?"

"Hi," I begin, and my eyes scan the neatly written chalkboard.

"I'll get one Caramel macchiato, one flat white, and a strawberry cake pop."

Her fingers speed across the screen of the register, nails

clacking against the screen as she quickly types everything in. The total loads up on the screen facing me. "Alright," she mumbles.

"Size?"

"Large for the Macchiato, medium for the Flat."

The screen loads accordingly, and I wait as the total amount hits the expected number. Grabbing my wallet, I hand the barista a waded ten and multiple folded ones, numerous Nickles resting within the bills.

"Keep the change," I mutter, and the cashier gives me a swift smile before messing around with the register. I walk toward a nearby table as she does so.

Sitting down, I watch as a man walks from the bathroom, a young girl clutching his left hand.

His hair is a duke cut, the color dark brown. Gray hoodie with matching sweats, and diamond studded earrings—Can't be older than 28.

"Daddy?" the little girl calls, tugging his arm. Her curly hair is in a low puff, butterfly clips pinned to her coils. He looks down at her for a moment before she continues speaking. "I want a cake pop," she demands, and he chuckles lightly before picking her up.

He places her onto his shoulders, and I watch as she points toward the menu, gesturing to what flavor she has in mind. Her father then walks toward the cashier and says her choice, and the girl wiggles in excitement as he speaks.

"4.50."

"Got it," he mumbles, digging into his pocket. He then mumbles under his breath before handing the cashier the money, to which she then gives him a rather unwanted statement: "You're short .75."

"That's all I have on me right now."

"If you don't have the remainder of the change, I'm afraid I can't sell to you."

"What?" I hear the child whine, placing her chin on his head. The man scoffs.

"Come on. It's just seventy-five cents, and it's not like I'm tryna scam you. I just don't have the change on me."

With no response, the woman shrugs.

I then reach into my purse, grabbing my wallet as I dig for spare change.

Standing up, I give a neutral call before walking toward the daughter-daughter pair, handing him the loose coins as I speak.

"Here," I request, and the man hands the money to the cashier. Without emotion, she types in the additional pay.

"Name?"

"Uhm, Aaron," the man stutters, his eyes still lingering on mine. He turns back forward, hands reaching for his daughter's before placing her back onto the ground.

She now stands by his side, lightly dancing along to the music that plays.

Hearing my name called by a worker, I walk towards the counter and grab the drink carrier and paper baggy. The employee hands the receipt to me, and I toss a kind grin before balling the paper and tossing it into a nearby trash.

As I make my way towards the door, my hand instinctively reaches for the handle before I'm interrupted by someone calling out to me.

"Excuse me."

Turning around, I'm faced with the guy I'd spoken to a couple of minutes ago.

"Thank you. You didn't have to."

For a second, my eyes scan his face, and I toss in a smile in the hopes of preventing it from seeming creepy. Shifting my stance, I continue speaking.

"You're good. I know how kids can be, especially towards sugar," I respond, which seems to earn a chuckle from him before I laugh along. Silent air sits between us before the bell over the door rings, signifying someone else walking inside. They pass us silently, and the man begins speaking again.

"Do you have kids?"

My phone buzzes in my pocket, and reaching for it, messages from my roommate, Zaara, accommodates my lock screen.

> On my way home now. Make sure you get me a large.

> Been out the house the entire damn morning.

I chuckle a bit at her message before rambling a response to him.

"Oh, no. I used to babysit growing up."

He nods firmly.

Tossing my hair over my shoulder, I tuck my phone back into my pocket.

"I'd love to continue this conversation, but I have somewhere to head to," I add. We both stand near the door, and I open it before moving out of the way as an elderly couple walks in. "Right, yeah, I get that. Thank you, again," he stutters.

"No problem."

Stepping outside, I'm barely a distance from the door when I hear it open again, the identical voice summoning me before I direct my attention to it.

"Aaron, you?"

For a moment, I find myself smiling, complimented by the exchange.

"Essence."

"Nice to meet you, Essence."

essence

. . .

THE DOOR CLOSES BEHIND US, and it didn't take long for Zaara to disappear somewhere out of my sight.

I feel like I'm back in college, wandering around some frat party until I can recognize someone familiar. Wandering into the living room, I observe the guys focusing on the TV, shouting as if a member of the team had lost. A few women stand along the back of the couch, cups or wine glasses in hand as they talk.

I continue walking, now heading toward the kitchen as everyone continues talking to one another. Stopping beside the kitchen island, my hands reach for a nearby bottle of white wine and a glass before being interrupted by a sudden appearance.

"Hey," a voice says, hands wrapping around my waist. Out of reflex, I knock my elbow back before turning around, finding a friend, Lamar, rubbing his arm.

"Shit, babe, I'm sorry," I say with concern, placing my glass down.

"You can't sneak up on me like that," I add on with an awkward chuckle. Taking hold of his arm, I kiss the spot I hit, causing a smile to appear on his face.

"You alright?" I ask, and he nods.

"Yeah."

Grabbing the bottle from the counter, I watch as he pours a shot of Hennessy into his cup. He hastily drinks it before carrying on with his conversation with me. "You look beautiful," he says, wrapping his arms around me once again.

This time, I don't strike at him.

"Thank you," I smile, giving him a quick peck. Moving beside me, Lamar places his hands on my hips the best he can before speaking.

"Have you seen Renee tonight yet?" he asks, and I shrug.

"Not yet. Knowing her, though, she's been on the patio," I respond. Watching as people walk around us, I lean against the counter.

"Got it," Lamar mumbles. Pouring another shot, he taps it down before tossing the plastic cup to the side.

"I'll be floating around if you need me, okay?" he pauses, waiting on my response.

His eyes meet mine for a moment, swapping words I can't find myself to send back.

"Okay," I murmur, and he nods before giving me a quick kiss on the forehead and wanders away.

Not too long after he does so, Renee walks in from the backyard.

Her eyes scan the kitchen for a minute before they land on me. I can notice the very moment they do, because the smile I've seen time and time again appears on her face.

"We're run through a couple rounds of karaoke," she offers, and I smile.

"There's $150 on whoever doesn't sound drunk. You in?"

I nibble on my bottom lip before nodding, and excited, she continues speaking.

"In the living room, fifteen minutes," she instructs. Looking away, I grab my glass from before and take a sip.

"Okay," I say.

"Meet you there."

. . .

I've known Renee for three years.

Of those years that we've been friends, I learned two things. One: She's one hell of a partier; and Two: Never accept a late night competition with her. Because it always involves alcohol, and I always lose.

Somehow, I'm still conscious.

"Let me sing another one," I mutter, words slurring together.

We've been doing karaoke for the past hour since charades, and man, am I ridiculous.

Pointing toward the TV screen, I direct Kylie to another song when Lamar comes from the kitchen. He places his cup onto the coffee table before taking both the mic and glass from me.

My laughter resembles much of a child's as I snatch it away, causing him to struggle as I do so.

Lamar lets out an awkward chuckle.

"That's enough for you," he mumbles, and I stutter.

"No."

My words come out more like gibberish as I continue to put out an argument. "I'm not done," I add.

"Ess, let's just sit down for a bit, alright? Take a break from singing," he responds, and I scoff.

Lamar takes a deep breath, and I sit down onto the cushions as I identify the frustration he seems to hold.

"Hand me the glass, and I'll do a refill," he offers, and I look at him.

Eyebrows furrowed, I hesitate before giving it to him.

"Thank you. Stay here, and I'll get your cup full again."

My mind attempts to break down his words, knowing that there's a catch to his sentence, yet I can't find it.

"You know where your purse is?" Lamar asks, and without speaking, I nod.

"Good. We can get it in just a second."

I roll my eyes at his recommendation before watching as he

wanders into the kitchen, listening as the others continue the karaoke round.

Allison, a friend of mine, stands up as music plays. The familiar melody concludes of the song *"Sandwich and a Soda"* by Tamia.

Yasmyn and I used to play it all the time when it came out.

Lamar comes back over, my refilled glass in hand.

"Here," he offers, and I grab it from his grip. Taking a sip, I lean back on the chair as I continue to listen to Allison sing.

"You ready to head out?" Lamar asks, gathering my attention back to him. "Yeah," I respond. He stands up, giving me a gesture before walking to the others.

The music cuts off, and I watch as Lamar's friend, Trae, stands up to do that bro hug with him.

Zaara spots me from the couch before getting up and walking over. "You alright? You want me to drive you?" she asks, and I shake my head no.

"I'm fine, Lamar's dropping me off," I ramble.

Digging in my purse, I grasp my car keys before handing them to her.

"Don't wreck my shit," I stutter, which causes her to chuckle a bit.

"I won't," she smiles. Giving me a kiss on the cheek, Zaara gives me a quick hug before wandering off, Lamar turning back around as he walks back over.

"You ready?" With him in front of me, I lie my head on his chest for a moment before nodding.

"Yeah."

"God," I mumble.

My head is throbbing, and the fact the curtains sit open

doesn't make it any better.

A deepened voice chuckles before speaking, "Morning."

Opening my eyes, the bed creaks from our movement, Lamar's face leaning towards me before his lips meet my cheek, giving me a kiss.

"How much did I drink?" I ask, now laying on my side.

"About two-ish glasses before you started acting wonky," he replies, his fingers moving in a motion around his head.

Rolling my eyes and groaning, my hands hit my face for a moment before I slide them down, moving closer to him. "Then about two more before I gave you a cup of water," Lamar adds. I roll my eyes, regretting the decision seconds later.

Lamar presses a few kisses along my neck before standing up and walking toward the window. Watching as he shuts the curtains, I thank him, and he tosses me a smile before walking into the bathroom.

The room is now dim, nothing but the bare sunlight underneath the curtain.

And just like that, I feel sick.

Springing out of bed, I rush into the bathroom, finding myself crouching beside the toilet.

Everything from the night before sits in the toilet bowl in front of me. Lamar comes over, his face scrunching up as the smell arouses throughout the small fitted room. My bonnet sits ruffled on my head before I sit there for a moment, unsure if what just happened was to happen again. Standing up, I flush the toilet, somehow becoming dizzy with the sudden movement.

This has got to be the most hungover I've ever been.

The sink runs from the bathroom, along with the sound of Lysol spraying in the air. I chuckle a bit, causing yet another wave of pain throughout my head. Glancing at myself in the mirror, I'm surprised by the sight of me in a white tank top and shorts.

"I changed you when we got here. Had to pull over twice because you kept gagging. Threw up once, the others were false alarms," Lamar comments, and with embarrassment, I shake my head.

"Fuck, I'm sorry," I groan, rubbing my temples.

"Nah, you're good. Didn't get in my seats. Got on your dress, though," he responds, pointing toward the right back corner.

My dress from the night before lays along the edge of my bathtub, a light stain around the upper chest area. It looks as if he'd attempted to rinse it a few times already.

"Thank you," I mutter, walking back into my bedroom.

"No problem," I hear him respond. Sitting on the edge of my bed, I rub my face a moment before hearing Lamar call out from the bathroom, "Could you toss me my clothes?"

Lamar comes walking from the bathroom about ten or fifteen minutes later, ready to head out.

"You good with me leaving? I can stay if you need me to."

"Lamar," I say, and he smiles. "I'm fine. Just bring me some saltines, a bucket, and a seltzer from the fridge before you leave."

A smirk pops onto his face before he walks into the hallway and towards the kitchen, and the sound of the pantry and fridge doors opening follows.

My phone buzzes against the night table beside me, the vibrations seeming to get louder each time.

Lamar then walks back in, a cup of water and a box of crackers in hand. "I can't find a bucket anywhere. There's no seltzer, and you guys only have a couple of saltines left. I still brought you the bag, though," Lamar says, placing the few things on the nightstand's surface.

"Damn it, Z," I mutter to myself, grabbing the water before taking a sip. It's her time to go grocery shopping this week, and somehow she still hasn't.

"Want a pot?"

"No," I mumble, placing the cup back onto the nightstand. "Those are the good ones." He laughs for a moment, and I admit, hearing what I just said, I laugh a bit, too. "Don't you have a bucket, though?" He asks, and I raise a brow.

"Where?"

"The Lowes one in the garage?"

I take a sip from the water, forcing myself to swallow. "I use that to wash my car," I sigh, and Lamar laughs. Placing the cup down, feel a little better. Laying back down, I close my eyes for a moment before continuing to speak.

"I'm good. If I've gotta throw up," My finger points towards the bathroom, "Toilet's right in there."

"Okay," he replies. Walking closer, Lamar leans over me before kissing me on the forehead. "Well, I'm good to talk later, at around four. Text me if you need me at all."

"Alright," I respond. I watch as he walks out the door and into the hall.

"Oh, make sure you don't throw up on the sheets, aye? I'm not gonna be here to clean it up," he jokes, and I roll my eyes before grabbing a small pillow and throwing it, hitting him in the middle of his forehead. He laughs a bit before grabbing my bedroom's doorknob.

His eyes meet mine for a moment, and even though he's a distance from me, I can tell there are words circulating in his mind.

Words that I'm not sure about, yet have an uncomforting feeling that I know what they are.

Lamar seems to notice he's been staring when he snaps back to reality, a smile appearing on his face as he speaks.

"Love you, Es," he calls.

For a moment, he stands, waiting for my response.

I let out an awkward laugh, unsure of how to feel.

Sure, I say those words to my friends all the time, but it's something about hearing it from Lamar that just feels different.

Like there's a different intention behind them.

Inhaling, I swat my hesitation aside and toss on a smile.

"Love you too."

essence

. . .

CHRISTOPHER STANDS in front of the building entrance when he spots me.

A grin appears on his face, and I toss him a smile of unease as I near him.

"Morning, Essence," he smiles, a rather sly tone hidden behind his words. "Morning," I say back.

He then opens the door, allowing me to walk in before he follows behind me.

A woman with blonde hair mans the front desk. Looking up from her computer screen, I recognize her face.

"Good Morning, Elise!" I exclaim, and she smiles.

"Morning, Essence! Morning, Christopher."

Her tone turns rather dull at the mention of Chris, and he gives her a quick nod before speaking.

"We have a photo shoot for 10AM?"

Elise quickly begins typing on the keyboard before writing something down on the notepad beside her. "Alright, yup, I see the appointed studio space right here. You guys got the number?" she asks, and Chris nods.

"Well, just meet everyone in there. The artists, stylists, and photographers are set and ready for you."

She then tosses on a tight-lipped smile as she closes off her sentence, and Christopher and I wander off down the hall, toward the studio.

The lights cast a dim glow, and we notice that most of the surrounding doors are shut as we walk down the hall.

"You ever thought about dying your hair?" Christopher asks. I glance at him and, unsurely, offer a small nod, my eyes busy as they scan the room numbers that we pass.

"Good," he mumbles, and we continue to walk down the hall in silence. Just as he seems to spot the studio room, Christopher brings us to a stop before speaking.

"They need to dye your hair."

Confusion fills my voice as I ask, "What do you mean, they need to dye my hair?"

I don't understand why my hair color is even relevant to the photo shoot.

"Jet black. They need to dye it jet black. It fits the shoot better, and I already told them it was alright with you," he adds, and I scoff.

"Chris, I told you before, you can't just make promises like that without asking me first. It's my hair," I respond, and I quickly regret it.

"Essence," he says, his voice firm. I shrink back instinctively, suddenly aware of his unwavering gaze. Reluctantly, I surrender.

"Fine," I mutter. "But it's temporary, right? A few washes and it'll be gone?" I ask, desperately hoping for some semblance of control over my appearance. Christopher hesitates for a moment before nodding, and I nervously bite my lip.

"Okay."

The room buzzes with activity, with stylists and photographers meticulously setting up their equipment. The smell of hairspray and makeup wafts through the air, adding to the surreal atmosphere.

You'd think that with the multitude of photo shoots I've found myself within, that I'd have at least gotten used to the sudden changes. I've had colored contacts, glasses, wigs, extensions, braces, even.

But I've never had to dye my hair.

A few photographers fix the lighting and cameras before noticing me, and they then wave over the director, Kiana, of the entire setup. She has her black hair in passion twists, and her jumpsuit is in a leather-type style.

"Hey!" she exclaims, and I smile.

"So we've got seven shots we need to get. We're gonna get this dye onto your head, then you can get dressed. That alright?" Kiana says, and I nod.

"Alright. Head on toward the hairdresser's area and she'll get you settled."

❤❤❤❤❤

Looking into the mirror, I find myself face to face with someone I don't recognize.

It's been years since I've seen this side of myself. Years since I've seen *this* Essence. The Essence before it all.

My waves still drape along my shoulders. Only instead of burgundy, they're streaked with black.

A natural color I thought I'd stripped away with the girl I was before, the girl I now sometimes beg to be once again.

The hairdresser hands me a towel, which I used to wipe my neck before placing it onto the counter beside me.

I keep staring at my reflection, somehow unable to let my gaze go.

"Like it?"

The woman's question snaps me back to reality.

"Yeah. It looks good on me. Fits my face," I stammer, and she smiles brightly. Grabbing my phone, I take a quick photo before uploading it onto my story, pairing it along with a 'Yes or No' poll that reads:

Jet Black. We like the new look?

It only takes a few seconds for people to respond, along with a few DMs.

"Essence!" I hear someone call. Looking up from my screen, I quickly shut it off before shoving it into my pocket and standing.

Looking toward the dressing room, the direction holds two hangers in front of Christopher, who sits on an armchair beside the door.

"Yeah?" I say, approaching them.

"All your clothes are on the rack inside. First take is in ten," Kiana says, and I nod as she quickly wanders off.

As I realize I'm now alone with Christopher, my heart quickly begins pounding.

Memories from times before flood my mind.

Memories I try to erase, and when I do, they're only over-written.

"I—" I stammer.

"I'm helping. You need to wear a zip-up dress in this first shot," Chris says, interrupting me. Without speaking, I nod, and he quickly follows behind into the dressing room.

"Unbutton," he mumbles, and I fumble with the buttons as I do so.

The fabric of my dress drapes along my skin as a grin appears onto his face, and he sits down on a nearby ottoman as he observes my body.

My breath quickens, and I feel as tears form in my eyes.

"Chris, I—" I stammer, but Christopher shakes his head at

my sentence, and I quickly shut my mouth before continuing to strip.

Slipping into the black Rib-knit the director had chosen, I fix a few folds within the material. Looking into the mirror, I quickly become startled as I spot Christopher, who now stands behind me.

His arms wrap around my waist, pulling me closer, and a shiver runs down my spine.

"Chris," I beg, trying to push him away, yet he only holds me tighter.

"Be quiet," he mumbles, and I feel a tear fall from my left eye.

"Please—" I stammer yet again, my voice trembling.

His lips meet my neck, leaving a trail of unwanted kisses, and I'm left standing here, helpless.

It feels as if time has stopped, as if I'm trapped in a nightmare that I can't wake up from.

This has happened before, too many times to count.

"Christopher," I whimper, but as he turns me around, he shakes his head once again.

"I would do nothing to hurt you, remember?" he states, his words contradicting his actions.

I nod.

"Never forget that."

Christopher's been my manager for the past six years.

Six miserable years.

I've endured this pain.

These unwanted moments and thought-staining memories.

He's also the reason I don't believe in love.

Producer of big-time movies, I could find nothing bad against him. All comments are good, and at the time that I met him, I couldn't help but spot him on my radar. So while he was my manager, he was also my boyfriend on the side.

I enjoyed being around him.

The way he smiled, the way he laughed, the way he made me feel.

He was everything to me.

Until he wasn't.

We spent all our time together, sharing our hopes and dreams, and laughing until our sides hurt. I felt like I had found my soulmate, the one person who *truly* understood me.

But two years in, minor disagreements turned into bigger arguments, slight mishaps turned into my mistakes, and slips of anger turned into physical altercations.

The one time I tried love, it proved all the things I'd thought about. All the things I've seen, heard, experienced—it was all confirmed.

And while I almost got out, there was just one thing in my way from truly escaping him.

The contract.

<h1 style="text-align:center">essence</h1>

. . .

OPENING THE DOOR, I find myself greeted by Aaron, who sits at the table nearest to the door.

"Based on your frequent party and invitation updates, I kinda figured you'd be quicker than that," he comments, a smirk arising on his face.

Displaying my annoyance, I smile before placing my purse in the empty chair beside him. I then sit in the one across as we sit silently.

"Well?" he begins, his tone bemused.

"What?"

"What're you in the taste for?"

I shrug in response before looking at the cafe menu. "I mean, there's not much to offer aside from caffeinated beverages, bread, and cake pops," I comment, and Aaron laughs.

"I mean, you said you could never say no to a croissant," he jokes, and with a smile, I roll my eyes. "Oh, fuck off," I retort, and Aaron laughs.

"Well? What's your choice?" Aaron asks again, and I lean into my palm. "I'll take that croissant, thank you very much," I smile, and he nods.

"Got it. Any drink?"

"Um," I pause, looking at the menu again. "I mean, I wouldn't mind a whipped Strawberry Frapp."

"Bet," Aaron responds, and I smile.

"I'll be right back, with your Frapp and croissant," he adds, a false French accent added on as he walks off.

Aaron comes back about five minutes later, a tray in hand.

"Got your two sweet objectives," he says, and I playfully roll my eyes before grabbing my things. Aaron grabs his coffee cup before placing the tray on a vacant table behind him. "So," he pauses, and I take a sip from my cup.

"You got any plans today?"

I give a scoff before speaking.

"Hardly."

Aaron responds with a rather sarcastic gasp before talking.

"You don't have another party to pamper and wander off to?" he comments, and I give him a look.

As I shake my head no, he nods again before adding, "I saw your stories Monday night."

Embarrassed, I cover my face quickly, a faint recall of the night crowding my mind.

"Oh, my god," I groan, and he begins laughing. Moving my hands away from my face, I listen as he speaks. "I mean, seemed like you had a hell lot of fun."

"I did," I respond, and he gives a slight interjection.

"Till dawn hit," I groan, and he laughs again. "Worst early morning hangover I've *ever* had," I confess with a light smile.

His chair shifts slightly as he moves, and I can see a faint smile appear on his face. "What were *you* planning for the day?" I ask, and he shrugs.

"I mean, I've got work after this," he responds, and I almost immediately apologize. "Shit, I'm sorry. If you need to head out—"

"No, you're alright," Aaron responds, and I give him an unsure look.

"I don't have to be there today until, like, twelve, anyway," he adds.

Reluctantly, I check my phone for the time.

9:57 AM

"So, you've got about an hour and a half?" I ask, and he nods.

"Exactly. You have my attention for two hours," Aaron responds. Somehow, that simple sentence seems to give me a feeling. A feeling I can't name—but it's not bad.

Leaving the two of us in silence, I begin to hum along with the audio of the music overhead.

"You wanna head somewhere in the meantime?" he asks, and I nod. "Where to?"

I shrug, "Anywhere."

"You like vinyl?" Aaron asks, which grabs my attention. "Yeah," I respond.

I watch as he nods slowly.

"Bet."

❤ ❤ ❤ ❤ ❤

Technically, it wasn't a lie.

Before Christopher and I started *anything*, I used to be all over town, searching for record spots to hit up. Played my music practically every day before my classes and work. It was my entire goal; to rack up a huge collection.

A year into meeting Chris, he said it hadn't been worth my time anymore. I had better technology. And even though he and I broke up a few years ago, I found myself never picking them up again.

"What's your vibe?" Aaron asks, and I chuckle.

"Vibe?" I repeat, and he nods lightly. My eyes scanning the room, I spot records of all sorts separated into different parts of the building. The back left corner honored cassettes, the center floor to R&B records, the front store for record players, and more displays throughout the room.

"Vibe," I faintly recite, slowly walking along the R&B. Rows of vinyl line the table, the covers displaying on the sleeves. Jhene Aiko's *Trip* album sits in the front row, and my hands firmly grasp it.

"Jhene, SZA, Brandy, Amerie," I recite, thinking of the different artists I listen to, the sleeves flipping in my hand as I stare at the back.

Aaron mumbles a bit under his breath when I direct my gaze towards him, witnessing as a faint smirk appears on his face.

"What?" I ask, confused. "Nothing," he shrugs, the smirk slowly growing into a smile. I roll my eyes as he walks toward my direction, swiftly coming to a stop in front of the third row as he searches through the labeled S's.

"Don't worry 'bout it. You said you like SZA?" he asks, and I nod. His hands continue sifting through the many sleeves, slowly and carefully; Sure not to scratch or smash the slender disks.

Pausing abruptly, I watch as he lifts SZA's album, Z.

"Holy shit," I chuckle in disbelief, now reaching for it. Placing it into my hand, I put the Jhene Aiko vinyl onto the others. "This may not be the collectible one, but *jeez*, I haven't been able to get one," I mutter, pulling the record from the sleeve.

"Honestly, like thank you," I continue as I slide it back.

"I haven't felt like this in a while."

I close the door behind me, the hinges creaking softly as it shuts.

Music blares from the kitchen and the familiar beat of the song *"Do It"* by Chloe x Halle echoes through the room.

Walking in, I watch as Zaara stands over the island counter, rapping along with City Girls before getting startled at my appearance.

"Fuck," she says, painful laughter in her voice. Pushing her thumb into her mouth, she places the knife she had in her hand against the counter.

"Made me nick myself," she says with a smile, giving me a teasing nudge.

"How's dinner going?" I sarcastically ask, placing my purse on a cleared counter. Sliding into a bar stool, I place my elbows on the table before leaning into the palm of my hands. "Absolute shit. Chinese?" she responds, and I laugh a bit before nodding. Zaara now stands in front of the sink, rinsing her hand before turning it off.

"You weren't home all day, so where'd you end up going?" Zaara asks, grabbing the cutting board she'd been using. Using a utensil to remove the chopped vegetables from the cutting board, she places them in a plastic bag and then places the bag in the fridge before placing her dirty dishes in the sink.

"Spent the day with a friend," I reply, grabbing my phone. Opening up Instagram, a flurry of likes pops up in my notifications.

"Need I check your tagged photos?" she teases, and I laugh.

"Nah," I say, still looking down at the screen. Walking back over, Zaara props her elbows on the counter before leaning against her palms.

"Who'd you hang out with?" she asks, brows furrowed. Raising my eyes from my phone, I rapidly switch it off before placing it with the screen facing down on the counter.

"Just someone new," I respond, crossing my arms. Her eyebrow now raised, Zaara leans closer.

"Who was it?"

"A friend, Z," I say, standing up.

"Want your usual?" I ask, grabbing my phone. A sarcastic chuckle releases from her mouth before she digs into a nearby drawer and tosses me a menu.

"Of course," she sighs, rolling her eyes.

Unlocking my phone, I open the phone app. As I get ready to dial the number, Zaara clears her throat, gaining my attention.

"I'm getting that name."

In a mocking manner, I chuckle before lifting the receiver to my ear.

"Yeah, we'll see."

essence

. . .

I HAVE the same dream every night and it scares me.

Ever since the shoot yesterday, my mind won't stop replaying what happened. The way Christopher's hands almost seemed to burn into my skin, the way he looked at me, the way his grip tightened with every move I made.

The names that once tasted like sweet honey left a sour taste on my tongue, and my thoughts whirled with sentences blaming me.

The way that it's happened over and over again. How every time it does, a piece of myself disappears.

A piece of who I am.

And I can't help but continuously think—what happens when who I am is gone?

What happens when that last piece of me is chipped away?

essence

. . .

I REMEMBER when I'd first moved down to New York.

I was a freshman in college and working to get my degree in culinary arts.

Sure, a simple program would've sufficed, but that degree was what I was working toward. The money Mama had given me months before was all spent on the impulsive purchase of a one-way ticket here, leaving me with absolutely nothing.

New York is expensive.

I figured that out the first week I was here.

Apartments can be almost $3,000 a month, and I hardly had that. So I worked as hard as I could to *at least* find a roommate *somewhere*.

In the meantime, I was staying in hostels with the little money I had.

One day during my shift at a diner I'd been working at, Christopher and I met. I forgot exactly what he had said, but it was something like practically offering to sign me at that moment.

And that was the beginning, that was the start of everything.

The start of *the* Essence Miller, the socialite.

. . .

The chilly water hits my face, and I quickly grab a towel to dry off.

A hear a knock on my bathroom door frame as I watch as Zaara lets herself in. "Hey," I say, drying my face. She sits on the counter before responding. "Hey. So what's Christopher want you to do today?" she asks, and I roll my eyes. Tossing the damp towel into the hamper, I apply my makeup. "Anything that doesn't involve changing my path," I say annoyedly, and Zaara laughs.

"Some invitation to a party tonight."

Zaara gives a rather fake groan before I continue speaking.

"Something for an upcoming influencer. Name's Tamera," I add, putting on foundation. Glancing at Zaara, I watch as she quickly pulls out her phone, seemingly to look at the girl I'd just mentioned up.

"Found anything?" I ask, and she nods before speaking. "She's 22, from LA, an actress for his upcoming movie, and is a frequent partier. She moved up from her neighborhood spots to the celeb ones since she's, you know, an upcoming actor," Zaara explains and I nod.

God, it sucks to watch more and more people collectively flock to Christopher. Knowing the shit he does, the shit he says, it's only a miserable hell. He keeps you compacted, keeps you silenced by mentioning the fact that he could ruin your life within seconds. If I could, I'd warn anyone—especially women —who's thinking about coming under his wing.

I finish up my base before starting the actual makeup look.

Zaara continues scrolling on her phone a bit as we sit silently. "Z," I call, and she looks up from her phone as her glance meets mine. "Do you ever miss how life was before Chris?"

She gives a forced laugh before looking back down at the screen. "I'm serious," I add. "Do you? How everything was before? How *you* were before?"

Turning her phone off, Zaara slides off the countertop. "Do I miss how I *felt* before all of this, how everything was before?" she pauses.

"Not at all. Life was hell. I appreciate where I am now—even what happens behind the scenes. It's better than where I was before."

♥ ♥ ♥ ♥ ♥

The street sits silently as Lamar and I walk outside, toward the car.

We spent the entire day together. Starting with the coffee shop, we wandered around Times Square for a bit before heading off to the class he found. It was cool. Made a tortilla wrap, and Lamar cut the vegetables we'd put inside.

"So, you have any other plans tonight?" he asks, hands in his pockets. "Got a party to head to," I mutter, irritated by the dreaded plan. Reaching his car, Lamar opens the door for me before I climb in.

Lamar gets in the driver's seat before putting the car into ignition and pulling off the curb. The sky's dimly lit by surrounding streetlamps and bare sunset. *"Int'l Players Anthem"* plays via. Bluetooth and Lamar raps along as Pimp C's line comes in. I nod along, scrolling on my phone as Chris sends me a message.

> Party starts at 8. Tamera plans for it to last to at least 1. Make sure it happens. Invite Renee, Dorian, Lamar, and Zaara. Post her invite to your close friends. Make sure a crowd gets there.

I sigh roughly before sending a thumbs-up emoji.

The song turns off, and Lamar turns the volume down a bit before speaking.

"You good?"

"Yeah, just irritated," I stutter, and he nods in agreement.

Turning the corner, the familiar surroundings allow me to realize we're close to the house.

"Have you ever thought about becoming a full-time chef?" Lamar asks, pulling into my driveway.

Putting the car in park, *"Hey Nas"* plays on minimal volume as we sit silently. "Yeah," I mumble, grabbing my purse. Checking the time on his car dashboard, I think about what to wear as it reads 7:37 PM.

"So why don't you?" Lamar changes his position to face me better. "I'm not talking about this right now with you, Lamar," I state, getting out. Walking up the porch, I hear Lamar shut his car door, quickly jogging toward me as I dig in my purse for my keys.

"Essence, I'm serious," he continues, tone firm.

"Lamar, I'm not talking about this with you. It's *my* business, *not* yours," I respond, looking at him. He stands quietly before I turn to unlock the door, leading us into the dark house.

Turning the corridor lights on, I quickly walk up the staircase toward my room, and I again, listen as Lamar follows. Now in my room, I toss my purse onto my bed and walk into the closet.

"I'll be ready in a few minutes. Entertain yourself in the meantime," I mutter, and the sound of the TV turning on sends his response.

Walking out, I struggle to zip the back of my dress.

"Lamar," I call. Sitting up on the bed, he then walks over. Moving my hair to the front, I feel the zipper slowly move up my back, the warmth of his breath against my skin giving me chills.

His touch sends shivers down my spine as I glance into the mirror, his eyes quickly doing the same as our gaze locks.

Turning around, I lean in for a kiss as he grabs me by the waist, pulling me closer. As our bodies press against each other, I wrap my arms around his neck, slowly backing up before feeling the counter hit the back of my waist.

Lamar then lifts me onto the surface, continuing to kiss me as I now lean against the mirror, his hands almost seeming to search my upper body.

A small ding exclaims from my phone, and with it sitting beside me, I push it from our view. As the phone continues to ring, I let out an annoyed sigh before moving back and reaching over to grab it. Glancing at the screen, a slight panic sears through me as I notice Christopher's name on it.

Looking into Lamar's eyes, they express impatience as I show him the screen before answering.

"Essence, where are you?"

Of course.

"On my way, why?" I stutter. Nudging Lamar, I slide off the counter before looking into the mirror and fixing any faults. "It's eight. Didn't I tell you to be here by now?" Quickly checking the time, I sigh roughly.

"Shit, yeah, that's on me. But yeah, I'm on my way now. Don't worry about anything, I'll be there in about fifteen," I add, now walking into my room. Grabbing a jacket off my bed, I slide it on before reaching for my purse.

"Alright, see you when you get here," Chris responds before hanging up. Rolling my eyes, I put my phone into my purse.

"Lamar," I call, and he walks out of the bathroom, head down on his phone before looking up.

"What was that about?" he asks, shoving it into his pocket. "Just wondering where I was at," I murmur. Walking closer, Lamar holds me still before leaning in for a kiss. For a moment, I give in but quickly snap back.

"Lamar," I murmur, knowing of the devious grin on my face.

"Essence," Lamar says with a smile. I nibble on my cheek a moment before giving him a quick kiss on the lips. Reaching for my hands, Lamar then holds them tightly.

Looking him in the eye, I notice his eyes seeming to search mine. Lamar stutters a bit before building up his words.

"I think I'm in love with you."

I open my mouth to speak, but nothing comes out. As I stare at him, my mind races.

"It wasn't meant to go this far," I mutter, and I watch as Lamar's expression immediately changes.

Fuck.

"No, I don't mean it like that, but like we *agreed*, this was a 'no-strings-attached' kind of thing."

Looking into his eyes, I can see the hurt and disappointment in them. Slipping my hands from his, I can't help but feel bad.

I led him on.

We went out, had dinners, and talked about things we couldn't talk about with anyone else.

"I'm sorry," I dimly say, watching as he hesitates before responding.

"Imma go on and head out."

"Oh," I sputter, unable to say anything else. Watching as he exits, I feel my eyes water, nothing but the sudden feeling of regret wandering through my mind.

"See you later."

❤ ❤ ❤ ❤ ❤

"Fuck Lamar."

The words exit Yasmyn's mouth, then are quickly sealed with a shot of lemon-lime tequila. I roll my eyes a bit before sipping from my cup.

"He knew what he was getting into. The rules were laid out from the beginning. Strictly no strings attached," she adds firmly.

"Yeah, but I feel bad. I was leading him on," I sigh, leaning against the counter. Yas nudges my shoulder before turning me directly toward her.

"Ess, you do not need to feel bad. Again, 'Mar knew what his ass was getting into. You told him from the jump, you weren't looking for love. He agreed to those terms."

I gnaw on the lining of my cheek before nodding, the lingering tequila now stinging the appearing sore. Grabbing the nearby Hennessy bottle, Yasmyn pours two tall shots, handing one to me before speaking.

"Now forget about that man for the night and *have fun.*"

The music is loud, and the place is packed.

"You see anyone you interested in?" Yasmyn asks, and I shake my head no. Yasmyn nibbles on her bottom lip as she searches through the crowd, eyes scanning every man that comes across. After a few minutes of searching, she walks off into the busy room, leaving me standing at the table alone.

"God," I mutter to myself. Sitting down in a nearby chair, I grab my phone before opening messages.

Nothing from anyone, not even Aaron.

We've spoken almost every day since we'd hung out, his words almost seeming to brighten up my day.

Would it be a good idea to invite him over?

Or would it be too weird?

Nibbling on my lip, I think for a moment before pressing his contact, quickly pulling up our chat.

> [TRUE.ESSENCE] HEY, I'M AT A PARTY RIGHT NOW, WAS WONDERING IF YOU WANTED TO DROP BY?

Turning my phone off, I tuck it into my purse before standing up and wandering back to the drinks.

Grabbing an extra cup from the stack, I pour a bit of wine inside. No idea of the kind or brand.

Taking a sip, my face scrunches up at the bitter flavor before I place it on the side. Turning around, I spot a face I've been dreading to see—Christopher.

"Hey!" he exclaims, reaching for a hug. I dodge it before giving him a bitter smile. Trying to walk off, I feel his hand lunge for my arm, tightening slowly for every moment I haven't turned back.

"What the fuck do you want?" I mutter, turning to him. His grip loosens as a sly grin appears on his face, much as if he were satisfied with my reaction.

"Just checking in on my *star girl*," Chris comments. I feel a hand grab my ass for a moment before I quickly pull back. Looking up at Christopher, I watch as that same sly smile reappears on his face.

And as he does so, it only adds to my building unease. Grabbing a shot glass, Christopher pours himself a shot before downing it, then reverts back to me.

"Three pictures before you leave. At least four stories."

"Fine," I snark, and his eyes narrow.

"You're helping out a beginner, Ess. Be a good citizen and stick around," he adds with a grin, then walks off.

I scoff a bit as I watch him leave, the reflecting burn of his grip continuing to sting my skin. I feel my phone vibrate in my purse, and I quickly grab it to find a response from Aaron.

[AA.MAAYERS18] GONNA HAVE TO SAY NO
TONIGHT. MY DAUGHTER NEEDS HELP WITH HER
HOMEWORK AND I'VE GOT STUFF TO FILL OUT
FOR THE NIGHT. THANKS FOR THE OFFER,
THOUGH.

I feel something in me dim slightly at his words, but I shrug it off before typing back a smiley face.

God, you'd think with as many parties I find myself at, I'd know how to start at least a conversation with a few folks.

Looking around, I try my hardest to find people I'd talk to, unfortunately finding no one but groups of try-hards and people I've never bothered conversing with.

Sometimes I just wish I could break the contract. Quit the

toxic management I've found myself in and find someone who values who I am and who I desire to be.

But I can't.

Even if I dared to try, Christopher has dedicated his entire being to making my life nothing but miserable hell. He's found shit to use against me and *will* make up shit to ruin my career.

And people would believe him, they really would. All because he's Christopher *motherfucking* Evans.

Christopher Evans could jump-start your entire career within seconds.

Christopher Evans could get you viral within *minutes*.

Christopher Evans does nothing *but* good for people.

Still, I can't do anything but sit and wait. Wait for the rest of the contract to end, and lose my dignity in the process.

Because if I lost where I am now, I have no clue where I'd be.

aaron

. . .

"FAITH'S HOMEWORK is in the purple folder. Make sure she gets it done," I declare, watching as Faith wanders inside.

Malia stands in front of the propped door, giving me a displeased expression. "I took care of her for three years. I know what needs to be done." Giving Malia a grin, I continue watching as Faith tosses her backpack onto the couch.

Looking back at me, she quickly runs back over before hugging me. Crouching, I hold my arms out before she jumps into my grasp, holding me tightly.

"I love you, Daddy!" she exclaims. "I love you, too, princess," I smile. Loosening my grip, I kiss her on the forehead before standing up, patting her shoulder as she wanders back inside.

"I'll pick her up Thursday night," I say, and Malia nods. "Alright. Text me the time you'll be down here," she responds, standing up straight before moving out of the way of the door. "Bye," I say, the door shutting slowly.

Before it closes, she waves and the simple sound of the latches locking quickly reaches my ears.

Every other Tuesday, I drop Faith off at her grandmother's house for two days. It was the only way I could get any kind of custody of her, especially with the unknowing location of her mother.

Gratefully, it's only for this year, so about five more months of this, and we're done with split custody. My daughter will be with *me*, and with me for good.

My phone buzzes in my pocket for a moment, a call from Essence engulfing the screen as I grab it. Finger pressing the green button, my ear is met with her bubbly voice.

"Okay, so there's a Menchie's not too far from that record place," she begins.

"Unless you want to try a new spot because I know there's a ton of other frozen yogurt shops along Central."

Walking away from the stairway, I begin along the sidewalk. "Let's try something new. Almost everyone's been to Menchie's," I mutter, my left hand reaching into my pocket for my keys. She sits silently, nothing but the sound of her nails hitting the screen.

"I found, like, four 5-star places."

"Name 'em," I respond, with my shoulder now holding the phone as I buckle my seat belt. The car turns on, and my phone quickly connects to Bluetooth. I place my phone on the cup holder and place my hands on the wheel.

"Okay, 16 Handles, Pinkberry, Emack, Sedutto, Amorino," she begins, mentioning nearby places. Her accent causes her to fumble on a few words, but I don't point it out.

"I thought Amorino and Emack were ice cream parlors?" I ask. "It is, the photos just look good," Essence replies. I laugh a bit before pulling out of the parking space.

"I heard some good things about Emack."

"Let me see the menu real quick," she then requests, now muttering as she reads the choices. "Nah."

"What?"

"The flavors seem good. I'm just not up for some ice cream."

"So, Amorino's is also out?"

"Yup."

Pulling in front of a red light, I pop my knuckles against the wheel as I hear Essence speak again.

"Okay, okay, I found a place. Pinkberry. The flavors look good, they have 5 stars, and the photos on Google are just too cute," she continues, light laughter in her voice.

"Yeah, I know where that spot is," I respond, my foot pressing the gas as the light turns green.

"Meet you there."

♥ ♥ ♥ ♥ ♥

Music plays on the speakers overhead, and I truly have no idea what it is.

The only familiar voice I can pin is Olivia Rodrigo—my sister Aanya used to watch High School Musical on repeat when we were younger. She was 13; I was 15, and I promise you, you don't know hell until you share a room with a HSM fan.

Non-stop movie replays and repeated lyrics, tunes, and references to the soundtracks only grow to drain one guy out.

Looking out the window, I watch as Essence's car pulls up to the curb, her curled ponytail bouncing as she steps out. She's wearing a short green dress, black heels, and a light corduroy side purse.

Her hair's the same darkened shade of black, pulled into a high curled ponytail.

Essence's hands constantly smooth at her sides, fingers tugging along the bottom as if she were in fear of peeking. She then walks up the concrete ramp before reaching the door and walking inside.

A smile gleams across her face at the sight of me.

"Okay, so I saw they have a Salted Caramel cookie crumble,

and I honestly want that more than *anything*," she gleams, and with a subtle smile, I nod.

Shoving my hands into my pockets, we walk towards the counter, standing behind a young couple as we wait.

"How's Zaara?" I ask, trying to strike up a conversation.

Essence looks up from her phone before responding.

"She's alright."

Quickly, she looks back down at the screen.

"That's good," I say, and Ess shrugs.

"Yeah," she mumbles.

Directing her attention back to her phone, she briefly casts a glance at me before switching it off and stowing it away in her purse.

"How's Faith?" she asks, which makes me smile.

"She's doing alright," I reply, and I watch as Essence shyly nods. We stand silently for a moment before I continue the conversation.

"So, your hair," I comment, and Ess rolls her eyes.

"I know. I've washed my hair too many times to count," she sighs. Her pointer finger on her right-hand fiddles with the rings aligned across her others.

"I think they used permanent dye."

"Permanent?" I repeat, and nibbling on her inner cheek, she nods.

"Christopher might've told them it's alright," Essence sighs. She licks her lips before looking up at the menu, adding to her sentence.

"But he loved the burgundy. It was the symbolism for a new phase in life, you know? Something new that I've never done before."

I think this shade looks nice on you.

The comment sits on my tongue as I abruptly fall silent because of the couple in front of us walking toward the machines. Stepping toward the cashier, she cheerfully greets

Essence and I's presence. She has brunette hair, tan skin, and freckles planted across her nose.

"Welcome to Pinkberry. How may I help you?"

Essence sits beside me, her hands grasping onto her cup.

As I grab a spoon Essence hands me, I quickly dig in and she does the same. "But about your hair," I comment, and Essence groans.

"Wait, wait, before you complain," I laugh. She kicks around a few pieces of gummy bears with her spoon before eating a scoop from her cup.

"I think the black suits you better," I say, and I watch as Essence pauses for a second. She licks her lips to hide a smile, which then causes her to smile outwardly, anyway.

"You hardly saw me in burgundy, Aaron," she coughs, and popping a scoop into my mouth, I shrug. Her smile continues to line her face for a couple of seconds before she manages a response.

"Well," Essence pauses.

"Thank you."

"What's something the media doesn't know about you?"

A silenced scoff escapes from Essence at my question.

We've been sitting in this shop for about two hours now, and we finished the frozen yogurt within minutes of sitting down.

"What?" Essence questions, and I raise my eyebrow before repeating myself.

"Exactly that—what's something that the media doesn't know?"

She leans back in her chair as she nibbles on her lip, clearly in thought.

"Well," She pauses. I watch as she crosses her legs before checking her phone screen and flipping it over.

"I'm awesome at cooking."

"I said something social media *doesn't*, Essence."

"I'm serious!" she says with a laugh.

"If I weren't so caught up with trying to keep up with the perfect image, I'd be owning a restaurant chain right now."

Uncrossing her legs, Essence leans forward, reaching for her cup.

"So, why don't you?"

"Don't want to," she mumbles.

"But you said—"

"That applies to if I weren't who I am now. If I were *just* Essence, sure, I'd try it. There would be no risk of frustrating anyone. No risk of losing everything. But if I change my path now, I'm at risk of losing every bit of success I've received. My manager would kill me, I'd lose fans, it's a whole thing," Essence interrupts, leaning back.

"I say make a move," I state with a shrug, and Essence gives me a strong expression. Clearing my throat, I shift the conversation.

"What's your favorite recipe?"

"Pretty much anything from my Mami's cookbook."

I smile at her response.

"A real favorite of mine is the Chile Relleno. It's a simple, savory dish that's easy to make and always hits the spot. The seasonings and vegetables she adds—," she pauses, seeming to gather her words.

"Just make it—," she pauses once again.

"I really can't describe it. You just have to try it."

I nod my head slowly, a small smile drawn on my face as I do so.

"It's been a while since I've really sat and hung out with someone. Someone interested in actually having a genuine conversation with me," she calmly says, adding a laugh of rather astonishment.

Surprised, I cock my eyebrow in confusion before speaking, "What do you mean?"

Her hand grazes her forehead as she gives me an expression that conveys both surprise and disappointment.

It's a look that says, 'Are you serious right now?'

"Aaron, do you *know* who I am?" Essence asks.

And for a moment, I almost nod.

"*Aaron.*"

"I'm serious. I don't *know* who you are. I mean, I know your name and what you're *known* for, but I don't know *you.*"

Essence rolls her eyes at my response before popping a glance out the nearby window.

"Then what am I known for?" she asks, exasperated.

"You're known for your media. Your appearance. What you do, who you do it with, where you do it," I respond, and Essence nods.

"Exactly. And you have no clue how exhausting that shit can get. How much it feels like I'm just running in a circle, repeatedly."

I inhale deeply as I watch her hesitate to continue speaking. Essence nibbles on her lip a bit as her eyes wander around my face, and her thumb fiddles with the silver ring on her finger.

"I appreciate having someone willing to just be here. I appreciate it a lot."

Essence tosses on an unsure smile before grabbing our empty cups and walking over to the trash can, where she swiftly tosses them inside. As she walks back over, she then grabs her phone and checks the screen, her body quickly expressing urgency not too long after.

"You got somewhere to head to?" I ask, and unsurely, Essence chuckles.

"I've gotta meet my manager someplace," she responds, and I nod.

Packing up her purse, she slides it onto her shoulder. I stand up from my seat, following along her side as she slowly walks toward the building's exit.

"It was nice having a break from reality for once, though,"

Essence sighs, and I smile. Standing up, I walk alongside her toward the door. "You should do that more often," I comment, and she smiles. "I should."

Now outside, Essence and I walk toward her car, where she comes to a stop before getting inside. I call her name, which gathers her attention as she looks up at me.

"Maybe you could come over to my place sometime and make something for dinner?"

An excited smile seems to play on her lips before she silently nods.

"I'll have to check my schedule and clear out a day sometime soon, but yeah, I'd like that." I can hear the excitement in her voice, clear as day.

"Would doing it at my place be better? You know, just to be sure you're not some psycho fan who's trying to kidnap me," Essence says, which causes me to laugh.

As she stretches out her arm towards the car door, she opens it and briefly pauses before moving forward.

"The amount of people who've tried that shit would surprise you."

I laugh a bit at her comment, and with a smile, Essence rolls her eyes.

"Well?" she states, and as I laugh, I nod too.

"Yeah. I'd like to come over for dinner," I respond, giving her a sly smile.

Essence rolls her eyes again before seeming to bite back a smile.

"Alright. We can plan stuff sometime soon. Maybe set something up for next weekend. Anything you in the taste for?" she asks, and shoving my hands into my pockets, I shrug.

"Surprise me," I smirk, giving her a sly glance.

Essence rolls her eyes before nodding, sitting in her car. As she shuts the door behind her and it automatically goes into ignition, she lowers the window.

"I'll text you the date before the end of the day tomorrow, alright?"

Smiling, I nod.

"Got it."

Essence smiles again before raising her window. I can still see the dampened smile through the glass, her face expressing pure excitement.

With that, she pulls back from her parking space and drives off, leaving me standing with a smile that I can't seem to wipe off my face.

aaron

. . .

"THIS IS a woman you met just four weeks ago, and you're already going to her house?"

Looking up from Faith's lunchbox that I've been packing, I give Andre, one of my best friends, a look.

"What?" he states with a smile, his tone rather defensive. I roll my eyes before shoving an empty plastic container into his hands.

"Put a couple of grapes in here. Second top drawer in the fridge," I point, and I hear the fridge open as he does so.

"Hey, I'm just glad you're finally knocking your walls down," Andre states, and I scoff. "Fuck off, 'Dre," I say, hiding my frustration with an unsure chuckle.

Opening a jar of peanut butter, I grab a knife and get some before gliding it across a slice of bread.

"I'm serious, Aaron. It's about time you've gotten out there forreal. I mean, when was the last time you really went out and had fun?"

I get ready to speak, but Andre quickly dismisses me.

"And not when Maeko and I had to force you."

Maeko is my other best friend. I grew up in a pretty fucked up home, but the two of them helped me manage.

Rolling my eyes, I stand silently, finishing up the PB&J as I cut the crusts off before putting it into a Ziploc bag.

"Exactly," Andre says, and I exhale roughly. "Andre," I groan, and I watch as he leans against the counter, arms crossed, as he gives me a silly look. Laughing a bit out of disbelief, I scoff.

"Man, quit playing around."

"Aaron, you know I'm not playing. You know how you are."

His commentary leaves me silent once again.

"Just promise me you won't toss this new interaction aside."

Zipping up Faith's lunchbox, I walk over to the fridge before placing it inside.

"Aaron," Andre calls, and I sigh

"Fine," I state. A sly grin appears on Dre's face as he reaches his hand out to give me a pound hug. Reluctantly, I give in.

"Promise, man," I say, and he nods.

"Good."

Walking toward the bar stools, Andre slides into the first one. "Now what's her name?"

❤ ❤ ❤ ❤ ❤

The bed springs creak lightly as I sit on the mattress, my phone in hand as I turn it on and begin relentlessly scrolling.

A few new photos on Essence's page pop up on my feed, each one giving a slight peek into her day, the latest being of her, Zaara, and Renee, gathered into a group photo. The caption reads:

Had an amazing dinner with las chicas! Cooked up a picante de camarón taco. @LarsMars89 @RightouslyRenee

I double-tap the post before scrolling on, quickly finding myself interrupted by a message from Essence.

> [TRUE.ESSENCE] MEET ME AT THE CAFE EARLY
> TOMORROW MORNING. WE COULD PICK UP
> BREAKFAST. ON ME.

A faint smile appears on my face as I nibble on my thumb before typing a response.

> [AA.MAAYERS18] YEAH, THAT'S ALRIGHT. I'LL HAVE
> TO DROP FAITH OFF AT HER GRANDMOTHER'S
> FIRST. BUT WHAT'RE YOU IN THE TASTE FOR?

> [TRUE.ESSENCE] FAITH COULD EAT WITH US, TOO.
> I DON'T MIND. I'D LOVE TO MEET HER IF THAT'S
> ALRIGHT WITH YOU. PLUS, WHAT KID DOESN'T
> LIKE BREAKFAST?

Chuckling at her comment, I hesitate for a moment before typing a reply.

> [AA.MAAYERS18] NO, IT'S FINE. I DON'T MIND
> DROPPING HER OFF.

It takes Essence a moment before typing a response, as the three dots linger on her side of the phone a bit longer than usual.

> [TRUE.ESSENCE] OH, OKAY. WELL, I'LL SEE YOU
> TOMORROW. I'D LOVE TO TALK A BIT LONGER,
> BUT I'VE BEEN ON MY FEET ABSOLUTELY ALL DAY
> AND I AM EXHAUSTED.
> [AA.MAAYERS18] LOL, ALRIGHT THEN,
> SLEEPYHEAD. SLEEP WELL.

Essence gives my text a quick tapback, which causes me to smile, before she sends me her reply.

> [TRUE.ESSENCE] NIGHT!

Turning my phone off, I place it face down on the nightstand before it buzzes. Grabbing it again, the display glows as a notification from Instagram sits on my screen.

{@True.Essence has liked your Instagram Post}

❤❤❤❤❤

Essence walks alongside me, her phone in hand as she takes a quick picture of her coffee cup.

"So, what's the plan for tonight?" I ask.

Essence comes to a stop, and it takes me a moment before realizing that where she's standing is right beside the restaurant door.

"It's a surprise, remember?" Her voice carries a playful undertone, and I can't help but smile a bit at her slyness.

"Right." I say, and Essence laughs.

"Mhm! But I can assure you it's amazing. Hint: You like spicy food?"

Essence and I head into the building, quickly greeted by the chilly conditioning inside. The music being played overhead is jazz, and groups of people sit together at separate coffee tables. A few people are alone, their laptops in front of them or books in hand.

It doesn't take long for someone to greet us.

"Welcome to Spot21. How many are we seating today?"

A guy with medium-length brown hair comes over, his fingers speedily gliding across the iPad's screen before looking back up at us.

"Two," I sputter, and he nods.

"Gotcha. Follow me."

Essence and I are brought into a separate room, where three other families sit around us.

Justin took our orders, since Essence and I had already known what we came in here for. Essence and I sit silently for a moment, and I watch as she takes a picture of the surrounding environment.

"You like spice, huh?" I ask, and looking up from her screen, a smile appears on her face as she nods.

"God, if *only* you knew."

I laugh at her response and nod, watching as she quickly uploads the image onto her Instagram before shutting her phone off.

"It's the only kind of food my mama really made. I mean, sure, she made a fair share of mild dishes, but spice is practically the only thing I grew up on."

I nod at her sentence, watching as she plays with the necklace that sits around her neck.

"*Well*, do *you* like spicy food?"

"Who, me?" I ask, and with a sarcastic smile, Essence nods.

"Duh."

I laugh a bit at her quirp before speaking.

"I mean, I like *some* spicy foods," I respond, and Essence nods again.

"I've got a feeling you're gonna like what I have planned," she continues, and I struggle to hold back a smile.

"Oh, really?" I tease, and she shrugs.

"But we'll find out."

Looking in the rearview mirror, I begin to back out of the tight spot, careful not to ding any nearby cars.

Essence digs in her purse for a moment before pulling out a compact mirror, along with a mascara wand.

"So, I've got all the ingredients needed at my place. Unless you wanted to make something like dessert?"

Essence carefully applies the mascara as she speaks, my eyes glued onto the road in front of me.

"I mean, I wouldn't mind something sweet. That's a pretty good combo. Sweet and Spicy," I say, and Essence smiles. Placing the two objects back into her purse, she leans against the middle console, her head placed in the palm of her hand.

"Maybe I could make something simple. Something that'll just give you a hint of sweetness. That sound alright?"

Coming to a stop at the red light, I turn to face Essence, who's only about an inch or two away from my face.

The intensity of the moment is palpable, and a wave of desire washes over me as I catch a whiff of her subtle perfume.

We exchange a knowing smile, my mind gradually becoming aware of the unspoken tension. Our eyes lock for a brief moment before I hear the honking of a car distantly behind us.

"Shit," I mutter, quickly pulling off at the notice of the green light.

Pulling out her phone from her back pocket, Essence unsurely points toward the AUX. "Yeah, I don't mind," I say, handing her the cord. She plugs it in, and her phone connects to the Bluetooth, a song beginning almost immediately. The display shows the song *"Si Una Vez"* by Selena, and I listen as Essence sings along.

As the song plays, I can't help but smile at Essence's enthusiasm. She sings with passion and energy, her voice filling the car with a warmth that makes me feel at ease. The song fades, and a different song plays almost immediately.

"Wow, you have a great voice," I say, genuinely impressed by her singing. Essence laughs and shrugs.

"Thanks, but I'm *nothing* compared to Selena."

I laugh a bit before turning the corner, and pulling into the neighborhood Essence resides in. "You like Selena?" Essence asks, and I shrug. "I haven't heard much from her," I respond, and it seems to almost shock her.

"Dios Mio!" Essence sarcastically caws.

"Selena is beyond amazing. I used to play her music *all* the time when I was younger. If I'm being honest, I probably know every song by her word for word."

Essence smiles as she finishes her sentence, and I can't help but smile as well.

Pulling into her driveway, I put the car in park before unbuckling my seatbelt, my eyes peering at the large house.

"You ready to get spicy?" Essence says with a grin, and with a smile, I roll my eyes at the hardly hidden joke. With my hand on the door handle, I give Essence a look before getting out.

And with a light chuckle in my voice, I say, "God, you have *ass* humor."

essence

. . .

AARON and I stand in the spacious kitchen, surrounded by an array of ingredients and utensils spread across the island counter. As I glance around at the organized chaos, I can't help but chuckle nervously.

"Sorry about the mess," I say, unsure of any thoughts Aaron may have. He simply shrugs, a genuine smile playing on his lips.

"Nah, don't worry about it," he replies, his demeanor putting me at ease.

Leaning against the cool surface of the fridge, Aaron's eyes follow my every move as I navigate the kitchen. With each item I retrieve from the nearby countertop, it's clear that his curiosity grows.

"So what's on the menu for tonight?" he asks, voice filled with anticipation. As I reach for a worn-out cookbook, a mischievous grin dances across my lips.

When I first moved out, my Mami handed me this book with all her family-fed recipes inside. Every single thing I've had growing up, *every little dish*, is all in here.

Anything Mami served was something she'd put her foot in, almost everything from scratch. If there was one thing I for sure know that we have in common, it's our love for the kitchen.

"Chile Relleno," I reply, my voice laced with excitement.

"That recipe I mentioned to you earlier."

Wandering toward me, Aaron looks over my shoulder at the now-opened cookbook. "You said you liked spicy food, right?" I ask, and without looking up from the page, Aaron nods.

Grabbing my phone, I quickly connect it to Bluetooth before opening a music app and pressing my playlist.

Selena's *"Besitos"* is the first to play, and I begin lightly dancing as I put my phone on 'Do Not Disturb'. It doesn't take long for Zaara, who sits in the living room, to realize what's happening, and once she does, she places her show on pause.

With an excited smile painted across her face, she joins in.

Looking up from the cookbook, a grin appears at the sight of Zaara and I dancing. Our laughter fills the air before I speak.

"You ready?" I ask, slowing down. He raises an eyebrow, causing me to walk over and grab his hands. I hold them tightly as I lead him into the Bachata, his body leaning into the movements almost within seconds. His feet, once hesitant, now glide across the floor with increasing confidence. I lead him into a turn, and to my delight, he catches on swiftly.

I prefer the traditional version of the dance. There's more footwork, movement, and energy weaved into it.

Well, that, and it can be a bit more physical.

"Move a bit more like this," I mumble, carefully leading Aaron's body in direction. He fumbles a bit, but once he catches on, he's back on the beat.

I bite back my smile as he does so, though I've got a feeling it lightly slipped anyway.

Aaron looks up from our feet, our eyes meeting one another for a moment before I break the exchange.

"You caught on fast," I stutter, and smugly, Aaron shrugs.

"I'm just like that," he comments, and I laugh. His ego is out of this world, yet it's scarily accurate at the same time.

Once the song fades, I realize Zaara had silently slipped off into the living room, leaving Aaron and I in the kitchen. She sits on the couch, propped along the back of the cushions as she watches the two of us talking.

Her face bears a knowing look, a look I see too often.

Rolling my eyes, I shake my head before waving her off, and as she lays back, Zaara raises her brows.

Turning my attention back to Aaron, I stammer, "Ready?"

My sentence startles him as he looks up from the seasoning bottles, his fingers fiddling with their tops.

An awkward smile pops onto his face, and he gives a response before we begin.

❤ ❤ ❤ ❤ ❤

"I swear if I drop one more piece of shell in this," Aaron mutters.

Looking up from the pot of oil, I watch as he struggles to use the shell method.

I chuckle at the sight before wiping my hands on my apron and walking over to help. Grabbing the eggshells from him, I put them to the side before grabbing the nearby mixer to stir.

"Stand by the pot," I request, pointing toward the stove.

"You want *me* to fry the peppers?" Aaron asks, and without looking up from the egg whites, I nod. His eyes swap between the pot and I, clearly unsure of what to do next.

Finishing up with the mixture, I grab the bowl of peppers before beginning to dip them into the batter.

"Need help?" I ask, and licking his lips, Aaron shakes his head.

"I just don't know how this is gonna work. Fried peppers?" he questions, and shaking my head, I smile.

"*Stuffed* fried peppers. And either way, just trust me, okay? This shit is fire," I respond, and Aaron raises his hands, a signal of surrendence.

"Okay, okay!"

A smile plays at my lips when I swap spots with him.

"You dip these and put them to the side. I'll fry. Make sure none of the cheese and chicken inside falls out," I begin.

Now standing beside me, I show to him how to do the process. "First, dip it into the flour mixture, then into the batter. Make sure you roll it around and coat it completely, otherwise, you won't get that crunch when you bite into it."

Grabbing a pepper, I do so slowly, using my fingers to make sure the coating is even.

"Once the tray is full, bring it to me, and I'll fry all the peppers," I say, ending my tutorial with a smile.

"Got it," Aaron replies.

The oil pops out as I drop the pepper I've just done, my hand seizing the tongs against the counter.

"That smells hella good," Aaron says, hovering over my shoulder. Turning to look at him, I bite back a complimented smile.

"I think I'm getting closer to the perfect flavor profile, but I'm still not there yet," I respond. Aaron takes a deep breath, once again inhaling the aroma before he speaks again. "Make sure you write what you're doing. I wouldn't mind recreating it."

I smile at his comment, something about it igniting something in me—something I haven't felt in a while.

"Don't worry, I'm noting every step for you."

After saying grace, we dig in.

"Holy shit."

Aaron's sudden words cause me to look up from my plate, concerned about where the shocked reaction had come from. Zaara takes a bite from her fork as she exchanges a glance with me, where a smile stays hidden behind her mouthful. Unsurely, I poke a bit at Aaron's words.

"What?"

He takes another bite before taking a moment and answering, "This is good."

I nibble on my lip a bit to prevent myself from smiling, yet still do so.

I take a sip of the wine Zaara convinced me to pour.

"Have you gone to culinary school?" Aaron asks.

As I give a response, Zaara quickly interjects, "She hasn't."

Aaron raises his eyebrow at me as I sigh roughly, trying my hardest to shoot Zaara a subtle, yet strengthening, look.

"No, I haven't gone to culinary school."

"You should. Not that it doesn't taste good, this is *amazing*," he pauses, and the fumble within his sentence causes me to laugh.

"The seasonings and flavors together taste phenomenal. If you ever decide to take the plunge and become a professional chef, you have a lot of potential."

I feel myself flush at his compliment.

Zaara nudges my elbow before giving me a look, one which I reciprocate back.

"Thank you. I've thought about it, but Christopher," I pause, unsure if I should even continue.

Looking up from my plate, I notice Aaron's face seeming to express his attention. I think for a moment before continuing to speak, my mind reeling with thoughts.

"With Christopher being on top of things, he sends me to parties and stuff, and I don't have the time. Plus, he said it'd mess with where I am now. It'd be a waste of time," I uncomfortably chuckle.

"Besides, it's not something I could do right now, anyway."

Zaara rolls her eyes before taking another bite from her dish. Aaron takes a large sip from his cup before speaking.

"Fuck him. Essence, you have literal talent. You're one hell of a cook. You have a genuine passion for this, and it's *extremely* clear."

I give an unsure laugh.

My heart wants nothing more than to agree with him. Yet I can't seem to. I can't get the words to form, can't get my mind to agree.

"Aaron, you don't understand. I'd lose everything—"

"No, Essence, *you* don't understand. It doesn't matter what anyone else says or what may fail. You're good at this, and you're happy when you do it. Quit the shit you hate and discover the shit you love. I believe you can do it. You just have to *try*."

❤❤❤❤❤

"Where have you been?"

Christopher's voice floods through the speaker, tone tense.

"I've been at dinner," I responded, walking down the hallway. "And you couldn't pick up my calls? Respond to my texts?" I sigh roughly, irritated by his behavior.

"Chris, a *friend* and I were cooking dinner. I put my phone on silent so I could—"

"God," he interrupts. The tone of his voice causes me to become defensive.

"What now?"

"It's just that I've told you repeatedly. Don't put your phone on silent. What if I needed to reach out to you?"

"You're speaking to me now, *Christopher*," I comment impatiently. A scoff emerges through his side of the phone, along with the sound of shuffling.

"This is the same fucking reason I left you."

His comment stings a bit, and my eyes water as I think of what to say.

"Well, fuck you," I stammer.

"Essence, if you're sick and tired of this shit, you know what to do," he snarls, and I feel his sly grin through the phone.

"*Fuck. You,*" I say slowly, which earns me nothing but a mischievous chuckle.

"Two years left, Essence," he pauses. Wincing, I realized I'd bitten down hard on my lip. The sharp silence between us is soon cut off by the sound of Christopher's voice.

"And I intend to make those two years a living hell for you."

essence

· · ·

EVEN WITH AS strong of a dislike that Christopher seems to have toward something that I enjoy, he brings that dislike down to a toleration when it benefits him.

Such as the casting party tonight.

During a meeting earlier in the day, he informed me of this dinner he volunteered to host. He hadn't thought about catering, but knew that I would take up the role—I'd have to. If I didn't, Lord knows what he'd do.

Ingredients lay scattered along the island's surface.

Between the bottles of wine that are meant for dinner and my bottle of god-forsaken vodka, I've found myself drunk for the night.

When Chris offered I make dinner, I knew that it would happen only under some circumstance, and it doesn't matter what to him—as long as I obey what he tells me.

The main course I picked is a Mexican dish called Pozole de Pollo o Guajolote, with both chicken and turkey added throughout.

It's a kind of stew and one I haven't made before. My eyes have been drawn to it, but I never fully endeavor my time toward it.

The sound of scuffling footsteps echoes behind me.

Raising my gaze, I observe Ivanna, a cast member, making her way into the kitchen.

A white shawl is tossed over her shoulder, the color pairing faultlessly with the cowl slip dress she's wearing. It's a milk chocolate shade, and she pairs white wrap-around heels to lock everything together.

As she moves closer to the island, she grasps a bottle of wine and sets it down.

"That smells delicious," Ivanna flatters, and I smile before adding a bit of Cumin and Garlic to the blend.

"Thanks. New recipe I'm trying out for tonight," I respond before grabbing the top.

Ivanna's skin is a rather cool golden, her coily hair always pulled back in a low bun. She's a producer alongside Chris for the upcoming movie—and one of the people I'm closest with that's within the cast.

I've known her for about five years.

Ivanna knows about my cooking, how well I am with a full pantry, and she endears me for it.

Putting a lid on the stew, I walk toward the cabinet before grabbing around 10 wine glasses, placing each onto the counter. With a glass and bottle in hand, she walks back to her spot from before, and before too long, the sound of the cork releasing from the bottle reverberates.

The full glass in her hand, she walks back to the pot. "I absolutely *cannot* wait to get a bite, Essence. Chris is talking about how great this recipe is, as we speak."

I smile weakly, feeling sheepish at the thought of him flaunting me off.

"It's something I haven't made, so I have no idea how it'll taste," I respond, walking over as I take the top off and stirring once again.

Stir clockwise every 5 minutes.

"Well, I'll be on my way. Just wanted to come to get a glass to wean my hunger," Ivanna continues.

Looking up from the pot, I speak.

"Let everyone know the food's almost ready. Give it about 15," I mention, and giving me a smile, Ivanna nods.

"Gotcha."

Walking into the dining room, I notice that the chandelier is dimly lit.

The new actress, Celena, sits at the head of the table, her legs crossed.

Celena's hair is styled in box braids, all of which are pulled back. She wears an off-the-shoulder black dress, paired with an array of gold jewelry. As she notices me, she tosses a smile with a wave, her nails as a French tip.

They're glossed, and rows of rings sit on each finger. Her skin has a definite darker tone than mine, and the matte maroon lipstick she wears looks gorgeous on her.

"Your hair," Celena points, and for a moment, I'm confused before I realize what she'd meant. "Oh, yeah," I laugh. Grasping a loose strand of hair, I tuck it behind my ear before continuing to speak. "It's taking a minute to wear off."

"I think black is an elegant addition to your character," Celena adds, and I bite back a smile as I begin setting out plates.

"It flatters you well. I think you should keep it."

As I finish setting the table, I sit down beside Christopher, who's quick to place his hand on my thigh. It takes a moment for me to react, and the moment I do, I regret it. With a quick motion, I push his hand away and look up at him. His eyes are intense, and I feel a shiver run down my spine. Christopher begins speaking to the cast, flaunting on about the process of figuring things out.

As the conversation continues, I feel as his hand slowly inches back towards my thigh.

I hesitate a moment before trying to push his hand again, but it does nothing but cause him to tighten his grip. My heart begins racing, and glancing around the table, I can't help but notice everyone's lack of attention.

Christopher cracks a joke and they laugh.

But I don't.

I can't.

Christopher's hand continues to rest on my thigh.

He loosened his grip a few minutes ago, meaning my demeanor must've given him *some* kind of hint. "Essence," I hear Naomi call. As I raise my eyes, I witness her taking a sip before carrying on with her words.

"This is absolutely amazing! The flavor is savory, seasonings hitting perfectly, and the breadsticks really complete the palate."

I take a bite from my breadstick, *wanting* to smile, yet unable to.

"Where did you get this recipe from?"

Moistening my lips, I steal a quick glance toward Chris, and he swiftly looks down at his glass before reaching for it.

"Something from my mom's cookbook," I respond.

"Never made this dish before. Added a few of my own twists, though," I add, and Naomi nods before taking another spoonful of broth. Christopher's phone buzzes against the table, and he quickly excuses himself before walking out to take the call.

I sense my body relaxing as he disappears, and I let out a silent exhale of relief.

"If you could recall the seasonings, Ess," Naomi pauses. Searching in her purse, she retrieves her phone before passing it to me.

"Type in your number. I'll send a message and have it locked in," she smiles, and taking her phone, I somehow manage to smile back.

Having finished my now-added contact, Ivanna lightly taps the table to gather my attention before speaking.

"Have you gone to culinary school? You'd enjoy your time there."

I sit silently for a moment before responding, noticing as Christopher walks back in. "I'm sorry, Josiah called to let me know of this little issue regarding editing, but we got it solved," he says. Adjusting his chair, he fiddles with the collar of his tux.

"But, uh, what'd I miss?" Tucking his hand underneath the table, he puts it back onto my thigh, causing me to slightly flinch.

"Oh!" Ivanna cheers, grabbing her wine glass.

"I just asked Essence if she's ever attended culinary tech."

Chris turns to me, and his eyes bore into mine, giving me a sense of discomfort.

"Uh, no," I uncomfortably chuckle, and a slightly satisfied grin displays on Chris' face.

"But I hope to within the future."

❤❤❤❤❤

"Thank you for coming," I gleam to Naomi, holding the door open.

"Thank you for having us! Dinner was amazing. Don't forget to send me that recipe," she winks before continuing to walk down the driveway.

Closing the door after me, I let out a rough sigh before entering the kitchen, where Chris is placing the dirty dishes in the sink. Turning around, he exhales roughly at my sight, his eyes full of frustration.

"What the hell were you thinking?" he begins, his voice accusatory.

"What?" I ask, trying to understand what he's referring to.

All of a sudden, my conversation with Ivanna, from earlier, flashes in my mind.

"Essence, I cannot tell you this enough. Culinary is a waste of time. I understand your passion for it, but you *need* to focus on the bigger picture and what will *benefit* you in the long run."

I stand silently, my breath quickening. I stutter, unable to speak. "It was just something I said. I didn't mean it," I sheepishly reply.

He exhales hard again, this time with a rather disappointed tone.

"Then what was in your history?"

"What?" I stammer, unsure of what he's talking about.

Closing his eyes, he takes a deep breath before opening them again and continuing to speak.

"You applied to that job."

Unable to breathe, I freeze.

"You went through my search history?" I ask, full of utter disbelief.

"I've told you over and over again, told you for years," he pauses, ignoring my question. "It's a waste of time."

Cornered against him and the counter, my jaw clenches in frustration.

"It's not a *waste of time*," I bark, my voice rising. "It never was. I've been working on culinary longer than you can imagine. Worked on my techniques, my competence, everything. And I let *you* take it all away."

Suddenly, I'm not pinned between him and the counter. I'm now in the center of the kitchen, walking with each word I say, every thought I make.

Tears fill my eyes, and the room blurs as my voice falters.

"Christopher, I've spent the past *six* fucking years intercepting nothing but pain from you. The non-stop parties, the aggression, the *harassment*," I snarl.

"And I'm fucking sick of it."

My voice shakes.

"You put me through hell, and I wouldn't *dare* lay a single fucking finger on you. I've given you all I had. *Everything*, I gave you everything, sacrificed everything *I* know to make this work, and you give me nothing but fucking pain," I yell once again.

Christopher inhales, eyes becoming cold. I glance at his hands, which he flexes into fists for a moment. Small regrets wander into my head, the fear of him touching me again floating into my mind as I continue.

"Chris, I fell in *love* with you and you fucking *broke* me. You took control of every little thing I did, made it feel like care, like passion," I sputter, "And for how long?"

His hands reach to grab my arm once again, but I smack them.

"Don't fucking touch me."

"Essence," he begins. He walks toward me, and I stay put.

"I did all of it to protect you. Can't you *see* that?" Narrowing my eyes, my breathing becomes ragged as I struggle to understand his words.

"Protect me?" I ask incredulously.

"Christopher, protect me from what?"

As I finish my sentence, I feel a sharp pain on my cheek, realizing what'd just been done.

My eyes become glassy as my mind replays the moment.

Chris hit me. He *hit* me.

The silence in the room is deafening as I try to process what had just occurred. The door hinges creak lightly, followed by the small moans from the floorboard before a hand touches my shoulder.

"Essence," Chris mumbles.

"Chris," I pause.

"I didn't mean to, you know that, right? I would never hurt you." Grabbing my purse, I struggle to breathe.

"Please," I stutter, my words fumbling, "Just leave me alone."

Getting up from the bar stool, I proceed towards the hallway that leads to the front door.

I hear a rough sigh before the following sound of footsteps, causing a rising panic to overtake my body.

I could've moved, could've stayed silent, could've hit back.

But I did nothing.

Rushing to unlock the door, I flinch at Christopher's touch as he attempts to keep me from opening the door.

"Fuck, Chris," I mutter. On the verge of tears, I place my forehead against the door before sighing and turning back to him.

"Let me *go*."

And just like that, he removes his hand from the door, allowing me to exit.

aaron

· · ·

CLOSING the car door behind me, I revert to the back, opening it before Faith hops out.

Her lavender-colored skirt flops in the wind as she stands, and I fix her hair a bit before closing the door behind her. Essence comes from the passenger's side, her hands smoothing the creases of her jumpsuit. It's a light blue color, the buttons a golden tone.

As she flips her hair to the side, Essence stretches out her hand towards Faith's and then firmly grasps both of our hands.

Our shoes crunch against the asphalt, the crackling sound soon cut off after stepping on the sidewalk.

Faith looks up from her feet, eyes glowing as she realizes where we are.

The banner reads 'Dreamland Pop-up', with the conventional neon pink unicorn mascot painted behind the words. Essence looks at me as well, her face expressing clear excitement as we walk closer to the entrance.

"Oh my god! I've been planning to come to one of these pop-ups for a while. Every time they have one, I'm busy and can't come," Essence says, obvious excitement in her voice.

I smile, glad I'm giving her a fresh experience.

"Well, then," I say, my hand reaching for the door handle. With the door swung wide, she and Faith enter, and both of them cast a quick glance around the busy rink. Walking behind them, the door closes as I release my grip. I gently touch Essence's shoulder, smiling as she turns around.

"Let's have fun."

Knotting Faith's laces, I help her stand before checking on Essence, who sits beside us, tying hers.

Essence stands but almost falls as she does so, reaching out for the bench.

"Shit," she mutters, paired with an exasperated laugh.

With my skates now on, I trail to her with my arms out, watching as she stands once again.

Grabbing on, Essence's nails dig into my arm as she attempts to steady herself. The spots she's latching on are *sure* to leave marks, plus they hurt like crazy.

After she finds a secure stance, I pay attention as her body relaxes and her grip loosens. She keeps her eyes glued to her feet, head down in a signal of trying not to fall. I skate back toward Faith before pulling her over.

"Daddy," Faith calls, tugging on my shirt.

"Yes, princess?" I ask. I fumble, peeking up at Essence in hopes she hadn't seen.

"Can you get me a push bar?" she asks, her hands in a motion referring to the trainer.

I nod before standing, calling Essence's name as she glances up.

"Hey, I'm gonna go pick up a trainer," I call, and she nods before waving Faith over. Faith sits, and Essence gives me a look. I smile, then skate over before helping Ess sit down.

"God, I don't know how I'm supposed to get out there on the rink, but it'll happen," she chuckles, and I laugh as well. She inhales before speaking.

"Hey, what's a trainer?" My finger points toward a nearby kid, clearly relying on one.

"Oh!" she exclaims, voice audit of her realization.

"The pushy things. Cool."

"I'll be back in a second, though. I'll make sure we get out there together," I chuckle, and Essence smiles before responding, "Alright."

She tilts her head toward Faith, and the two speak as I walk away.

Now on the rink, Faith stays close to us, but far enough to skate on her own.

Essence stumbles a bit, and I listen as she chuckles.

"Shit, I just," she pauses.

"You're good," I laugh.

"Focus on your stance, that's your foundation," I add, holding her shoulders as she wobbles.

I skate to her left, keeping an eye on her as she looks downward. Her hands reach out for me, freezing as she realizes my disappearance.

As Essence turns towards me, her eyes relax before she makes a move to hit me.

"What was that for?" I laugh. Essence stumbles, her skate wheels squeaking as she maintains her balance.

We pull to the side, Faith following, as we stand against the wall.

"Want me to teach you?" I ask, and holding back a laugh, Essence nods. Her fingers fiddle with one another, causing a small smile to appear on my face.

"Okay, bend your knees a bit, lean forward," I respond, holding my hands out for her to grasp. She hesitates for a moment, but holds on.

Ess's head tilts downward, all focus reverting toward her stance and posture.

A song by Montell Fish begins, and people scatter away from

the rink as couples take over. Essence doesn't notice, her eyes continuing to stay focused on her feet as she stands stably.

I turn my attention to my side and briefly observe Faith as she skates in place.

Essence's grip still tightened on my shoulder, she begins to get the hang of it.

"Holy shit," she mutters. Looking up, her hand loosens as she manages her balance.

We make our way around the rink, side-by-side, Essence's hand clasped in mine.

Faith skates beside us, a few feet away, with the occasional glance in our direction. Now and then, Essence stumbles, and I can feel her tense up in my grip. She chuckles, and I give her a reassuring squeeze.

"My bad," she says. I laugh, trying to encourage her.

"You're doing great," I say.

"Just focus on your posture. That's the key to keeping your balance."

I grip her shoulders as she maintains her balance, making sure she doesn't fall. Almost as if she intended it, Essence trips.

"Aaron!" she calls, groaning.

I laugh, and a sly grin appears on her face.

"Help me up, would you?" Essence states, and as I lean over to help, she pulls me down with her.

I tumble beside her, listening as she combusts with laughter at my impact. Faith skates over, laughing as well, before helping me. Essence sits up, a bright smile on her face as she stands up. I slip a bit as I gather my balance.

"I saw that," she laughs, and I roll my eyes before placing my hand against the nearby wall. "I'm starving," I mumble, stance ready as I try to skate toward to exit. Essence grabs my hand before I'm able to get away.

"One full round. All of us, Faith in the middle," she states, a smile perking across her face as she finishes her sentence. I gaze at Faith, her eyes pleading as they patiently await my response.

My eyes observe the rink, witnessing people returning one by one, and I shrug before responding.

"Why not?"

♥ ♥ ♥ ♥ ♥

My hand messes with the radio knob before finding a station with good music.

"Tonight was fun," Essence sighs. She faces the window, which is open halfway, as the chilly breeze flows through her hair.

"Yeah," I respond.

"I Need You" by Alicia Keys plays on the radio, and I tap my fingers against the wheel along with the beat.

My eyes glance in the overhead mirror, spotting as Faith falls asleep. I listen as Essence hums along, which I find soothing. We stop at a red light, and Essence turns to me a moment before opening her mouth to speak.

She hesitates for a bit before deciding against it. Unsure of what that may have been, I don't push into it. The green light from the streetlight reflects against the windshield. Pushing the gas pedal, the car swiftly accelerates before smoothly returning to its original pace.

I shift my gaze to Essence, noticing her now positioned in front of the window.

"What were you about to say?" I ask, turning the corner. We're only about ten more minutes away from home. She turns to face me, her eyes darting to the corner as she thinks.

"Nothing," Essence responds, and we sit silently. I turn the radio volume down a bit before speaking.

"You sure?"

Directing her gaze towards her lap, she fiddles with her nails while nodding. Inhaling, I secure my grip on the steering wheel before turning the corner.

"I applied for the school you sent me a couple of days ago," she says, voice unsure.

Suppressing a smile, I contemplate how to reply.

"And I didn't think of anything, I just kind of did it," she adds. Essence's elbows now rest against the middle console.

Pulling into the parking lot, I put the car in park before turning toward her, her eyes looking into mine.

We sit quietly in the dimly lit car, nothing but the overhead streetlight illuminating the cramped space. I glance over at Essence, who's staring out the window, lost in thought.

"I'm proud of you," I mumble. Shifting her gaze towards me, a subdued smile emerges on her face.

"Thanks," she mutters. Her hands sit in her lap, thumbs tossing around one another. "Essence," I pause, and she looks up at me, waiting for me to continue speaking.

"I want you to know I'm here for you," I say, which causes her to smile.

"Always."

Silence falls upon us again, Essence's eyes peering into mine as we don't speak.

Her elbows against the middle console, Essence leans close to my face, licking her lips as she does so. I replicate her posture, and we now sit an inch apart.

Her eyes lock onto mine, giving me an expression I can't quite decipher.

A strand of hair falls upon her face, and I move it out of the way. As I do so, I hesitate a moment before pulling her face close, closing my eyes as she gives in.

Her soft, full lips meet mine and I feel an electric surge of pleasure course through my body. I can taste the sweetness of her breath, mingled with a hint of peach.

As our lips part, I can see the skepticism in Essence's eyes.

She's hesitant about what had just happened. Honestly, I can't put a label on what just happened, either.

Her expression's a mix of surprise and uncertainty, and she unbuckles her seat belt.

"I," Essence stammers, reaching for her purse. Her hand grasps the door handle, and it opens a crack as she speaks.

"I have to go. Zaara's waiting for me."

essence

· · ·

AARON and I haven't spoken in a week and a half.

He hasn't texted—or called—and honestly, neither have I.

The past week has been nothing but Netflix binges and mindless Instagram scrolling. I've had no energy to dress up—let alone leave the house.

My phone buzzes underneath the blankets beside me, and my hands ruffle around for the insignificant item. Grasping it, I catch the eye of nothing but a spam email.

My heart sinks a bit, as my mind hoped for a message from Aaron asking for us to hang out. If there's one thing I've got to admit, each buzz I hear has me hoping it's him.

I do.

Whether it be sending me a picture, a quick check-in, or asking to hang out, I hope for anything.

Zaara and Maya sit in the living room, laughing and joking as the TV sits on pause.

Zaara's trying hard to convince Maya to move in, and it's not like I have complaints. The house is huge; the bills are expensive, and we've got about four vacant rooms—Maya's free to join us anytime.

The floorboard creaks as I walk in, causing Zaara to turn around, spotting me walking in.

"Well, if it isn't the little sleepyhead," she smiles, her voice teasing. A faint grin pops onto my face, and I sit down on an armchair not too far from them. Zaara sits beside Maya on the couch, a half-full wineglass in hand as she takes a sip.

"You know what you need to do?" Zaara asks, beginning to stand. She places her glass on the coffee table.

"What, Z?" I ask. Grabbing my hands, she pulls me up, causing me to stand.

"A girls' night out."

"Oh, no, I'm fine. I've got a party to head to tomorrow, plus, we just went out last week," I respond.

"Blah! That was last week!" Maya exclaims with a laugh, and I roll my eyes with a smile.

"Come on, Ess. Lavo is having singles night tonight, and I'm *sure* you need something," Zaara pauses, tossing a smile onto her face before continuing to speak, "Or some*one* to cheer you up." I roll my eyes, stifled laughter escaping my lips at her reference.

"I invited Yasmyn, Renee, and Jasmine," Zaara rambles, and I sigh.

"Zaara, not tonight."

"Essence, you've said that all week," she whines. I chuckle, my mind thinking back at the many times I *have* said that.

"Fine," I grunt, giving in. "Just for tonight."

"Just for tonight," Zaara repeats with a smile. "And next week you'll leave me alone?" I add, and she gives me a look. "I'll give it a try," I say with a smile, and as Zaara holds up her pinky finger, I can't help but laugh.

I know Zaara too well to believe she'll leave me alone next week. But for tonight, I'll let her have her way. After all, we've been friends for years and it's hard to say no to her.

Plus, it's not like I have any other plans for the night.

❤ ❤ ❤ ❤ ❤

We pull onto the busy street, and my eyes watch as Yasmyn pulls closer to the nightclub's building.

Renee sits in the passenger's seat beside her, applying her mascara as she looks in the sun visor mirror. Zaara and Maya sit in the backseat with me, singing along to *"Pon De Replay"* by Rihanna, which plays within the playlist Yasmyn made. Her eyes glance at the rearview at me, a quick smile appearing on her face before I roll my eyes and smile back. Grabbing my phone from my purse, I check the time.

9:57 PM

Yasmyn pulls onto the curb close to the building, and my eyes watch as she puts the car in park.

After exiting the car, Renee walks alongside me, while Yasmyn and the others stay ahead.

"You have any specific plans for the night?" Renee asks, and I shrug.

"I was just dragged along," I chuckle, and she rolls her eyes with a smile.

"Well, I know for sure that I intend to get blazed before the end of the night."

Looking around the busy sidewalk, I listen as people converse with one another, zoning out as I spot a familiar person. Someone taps my shoulder, snapping me back to reality.

"You got any hookups in plan?" Yasmyn asks, and I laugh.

"Ha ha, *hilarious*," I blow, and she smiles.

"Just here to get some drinks and maybe lay out with some guy," I respond.

Looking back in the direction I had been just a moment ago, I noticed that the person I'd spotted disappeared.

"You've gotta settle down sometime soon, Ess," Yasmyn says, nudging my shoulder.

"Find a man to fall in love with."

I scoff at her sentence before rolling my eyes and tossing a reply.

"Yeah, sure."

The line moves a bit as Yas groans.

"Oh my god, Essence. You can't just stick by what Christopher did and use that as an excuse to not try again."

For a moment, I can't help but feel hurt at her words.

Everything he's done has led me to nothing but pain, yet somehow that's overlooked by every other person who's met him. They see the pain, the tears he exerts from me. But still, they expect me to nustle up to him and forgive him.

But I can't.

Not for what he's done. And experiencing it time and time again?

I can't open up, even if I wanted to.

I sigh before giving Yasmyn a response, one that I wish could be replaced by a quick snap at her statement.

"Yasmyn, it isn't an excuse. I'm just not interested in something long-term."

"That's what you've said for the past 10 years, and look where it's gotten you," she sighs. "Not all men are like them, Ess. Never think they are," Yas adds, and licking my lips, and I think of what to say.

A sentence comes to mind, and I almost bite back on my tongue about it when my mouth moves quicker than my mind can think.

"Well, that's hard to believe when you've been hurt every time you fucking try, isn't it?"

Reaching the entrance, we flash the bouncer our IDs before heading inside, immediately surrounded by loud music.

Tinashe plays overhead, and my ears are unable to recognize the song's lyrics as people sing and talk over the audio. I feel a tap on my shoulder before turning around.

We stand near a wall, and I lean against it as she speaks.

"It's been some time since I've been a wing woman," Yasmyn sighs. I force out a chuckle, eyes scanning the packed space.

"Where'd the girls go?" I ask, and she does nothing but shrug.

"Lord knows where Renee heads to. Zaara and Maya headed to the bar," Yasmyn responds, glancing in their direction.

"Anyway, what are you looking for? A *healthy* relationship?" Pausing from my scope, I give Yas an unamused look.

"You're one to talk," I snap, and she shrugs.

"Just throwing it out there."

Rolling my eyes, I shuffle toward the bar, sitting on an empty stool before calling the bartender. She has light skin, her hair in goddess braids and she gives me a smile. "Vodka on the rocks, please," I request, and she nods before doing so.

Yasmyn sits beside me, a smile drawn across her face. "Okay, two guys sit to the far left, and one of them is checking you out," she points. My eyes dash over, and just as she said, there sit two guys.

I chuckle for a moment, the bartender sliding my glass to me.

"You just expect me to walk up to them and just say something?"

"Duh."

Placing the half-empty glass on the counter, I turn around on the stool before getting up and heading toward the two. I sense her excitement as I walk, but my unease doesn't pass.

If I'm being honest with myself, I don't want to be here.

I don't wanna be at this bar, flirting with random guys, hoping one of them is down for a quick fling. I've been doing this shit for years now. Suddenly I don't feel so up to it anymore.

The guy I walk over to has a bleached high-top cut.

His skin is a caramel tone—one that reminds me of Aaron's—and a silver nose ring on the left nostril. Sitting down, I watch as a tired smile forms on his face, hand waving the bartender over before I decline.

"Not here for anything," I mutter, leaning against the counter. The guy chuckles a moment before speaking. "Okay, then. Just wanted to say what's up." I scoff before rolling my eyes. Glancing in Yasmyn's direction, I watch as she ignores the man speaking in front of her.

"Tyler, and you are?" My attention reverts to him as I respond, "Oh, uh, Essence."

He takes a quick shot.

"Pretty name. Essence," he recalls, and I nod. "So, if you're not here for anything, what're you doing here?"

Honestly, Tyler, I don't even know myself.

"Just wanted a night out," I lie. Tyler nods, calling the bartender over before ordering another drink.

"Okay, then. I'm guessing you're here with little Miss Cupid?" he points toward Yasmyn. I chuckle before asking, "What?" The bartender comes over, yet again, and hands him a glass.

"Yeah, she came over here earlier, asked if I could speak to you."

God.

"Oh," I mutter. I know it's from the bottom of her heart, but sometimes Yasmyn just *doesn't* listen. "Yeah," he adds, taking a sip. "Well, it was nice meeting you, Essence," he states, beginning to stand up.

He grabs his glass before adding, "But I'd like to enjoy my night."

"Sure, then. *Enjoy your night,*" I mock, and he lets out a scoff before walking away. With him now gone, I find myself feeling even worse.

And it's not just because of our brief conversation, but because of the way I've been feeling. The way Aaron hasn't spoken to me once, and the way I haven't bothered to reach out, either.

I should've stayed inside, watching *"Put a Ring on It"* while coddled up in blankets. I know I'm here with the girls to have a good time, but I just feel lost and confused. Tyler's question about why I'm here hit a nerve, and it was obvious I didn't have a straightforward answer.

I walk back to Yasmyn, whose face changes the moment she notices me walking over. "Well, what did he say?" she asks, voice expectant. I smile, my mind not wanting to disappoint her.

"Yeah, just said he wanted to speak to me. Thought I looked nice," I fib, and her face drops.

I sit beside her, leaning against the counter before she speaks. "God, that was weird. Okay, well, there's another guy I want you to speak to," she adds, and I groan.

"Yasmyn," I whine, feeling like a child. Not how I wanted to spend the night. My eyes revert toward the counter, thoughts desiring for me to disappear.

"Just this guy, then we can dance, okay?" I sigh before looking up. "Where?" I ask, and her sly finger points back to where we had stood before—a familiar face sticking through the crowd.

Aaron.

Shit.

A smile pops onto Aaron's face as he notices me, eyes almost seeming to admire my appearance before turning away. "Him?" I ask Yasmyn, pointing toward him. She shakes her head no before moving my head toward someone else.

The man I'm looking at has a clean fade, his skin a darker tone, and diamond piercings in his ears.

How'd I not see him earlier?

Was that him I spotted outside?

Did Yasmyn speak to him?

What was that look he gave me?

Stuttering, I respond to Yasmyn's lingering offer.

"Fine."

❤❤❤❤❤

Scoping through the crowd, my eyes scan each person, trying my hardest to spot Aaron once again. Without looking, I bump into someone, their drink spilling along the top of my dress.

Could this night get any worse?

"Shit, I'm so sorry," the voice says. It's familiar, but my mind straggles to put it to thought as I close my eyes. I inhale before opening them again and speaking.

"It's alright, you're alright," I mumble. Looking forward, Aaron's face comes into view.

Fuck.

His face expresses what I'm thinking as he realizes.

"Oh, Essence," he begins. I smile, mind unable to erase the vivid look he'd given me. "Hey," I reply. We stand for a few seconds before speaking again.

"So, you want a drink?" Without hesitation, I nod, and he leads us out of the crowd as we approach the bar. "Anything specific?" Aaron asks, and I try to speak, but nothing comes out. Instead, I shake my head no.

"Alright, then. I'll pick both of our drinks. That okay?" I nod, and he calls the bartender over.

Shit, I wanted to be near Aaron so badly, and now that I'm *with* him, I have nothing to say. It's as if my entire mind went quiet. He clears his throat, causing me to snap back from my thoughts.

"How've you been?" I ask, my voice fumbling.

It shouldn't be this difficult to speak. I shouldn't feel so clammy about what he may say. I shouldn't—

"I'm good," he responds, interrupting my thoughts. The bartender slides our glasses over, a smile on her face, before walking away.

I take a sip, the immediate taste of mint engulfing my mouth.

"God, it tastes like I just ate toothpaste," I grimace, and my reaction causes Aaron to laugh.

His laughter calms me. Grabbing a napkin from a holder, I spit the bitter liquid into it.

"How's Faith?"

"She's good. Went with Malia yesterday morning," he responds, and I nod. "Two more months and she's locked in with me." I can sense the joy in his voice as he says this, and it causes me to smile. I take another sip, this time the mint less noticeable.

"We can hang out sometime soon if you want," he begins, and I nod.

"Yeah."

That night from last week replays in my head again. The way he looked at me. The way I felt.

How we *kissed*.

"Where you wanna head to?" Aaron asks, and I think for a moment before replying. "We could head to the movies," I suggest, trying to keep my voice steady. The thought of spending time with him again makes my heart race.

"Cool. What time of day?" he asks. I shrug, my finger moving around the rim of the glass.

"We could do something earlier in the day, then head to an afternoon showing. Saturday cool?" I respond, downing the last bit within my cup.

"Yeah, I can do that."

aaron

. . .

ESSENCE LOOKED FUCKING AMAZING.

Her hair framed her face in a way that accentuated her features, and it was styled perfectly. Her makeup was flawless, and her dress—*oh*, her dress. The black shade gave her a rather attractive look, and the fabric hugged her curves in all the right places.

Essence had to have been avoiding me until Thursday night. I'd gotten no messages, no calls, no signification of her presence, nothing. And sure, I've been doing the same, but the moment we'd seen one another, it was as if I couldn't focus on anything but her.

It was only a matter of time before we'd bumped into one another. And once we had, we were inseparable. We'd spent the rest of the night drinking and catching up.

She mentioned booking a couple more shoots, attending a few parties, and helping Christopher with the cast. Her hair was still a darker tint, so I'm guessing the color seemed to grow on her.

I left a couple more shots in while she stayed. I hope she didn't drink more than she could handle, and more than anything, I hope her friends looked out for her if she had.

I hear my phone ring as I wake up, but my head lifts to find nothing.

It continues to ring in the distance, and I stand up as I remember where I had it last. Walking into the kitchen, I find it, vibrating against the counter before I grab it.

"Hello?" I speak, and Essence's voice follows, "Hey, where are you?" I stand confused for a moment before looking at the clock on the oven.

"Shit," I mumble, reading as the time reads 12:45.

My mind slurrily recalls my assurance to her of me picking her up at noon.

Yet here I am, hardly present.

"Essence, my bad. I overslept. I'll pick you up around 1:15," I respond.

"That's good. You're alright, I understand," she chuckles. I chuckle back as I shift through my closet. "They had me out there till, like, three," she adds with a chuckle.

"You weren't driving, were you?" I ask, and she dismisses my question.

"No. Zaara did. She stayed sober the entire night."

Essence's continuing sentence seems to bring me ease as I wander back toward my bedroom. "Okay, cool," I say, turning the shower on. "What're you doing now, then?"

"Oh, watching some shit on Netflix," she responds, and I chuckle.

"What?" she asks, her voice playful. I can almost picture her mischievous grin on the other end of the line.

"Nothing," I respond, a smile tugging at the corners of my lips. We fall into a comfortable silence, the sound of her show faintly audible in the background.

Essence clears her throat before speaking.

"What about you?"

"About to take a shower," I respond.

"Oh," she comments, which makes me laugh a bit. Wandering toward my dresser, I dig around in my drawer as a muffled sigh releases from her side before being followed by shuffling.

"Well, I'm still here on the couch," Essence jokes. "Got it," I smile.

"See you when you get here."

"Yeah," I reply, tossing my clothes onto my mattress.

"See you soon."

❣❣❣

As I pull into the driveway, it doesn't take Essence very long to come out after I text her of my arrival.

She exits the front door, waving to her roommate inside before locking the door and wandering toward the car. As she settles in, she secures her seat belt before motioning for me to begin moving.

The radio's turned to a faint volume, and the familiar tune of the Arctic Monkeys plays through. I mouth along as I drive through the large neighborhood.

Essence scrolls on her phone for a moment as we sit. She takes a couple of pictures, one including me, and uploads them to her story. It takes a moment before we speak.

"So I was thinking," she pauses, opening Safari. *"No Time to Die?"*

Essence unsurely offers the movie selection as I turn the corner. "My sister said it was good," I shrug. "What time is it on showing tonight?"

Approaching a street light, it turns red before I quickly glance at her phone screen. A chart of screening times illuminates the display.

"Two times. 7 PM and 10 PM," she reads, and I nod. Watching as the light turns green, I press the gas. Essence continues to scroll through her phone a bit before speaking.

After a moment, she looks up at me with a mischievous smile.

"I'd say let's pick the 7 PM showing. I like it when it's crowded," she suggests. I let out a chuckle, intrigued by her reasoning.

"Why? Don't people recognize you more?" I ask, and turning her phone off, Essence shakes her head.

"Not really. People in crowded theaters are so focused on their own experiences that they hardly pay attention to others around them. *Especially* teenagers and couples. They're more concerned with having a *good* time, getting caught up in the atmosphere of the *movie*," she explains, with a hint of amusement in her voice. I find myself laughing at the image she paints.

"People actually—"

"*Yes*," Essence interrupts and a scoff of unbelief escapes her mouth as she speaks. "And it's disgusting. I used to work at a movie theater down in Chicago," she pauses. "You won't believe the *shit* you'd see with a UV light."

Essence gives a false gag at the closing of her sentence, and I can't help but laugh as I imagine a teenage Essence cleaning up behind a large group of people.

"You actually worked at a movie theater?" I ask, my tone full of disbelief. "Uh, yeah," Essence scoffs.

"It was one of my first jobs. Why? You can't believe *the* Essence Miller *actually* worked?"

I laugh at her comment before shaking my head.

"Nah. Just can't see you working at a *theater*, of all places." Essence rolls her eyes playfully before responding.

"Where do you think I learned how to give those wack ass smiles?"

As if on cue, she flashes a perfectly rehearsed fake smile, causing us both to burst into laughter.

My eyes scan the street we're on, people walking along the sidewalk, and busy restaurants along the side.

"As long as we stop someplace to get the snacks first," I say before pausing, which causes Essence to laugh yet again. "I'm cool."

"You brought a tote bag in that case, right?" Essence asks, her eyes sparkling with mischief. I scoff playfully, rolling my eyes. "Uh, 'did I bring a tote bag?' Of course, I brought a damn tote bag," I respond, unable to hide my amusement.

Essence rolls her eyes, but a smile tugs at the corners of her lips, a silent acknowledgment of our shared quirks and traditions.

"7 PM's good?"

"7 PM's good," I recite, and Essence nods before speedily typing away at her screen. The screen then changes to a confirmation before she turns it off and tucks it away.

"Well then," Essence pauses. Essence lifts her sun visor, glancing at the mirror before adjusting her ponytail slightly.

"What's the plan for now?"

❤ ❤❤❤ ❤

"Where are we?"

Essence sits up from lying against the window, her eyes wandering around the world around us. I smile mischievously, enjoying the suspense.

"It's a surprise," I reply, my voice filled with a hint of mystery. She lets go of a tired laugh before exhaling.

Scanning the unfamiliar surroundings, Essence's exhaustion seems to dissipate, replaced by a sense of wonder.

We both step out of the car, the sound of crunching gravel beneath our feet filling the air. Essence slings her purse over her shoulder, her eyes narrowing as she takes a closer look at our surroundings. Recognition flashes across her face as realization dawns on her.

"We're at the aquarium?" she asks, a playful smile dancing on her lips. With a sly grin, I shrug.

Rolling her eyes playfully, she quickly snaps a picture of the aquarium building. After taking the photo, she adds a filter, finds music, and tags the location to the image before posting it to her story.

I scoff at the sight, and she quickly looks up from her screen before tucking the phone away.

"What?" she asks, and I shake my head.

"Nothing. You ready?" I respond, and hesitantly, she nods.

As we approach the ticket counter, I can see the excitement in Essence's eyes.

"Two tickets, please," I request. The staff member efficiently hands us the coveted tickets, and I swiftly insert my card into the card reader, eager to begin our escapade.

Handing Essence her wristband, I swiftly secure mine before glancing toward her, quickly finding myself amused as she struggles to put hers on. Suppressing a laugh, I watch as she rolls her eyes before joining in the laughter.

"You could help out, you know," she comments, and I chuckle in response, stepping forward to assist her.

Standing side by side, we take in the bustling scene around us. Families chatter excitedly, children dash around with boundless energy, and parents intermittently scold their little ones for their exuberance.

Couples and teenagers converse quietly or share hearty laughs, adding to the lively atmosphere.

Essence looks around the area, the scent of saltwater wafting through the air as she does so. Taking hold of her phone, she quickly captures another photo. "Essence," I call out, my voice tinged with a hint of frustration. She momentarily ignores me, her focus fixated on the digital world within her phone.

Finally, her attention is wrestled away, and she looks up at me with a mixture of curiosity and guilt.

"Do you *ever* stop posting?" I ask, unable to hide my exasperation. She nibbles on her lip, contemplating her response before reluctantly sliding her phone into her back pocket.

"Christopher set this schedule for me," she explains, her voice tinged with a touch of resignation.

"I have to post like 15 stories today."

I scoff at the mention of Christopher, something I haven't noticed I'd done until Essence pointed it out. "What?" I ask, confused.

"You. You sighed, scoffed, or whatever," she responds, and I exhale roughly.

"Fuck Christopher, okay? Ignore him. Don't do anything he wants to do, even if it's just for today," I say firmly.

Essence looks at me, her eyes searching for guidance.

"Ess, what do *you* want to do?"

essence

. . .

SHUTTING THE DOOR BEHIND ME, I feel a faint smile appear on my face as I watch Aaron's car pull off.

After spending two hours at the aquarium, Aaron suggested we just wander around the city, so we did. For the first time, I had a friend that I could just hang out with and relax with—other than Yasmyn.

I showed him places I used to visit all the time when I first moved down here, places that somehow held special places in my heart. The faded memory of the person I used to be before now.

Licking my lips, I kick my shoes off and place my bag onto the ground when I walk into the kitchen and find myself startled by Christopher's presence.

"What the *fuck*, Chris?" I exclaim, placing my hand on my chest.

He sits at the kitchen table, my laptop on the surface beside him. My breath quickens at his mischievous grin and can feel the smile that was on my face just seconds ago fade away as I slowly walk over before standing next to the chair across from him.

"What do you want now?" I groan, and Christopher lets out

an uneasy laugh before sitting back and flipping the laptop screen over toward me.

"I want you to *withdraw* your application," he responds.

The screen displays the terms following what happens if I take back my requisition—including that I wouldn't be able to apply again until next year.

Looking up at the screen, I watch as his expression morphs into one of satisfaction.

He thinks I've given in. I can tell that's what he thinks.

But I haven't.

Breathing in, I gather a bundle of false confidence. "If I don't?" I state, my eyes landing on his. Christopher's face changes, much as if he hadn't expected my response. He clears his throat before answering.

"I *end* the management contract," he says, his voice cold. His eyes exchange dominance, something that I've only grown to notice over the years. While I know his declaration should bring me ease, it seems to leave me feeling anything but that.

The current house I've lived in for the past five years is *owned* by Chris. When I first signed the contract, he stated that Zaara and I would only live in it for as long as we were under his management. And with that being told, all we' have to do is bring in enough to pay rent.

If he or I were to end the contract between us, *I'd* be kicked out. No warning, extensive time to pack or anything. A time and day to be out, and I'd have to oblige.

All because of that damn agreement.

A scheming smirk reappears on his face as he seems to notice my expression.

"Reconsidering?"

Clenching my jaw, I bite back a sly remark, knowing that whatever may come out will do nothing but cause the situation to become worse.

Sure, I've got enough money to get a house of my own, but that's for right now. Christopher could make up any financial exchanges if I leave, plus Lord knows where I'll end up with this new faith toward the culinary field.

Any education is a shitload of money, and without the consistent stream of income I've leaned on for years, I may as well be on a jagged edge.

Nibbling on my lip, I continue to think more about the situation, watching as Christopher becomes more and more impatient.

Then again, there's the past few years. The years of abuse, harassment, both sexual and physical. Years of nothing but pure pain. I've hidden it all, keeping no one else in mind but Christopher.

I swallow the knot that sits in my throat, and Christopher lets out an irritated cough.

"Essence, decide or else I do it *for* you," he states.

For a moment, he shifts in his seat, causing me to move a bit, unknowing of his upcoming move. The moment he notices, he lets out a little scoff, paired with a smirk. That smirk, the smirk that he's had for as long as I've known him, the smirk that only expresses the worst.

My eyes then dart between him, the laptop, and his hands.

Always his hands.

"I—" I stutter, and as the words exit my mouth, Chris raises an eyebrow, his finger swirling along the mouse pad as he waits.

I let out an uncomfortable chuckle, trying my hardest to ease the fear that sears through my veins.

Closing my eyes, I take a deep breath.

I can't see anything but the woman I used to be before this all. Before the bruises, the tears, and lies. I had a goal, and I was determined to reach that goal, yet I somehow trailed along another road on the way there.

Now that I'm here, I realize this is my break.

This is my way out.

My way back to who I used to be.

Opening my eyes, I watch Christopher slide the laptop over, a grin appearing on his face as he does so.

I chuckle, amused at his audacity. He must think I'm a fool.

Well, honestly, I *must* be since I'm still here.

Taking a deep breath, I prepare for his reaction as I speak.

"I'm not taking back my application."

Chris then stands, and I feel my body tense up as he does so.

My mind spirals, the memories of his hands on me flashing through my mind.

He nears me, his fists curling into separate balls. His eyes burn into mine, giving me that eerie feeling I've felt since the start of it all.

He's now not even a foot away from me, our gazes glued to one another.

Shaking his head, Christopher chuckles with frustration, muttering to himself under his breath before he speaks.

"I want your shit gone by *sunrise*."

Nervously, I nod. I keep my eyes on his hands as I go to grab my laptop. Gripping it tightly, I quicken my pace to walk into the hallway, in fear of what may do with my back turned. Maybe he'll grab my hair, push me, or pull me close.

Each thing being what he's done once before, and I know he wouldn't be afraid to try again.

The assaults, the tightened grips, the sexual harassment.

As I near the staircase, I can feel Christopher's angry gaze burning into my back. My heart races with fear, but I remain calm and composed. Reaching the staircase, I turn around to face Christopher one more time.

He still stands in the kitchen, his eyes fixated on me.

I can see the anger and resentment on his face, and for once— it doesn't scare me.

essence

· · ·

BOXES SIT IN THE BACKSEAT.

Dry-cleaning bags, purses, shoes, clothes, and more of my necessities sit scattered throughout. Bottles of vodka, tequila, wine, and cheap-ass brands of Hennessy sit in the passenger's seat beside me.

Sitting up from my lowered seat, I watch as the sun slowly sets, the shadow casting across the empty parking lot I've found myself in.

Blankets lay wadded across my lap, and a compacted pillow sits on my headrest. My phone sits in the cupholder, shut off completely for all I care.

Shut off from everything.

No messages, no calls, no emails, no notifications. Nothing.

And quite frankly, it feels amazing.

Amazing to somewhat have a connection with my older self. I mean, here I am, living in my car for all I know, back to square one. My funds have been lowered, not to a matter of diminishment, but enough to notice a difference.

Enough to know that I need help.

Enough to know that I can't do this on my own.

I need Christopher. I need his management, even with all the shit I go through. I need his publicity, his events and planning, and his consistency. Stuff I don't have.

Stuff I can't find.

Laying my head onto the steering wheel, I think back over the past two weeks.

The extermination and what lead up to it. The way I didn't go back. The way it felt so good. And of course, the way I've been living in my car since then.

Inhaling deeply, I close my eyes for a moment, my memory giving me a quick rehash of what happened that night going through my mind.

"Fuck!" I yell, hitting the wheel abruptly. My breath quickens, tears welling in my eyes as I try to think.

Looking around the parking lot, I can't help but feel a sense of hopelessness wash over me.

I had everything I needed. Everything. All for it to just be gone within seconds simply because of a foolish thought that some stranger put into my head.

Who did I think I was, giving that shit a try?

I know Christopher better than anyone. I knew how he would react if I even tried ever so slightly to delve on my own, yet I did. And here I am.

On my own.

I feel my breathing become shallow, and slight tears fall down my cheeks as I try to compose myself.

Within seconds, I break down. All the feelings I've been holding in for the past few years, everything, exit my body. All the times I'd been manipulated, coerced, hit, and touched.

Every little moment comes back into thought.

Wiping my face, I stumble over my phone.

Turning it on, it takes a moment before it connects to a nearby service tower, and the moment it does, my phone immediately blows up.

Notifications from Instagram, Twitter, Facebook, and

YouTube shoot down the display. Messages and missed calls align my screen. Multiple of them are from Aaron.

I read only the recent ones.

> Hey, I was wondering if you wanted to come over and watch Scary Movie 2 TN?

> Faith has a field trip upcoming. Mentioned she wanted you to come.

> You alright?

> Text me whenever.

His texts go from an array of excited news to depleted messages, and I quickly hesitate before sliding back toward the main screen.

Yasmyn, Renee, Zaara, and Maya are my other notifications. They all sit at the top of the arrangement, their latest messages being a mix of dates.

Reading a few of theirs at a time, I pull up Yasmyn's contact. Taking a glance at the time, I watch as it turns to 8.

Yasmyn's usually off getting drunk or high around this time; at least, knowing her character. Turning my phone off, I sigh roughly before tucking it between my thighs.

I stare blankly at the screen, my mind whirling with thoughts.

What do I even say? I've practically left him on delivered for the past two weeks. Why would he even want to hear shit back from me?

Nibbling on my bottom lip, my hands type away at the screen, faster than my mind can even comprehend.

The unsent words sit within the text bar, waiting for them to be passed along.

And without hesitation, I press send.

Could I stay with you for a bit?

I've never had alcohol problems.

Never been prone to drinking in the middle of the day, multiple times in a row without break, or even using it just to bury my sorrows away.

At least, I think.

But it's like everything hit me all at once. Christopher dumped me off, I've been kicked out, and I have no job, support system, or backup plan.

Everything hit and it hit *hard*.

And the only thing I've been finding easy the past couple of weeks was something as simple as picking up a bottle.

No matter the consequences, I can't help it.

All thoughts fade.

All emotions and feelings.

Everything that's happened floods out of my memory.

And damn it, it feels fucking amazing.

aaron

. . .

IT'S BEEN over ten hours since I sent a response.

Not a single word or even 'Read' from Essence.

Sighing roughly, I place my phone into my pocket before pulling into my job's parking lot, quickly greeting a crowd of workers.

Putting the car into park, I grab my jacket from the passenger's seat and slip it on before getting out.

A light grey Tesla sits unevenly parked, taking up almost six spots, as many people stand aside on their phones in irritancy.

"Shanice!" I call, and my partner turns around. Moving away from the car window, she pushes her coily hair aside before walking over.

"Hey, what's going on?" I ask.

"Came up here this morning to this damn car in my spot," she responds, frustration clear in her voice.

"Is a person inside?" I ask, peeking through the back window.

"Yeah. They're knocked out."

Nodding, I walk away before treading toward the driver's window, finding myself shocked as I spot a familiar mirror key chain.

"Essence?" I say without thinking, my breath fogging the glass.

Knocking on it, I quickly find myself stumbling to get her awake. "Fuck," I mutter. Pulling out my phone, I dial her number. Sure enough, her phone buzzes rhythmically in the cupholder.

"Shit," I say, turning my phone off. Shoving it back into my pocket, I hit the window a bit harder, careful not to break the glass.

"Essence!" I say louder, and I watch as movement occurs inside. Her head moves around, glancing at the small crowd of employees standing around, watching as she sits up. She looks groggy and disoriented, but slowly starts to come to reality.

Putting the car into the ignition, she pulls back before heading to a nearby empty spot. I follow behind as she parks, heading toward the passenger's side before opening the door and sitting inside.

"What the fuck?"

Essence inhales deeply before laying her head against the steering wheel.

"Essence, what happened back there? Why were you *here*?"

"I don't know," she murmurs. Her messy hair sits in a low bun as she moves her arm underneath her face. Looking around the car, I spot boxes, clothes, shoes, and purses tossed in the backseat. A few clothes sit on the ground beside my feet, along with multiple half-empty bottles of Vodka.

"Did you sleep here?" I ask, but Essence rolls over my concern.

"Did you see my message?" she asks.

"I did, and I responded," I reply, but quickly switch back to my question.

"Essence, did you *sleep* in here?"

She doesn't answer, instead, stares out of the front-facing window. Her eyes seem dimmed, lifeless, and bored.

Almost as if the Essence I'd known so far had just walked up and left.

"*Essence.*"

"Yes," she sighs exasperatedly.

"*Yes*, I slept in here. Hell, I *live* in here."

"Why? Did something happen?"

Looking at Essence, I watch her gaze head-on toward the distance.

"Essence, please."

"Because I have nowhere else to stay, *Aaron*. Christopher found out about the application, put me in a verbatim between him and my wannabe career, and I chose culinary. Chris fucking kicked me out, *Aaron*. So I'm here because I have nowhere else to go, *Aaron*. You happy?"

Her sentence had been broken up with the light cracks of her voice, continuously pushing through. I look at Essence, and I watch as her eyes go from the calming, warming, and welcoming woman that I met to someone unable to recall what's going on in their life.

Someone who'd had it all, just for it to be taken from their grasp within seconds.

"Okay, then," I say. We sit silently in the car, watching as more workers pass by. Essence continues to lie on the wheel, her eyes open as she stares on in the busy city.

A couple walks by, hand in hand, and I watch as she reverts her attention in a different direction.

"Aaron, I'm losing everything. I lost my home, my management," she pauses to take a deep breath, only for her face to express pure regret.

"*God*, I can only *imagine* the shit he's saying about me online."

Sitting up from the wheel, Essence leans over the middle console to reach for a nearby bottle. The weight of her troubles seems to hang heavy in the air.

With a slight tremor in her hand, she twists open the cap and takes a long, desperate gulp from the bottle.

But before she can reach for her phone, I intervene, gently but firmly stopping her from making another impulsive decision.

"Aaron."

I can see the pain etched on her face, the exhaustion in her eyes.

"Don't," I warn, and she lets out a heavy sigh.

Going to take another sip from the bottle, I hit that as well, watching as it pours into her lap, quickly causing her to sit up.

"What the *fuck*?" Essence exclaims, her anger mixed with confusion.

"I'm not going to sit here and watch you drown your life's sorrows over shit you can easily fix," I state, and she scoffs.

"Then don't. I never asked you to come and save me," Essence comments.

The bottle now sits in the cupholder, with hardly any liquid left to scour.

Laying her head back against the steering wheel, she sits slumped over the surface before breaking down.

The hair from her bun falls across her shoulders, and the sobs that escape her mouth are cries I'd never heard from anyone.

"Damn it," Essence mumbles, wiping her face with her hand. Reaching over the console, I pull Essence close, allowing her to lie against my shoulder. Another sob leaves her lips, and I can't do anything but hold her.

Hold her until it all fades.

Hold her until what she feels is gone.

Hold her until the pain goes away.

And really, I wouldn't mind.

No matter how long it takes.

aaron

. . .

THE MOMENT MALIA opens the door, I can see it on her face.

Essence stands beside me and hands her pockets as we stand. I clear my throat, which seems to snap Malia's thoughts back to reality. "Um, Essence," I introduce, my hand motioning to Ess. She waves before tucking her hand back into her pocket. Malia nods. Clearing my throat, I say, "Faith."

"Right, yeah, Faith," she stutters, moving out of the doorway.

Gracie's Corner plays on the TV, and Faith sits on the ground as she sings along. Markers sit around her, and sheets of drawn on paper sit scattered across the coffee table. Essence sits on the couch, her face clear, as she has no clue where to sit.

"Faith," I call, tapping her back. She turns around, and her expression brightens.

"Daddy!" she cheers, leaping up to hug me. I kiss her on the forehead as I cling her tightly.

Letting go, she bends over before grabbing her coloring sheet.

"Nana and I were drawing," she expresses, holding the page to my face.

Glancing over at Essence, she smiles, a glow appearing in her eyes I haven't noticed until now. My eyes dart back to the page, trying to piece something together from the wound-up scribbles.

"It's you, me, and Essence," Faith begins, her finger pointing toward each person.

With her identification, everything snaps together. "It's us at the skating rink," she continues. Essence wanders over, and Faith shows her the paper.

"Aw!" Ess exclaims. "Faith, I love it. It's beautiful."

"Thank you," Faith responds.

"Well," Malia says as she walks over, Faith's school bag and sleepover bag in hand. "We got her homework for the week done ahead of time, and she has an upcoming field trip that I paid for."

"Thank you so much, Malia," I respond, and she smiles. Essence grabs the sleepover bag before handing Faith her backpack.

"No problem. Aaron, I need to speak to you," Malia adds, her eyes sticking onto mine.

I nod, following as she leads me to the dining room.

Malia shuts the door behind her before sitting in a chair, her hand extending across as she offers one to me.

"No, thank you."

"Aaron, you're going to want to sit down for this."

"Malia, I'm fine," I insist, and I watch as she gives up. She pauses for a moment, then inhales before speaking.

"I sent in papers for full custody."

The words repeat in my head for a moment.

Full custody?

Glancing up at Malia, she stares at me with a mixture of concern and sympathy.

"Malia," I mumble, my mind continuing to process. Taking a deep breath, I try to compose myself before responding. "I don't understand," I say, my voice shaking.

"Why would you do that? I've been doing all I could to make sure she's fed, loved, bathed, and cared for."

Malia's expression softens as she leans forward in her seat. "I know you have, Aaron. And I'm not saying you're an inadequate father. I just want to make sure she's able to stay in a stable home."

"Malia, she *is* in a stable home. I keep the bills paid in time, I get her to school every day, I keep her fed, I make sure she's *loved*," I ramble. "Faith's fine in my hands. There's no need to get full custody. Just one more month of this, and it'll be over. If this is about that one time with the bills, I promise that'll never happen again. I get this big promotion—"

"Aaron, the only way we can settle this is in court. I'll hire a lawyer for you if you need," she interrupts.

My jaw clenches, and my mind thinks of what to say. "Malia, *please* email and say we haven't spoken about this. You're supposed to talk to me before you send in a petition like that."

"I'm not required to if I'm concerned about her safety."

"Her safety?" I repeat.

"Yes."

"Malia, please tell me what's going on with her safety. I don't spank her for discipline, let alone hit her. I feed her, have alarms in the house, am careful about people I let in the house—," I pause, and her eyebrows raise.

"You just met Essence. I've seen her in your posts, and Faith talks about her all the time. You brought a stranger you just met into your home?" I sigh.

"Okay, I get that. I slipped up, but she's no one to worry about."

"And not to mention her name all over the media. Have you seen what that man, Christopher, has been saying about her?" Malia's comment piques my attention, causing me to veer the conversation.

"Wait, wait, what's he saying?"

"Aaron, don't play dumb."

"I'm not, Malia. I swear I'm not. Just tell me what he's saying," I respond, and she sighs roughly. Malia seems to recollect her memory for a moment as she darts her eyes in the opposite direction.

"That she'd broken the contract for the sake of not getting her way. She's bad for business."

I bite back a snark at her comment as she continues.

"Which is why she shouldn't be around you, yet alone Faith."

Small fragments of what happened this evening flash through my mind.

The way Essence hadn't been able to even know what happened.

"She's not a threat at all, Malia. Trust me."

❤ ❤ ❤ ❤ ❤

After slipping Faith's bonnet on her head, I walk back toward the doorway, turn her light off, and shut the door.

Heading into the living room, Essence sits kicked back on the couch, somehow already in what seems to be her pajamas. She sits on the right side of the sofa, lying against the armrest as she scrolls through shows.

"When did you change clothes?" I ask, sitting down. Her feet lay against my side, and I notice her hesitation before slipping them behind me. I chuckle a bit at her decision. "Right when we got here. Wanted to get out of that damn bodysuit," she says, light laughter in the middle, and I laugh a bit as well. Leaning back, I make sure not to lie on her feet.

"What was that thing with Faith's grandmother about?" Essence asks. She stops scrolling, and I tense at her question.

"What was this morning about?" I snap, and Essence sighs before continuing to scroll.

She sits silently even so, as if she's thinking.

"The fucking contract was the *only* thing keeping me intact. The house was in it, my assets and values. And I swear the car was, too, but I kept that shit. Then Christopher demanded he take like, 25% of my current balance and 30% of my income *because* I ended it, or else he'd bring me to court. And we all know he'd win."

"Don't you have, like, a shitload of money?" I ask, and she scoffs.

"You can't rent or buy a place last minute like that," Essence sighs again.

"Even if you could, do you know how long it takes to get that shit under your name? Minimum, six weeks. I can't live in a car for six weeks, Aaron," she adds.

Nudging her shoulder, I give her a look. "You're not living in a car. You're living here," I say, and she shrugs. "And you will be until you can get back on your feet. Okay?"

Essence nibbles on her lip for a moment before nodding.

"Now tell me, what was that thing with Faith's grandmother about?"

"Nothing," I respond, switching positions. Giving me a face of attitude, Ess sits up, her legs now contracted against her chest as she leans toward me.

Placing the remote beside her, her attention reverts to me. I sit, my mind replaying the conversation, remembering the way Malia just seemed to not even bother listening to what I had to say.

What she'd said Christopher had been claiming the past couple of weeks. How much of an obvious lie they all are, *yet* he still gets listened to. I just don't understand. Why didn't she speak to me? Why didn't she just ask what was going on? If she had such concern for Faith's safety, why didn't she *ask*?

"Aaron," Essence repeats, and I snap back from my thoughts.

"She wants full custody," I mumble, and Essence freezes. "She what?"

"Malia applied for full custody and there's nothing I can fucking do about it," I add, my tone growing more and more tense.

The cushions shift a bit. Then I feel Essence's body against mine.

Looking away from the wall I'd been staring at, I turn to find Ess leaning on my shoulder, legs held between her arms.

For a moment, we sit in silence, my mind still reeling.

"I just don't understand why she would do that. Faith loves being with me, and I love *having* her with me," I say, frustration clear in my voice. Essence continues to sit, to sense the tension in the air, and I appreciate her silence.

"You'll figure it out. I know you will. Aaron, seeing the way you treat her, the way you try to give her the world, no matter what's going on," Essence pauses, sitting up.

"Malia's a fool if she thinks you're anything but a good father."

And for a moment, I almost tell her.

Almost tell her what he's been saying, and how far it's gotten.

But I don't.

I can't.

essence

. . .

"SURE, Aaron's cool and all, but don't get too comfortable," Yasmyn says, sitting down beside me.

Her couch sinks underneath her body, and her face expresses comfort as it does so. Handing me a wineglass, she takes a sip from hers.

"You can't stay there forever."

I roll my eyes.

"I'm not planning to," I say, turning to my side. My legs now lay underneath hers, which are crossed.

"I just need some time to get myself gathered. I applied to the school a few weeks ago. I'm just waiting for a response." Yas clicks her tongue before taking another sip.

"I'll search for a new place around here. That good with you?" I sarcastically say, and she clicks her tongue in satirical judgment.

It's been a couple of weeks since I moved in with Aaron and Faith.

We'd set some rules, a few basics. No bringing people home unannounced, keep your side of the room clean, keep it light with the noise, etc. Just a few ground rules to express boundaries.

"I'm just so proud of you," Yasmyn says with a growing smile. The glass meets my lips as I grin.

"I'm serious, Es. You can do what you've *always* wanted to. Go to culinary school, become a chef, or whatever," Yasmyn adds, and I chuckle.

"I guess so, yeah."

"There is no 'I guess', Essence. You can do you."

Nibbling on my lip, I hold back a smile.

"Plus, everything going on is a new beginning. And you know what a new beginning means?" Yasmyn says, her voice pitch getting higher.

"Oh god, Yas, no," I groan, already anticipating the direction the conversation is taking.

"Please? It wouldn't hurt to try," she adds. Pursing her lips and giving a fake puppy dog face, I groan before giving in.

"Fine."

"Yes! I've been waiting forever to say this," Yasmyn pauses, reaching for my phone before she continues, "Let's get you a Hinge profile set up."

I feel my eyebrows scrunch up as Yasmyn continues to go through my photos.

We've been scrolling through my album for about an hour now, searching for pictures that fit my profile.

"Are you serious?" I ask, trying to mask my slight eagerness. Yasmyn nods, a mischievous glint in her eye.

"Why not? It could be fun. And who knows, you might catch your ass a man who's worth your time," she teases, shoulder shrugging in my direction. Placing my glass beside hers, I roll my eyes.

I hear her coo, and I quickly lean toward the screen to find a full-body picture of me. It's from about two months ago, and I was wearing this silver sequin slip dress I had gotten for a launch party.

The straps were silver chains, and the fabric stopped around my middle thigh. I still have it, I just don't wear it much now.

"You look amazing in this picture, Essie. You still got this dress?" Yasmyn asks, and I nod.

"Wear it again. It looks amazing on you."

Her compliment makes me smile as she presses it and uploads it to my profile. A notification almost immediately pops up on the top of the screen. Something about someone matching with me.

"Yasmyn, we haven't even set anything up yet," I point out, and she just swats my hand away.

"Give the man a quick look!" she exclaims, patting my thigh as I annoyedly groan.

Pressing his profile, it loads up to a picture of a guy standing in the middle of a crowd, a little child on his hip, and another girl standing beside him. He's probably a light-ish shade of chestnut, his hair in two-strand twists. It fits him moderately well, and his clothes look nice.

"Name's Joshua. 29, doesn't live far from Central Park, and loves music," Yasmyn says, reciting his bio. Yasmyn presses accept before handing the phone to me, the screen illuminating the fact we'd matched, instantly leading me to the PMs.

JOSHUA KISYN | HEY!

"Text him back!" Yasmyn ushers.

Hesitantly, I do so.

ESSENCE MILLER | HI.

JOSHUA KISYN | HOW YOU DOING?

ESSENCE MILLER | I'M DOING ALRIGHT, HOW ABOUT YOU?

"'I'm doing alright'?" Yasmyn reads, and I shrug.

"What the fuck else am I supposed to say?"

"I don't know, something better than that, that's for sure," she says before standing.

"*God*, I need some wine."

❤❤❤❤❤

"What do you usually do for Halloween?"

Aaron looks up from his laptop screen, his eyes narrowing to mine as I stand in the doorway. Faith lies beside him, her little hands fiddling with the TV remote.

"Not much of anything. Why?" Aaron answers, his tone dismissive. Intrigued, I give him a sarcastic gasp before walking over and settling on my side of the bed.

As I reach for my phone and plug it in, I lean against the headboard. Faith crawls over and nestles on my lap, eliciting a smile from me. "You do nothing?" I press Aaron, bringing back the topic of Halloween.

He nods before continuing to type away at his keyboard. "Why?"

"Why what?" Aaron asks, and I nod.

"I mean, I did nothing when I was younger. It was a combination of choice and not feeling obligated to take part," Aaron explains, his fingers still dancing across the keyboard.

"Plus, there was always the pressure to come up with a creative costume and take part in all the events. It just didn't appeal to me, I guess."

I roll my eyes in response. "Halloween's overrated," he adds, almost nonchalantly. I shake my head in disbelief.

"No, you're wrong. Halloween is, and, *underrated*. Skipping a day where your kid can get unlimited candy is what's overrated."

Aaron laughs at my comment.

"I get candy from school on Halloween," Faith chimes, and I give Aaron a look.

"Oh come on. How's an entire *school* building replacing the glorious honor you're *meant* to give your daughter?" I joke, and he rolls his eyes.

"I just never was a fan. Especially of the matching costumes," he admits with a sigh.

Sitting up, I can't resist teasing him once again. Letting out a playful gasp, I cause Faith to roll off me, bursting into laughter.

"Oh my *god*, you're a hater," I retort, and his laughter only confirms my observation.

Shutting his laptop and sliding it aside, he stands.

"I'm not a *hater*," he defends himself, trying to maintain a serious expression. Raising an eyebrow, I can't help but give him a skeptical look.

"You're *not*?" I tease. A smile cracks on his face, despite his attempts to hide it.

"Nope," he states.

"Well, then," I pause. Grabbing the remote from Faith's grasp, I gather her attention before finishing my sentence.

"We're matching costumes this year."

Aaron raises an eyebrow at me, his eyes expressing muted excitement.

"Essence, Halloween's in a week. There's no way you'll remember that," he chuckles.

I smirk, a mischievous glint in my eye.

"Oh, I'll not only remember it, but I'll make sure it's a Halloween *to* remember," I reply.

"Just watch."

aaron

. . .

ESSENCE EXITS the bathroom dressed in a thigh length light green sequin dress, the straps silver chains.

Her hair's pinned in a low bun, face framed with silver diamond tassel earrings. "Where you going?" I ask, slipping off the bed. She smiles at me as she struggles to put on an earring backing.

"Going on a date," she says, and scrunch my eyebrows at her response.

"A date?" I repeat, and she chuckles with a nod. Walking toward the full-body mirror, she gives herself a quick look before walking back into the bathroom, and I follow.

"Who're you going with?" I ask, steady behind her.

Grabbing her mascara, Essence applies it as she gives me a scoff.

"Who's asking?"

"Me, I am. Who's the guy you're going with? Not that guy Lamar, right?"

"Nah," she mumbles, focusing on her mascara. "Yasmyn signed me up for Hinge last week, got me matched with a guy named Joshua, and now we're headed out for dinner," she shrugs. Standing straight, Essence turns toward me.

Popping me a smile, she adds, "Nothing big."

Waltzing back into the bedroom, she digs in her dresser drawer before pulling out a pair of stockings.

"Where at?"

"Why, does it matter to you?" she asks.

"I just wanna know where you're gonna be. What if the guy you're meeting with is a crazy serial killer?"

"Oh, come on," she scoffs, giving me a look. "What's the probability of that happening?" Essence asks, and I shrug.

"I don't know, but it's possible, Ess." She rolls her eyes at my sentence. After slipping the tights on, she stands up, grabs my arms, and holds me tightly before speaking. "Aaron, do you know how crazy you sound right now?"

"*I* sound crazy?" I bleat, and she rolls her eyes with a smile.

"If I didn't know better, I'd say you sound jealous, too," she teases before walking out of the room.

I scoff at her sentence before crossing my arms and following behind her. Now in the kitchen, Essence grabs her car keys from the wall hook. With her coat, scarf, and clutch in hand, she pauses a moment before facing me.

"I'm not jealous, Ess," I say, reacting to her comment from just seconds ago. Her eyebrows raise, and I watch as a smile snags at her lips.

"Essence."

"Okay, okay!" she exclaims, holding her arms to surrender. Retreating toward the front door, she lowers her arms.

"You're not jealous."

Hand now on the doorknob, Ess opens it a crack.

"I'll be back before midnight."

essence

. . .

I'VE BEEN SITTING at this table *alone*, for the past hour and a half.

Digging into my clutch, I check my phone for what feels like the thousandth time.

No messages.

Leaning against the table, I cross my arms before sighing. I can't believe I'm being stood up right now. All the conversation we've had, all the flirting, the apparent interest, all of it just for him to dodge out last minute?

Staring at the empty chair across from me, I hesitate before getting up. Maybe he's just running late. Maybe he got held up at work, or traffic got in the way. My phone buzzes against the table. This time, there's a text from him.

JOSHUA | SORRY, GOT HELD UP AT WORK. I KNOW
THIS IS A LONG SHOT, BUT DO YOU THINK WE
CAN STILL GO FOR DINNER TONIGHT?

Reading the message, I sigh before typing up a reply.

ESSENCE | STAYED HERE HOPING YOU'D COME
EARLIER.

JOSHUA | AGAIN, I'M SO SORRY. I WISH I'D SENT
YOU A MESSAGE WHEN I FIRST GOT DELAYED.

ESSENCE | HOW FAR ARE YOU?

JOSHUA | ABOUT 15 MINUTES.

Inhaling, I throw myself off guard by the message I send him.

ESSENCE | YOU'VE GOT 30 MINUTES, ONCE YOU
GET HERE, TO IMPRESS ME.

JOSHUA | BET. CHALLENGE ACCEPTED.

Before turning my phone off, I check the time.

10:57 PM

I lick my lips, unsure if even giving Josh a shot is even worth it.

Maybe it will, maybe it won't, but I'm willing to take the chance and find out.

❤ ❤ ❤ ❤ ❤

Someone clears their throat before sitting down. Looking up from my phone, I smile as I notice it's Joshua.

"Hey," I say.

"Hey," he responds. "I can't say sorry enough. I meant—"

"It's fine, don't worry about it," I interrupt, and Josh nods. The waitress walks over, notepad in hand.

"Hello, my name's Brianna and I'll be your server for today. What can I get you two to drink?"

I nibble at my bottom lip before answering.

"I'll take *another* Cranberry Martini," I comment, and Josh's eyes revert downward toward the menu.

"I guess I'll take the same," he stutters.

"Gotcha! I'll be right back with two Cranberry Martinis."

"So," Josh begins. "You apply for that position you were talking about?"

"No, not yet," I respond.

"Oh, okay."

The drinks come out as we sit silently.

"Alright, are we ready for our order?" Brianna asks, and I give a glance at Joshua before he nods.

"Yeah. I'd like the grilled steak, medium rare, with a side of mashed potatoes," I say, pointing toward the menu number. The waitress then smiles as she writes my order down.

"And for you?" she points toward Josh.

"Grilled Salmon with a Cobb salad, please."

Joshua and I spend almost the entire dinner talking.

From updates on my current public life to updates on his acting and pending films, we're doing pretty well. Everything has been just as they were on text. Our conversation, our compatibility, our interactions—It had all been the same.

"Are you and Christopher still talking?" Joshua asks, clearing the air.

Irritated, I roll my eyes.

"Oh my God," I say with an aggravated laugh. Josh gives me a look of confusion.

"I'm just wondering," he shrugs.

"Why? Tryna see if you could get a quick shot at him for something?" I snark, and I feel my eyes swell with tears as he sits.

"Oh my *God*," I repeat. Standing up, I grab my coat from my chair before reaching for my clutch.

"Essence, please," Joshua says, reaching for my arm.

"Let me fucking go," I say, snapping my arm away. "I can't

believe this shit," I mutter. Slipping my coat on, I reach into my wallet before grabbing cash and slamming it onto the table.

"No, *Joshua.* Christopher and I are *not* talking," I say. "And we *haven't* for *a month.*"

He sighs. "Frankly, it's none of your business anyway," I add with a steady voice. "I'm sorry. I was just wondering if you could put a quick word—"

"*Goodnight,* Joshua," I scoff.

"I'll text you tonight," Joshua adds.

Please don't.

I keep myself calm until I reach my car.

I open the car door, sit down, and take a few moments to gather myself before starting the engine.

What the fuck was I thinking?

Giving myself a chance this early in my situation? It's only been two months, two months. I should've known I was only bound to have an encounter like this.

While being and interacting with Chris, I gained a reputation for meeting with people and "recruiting" them for his upcoming productions or projects, and it seems like that aspect of my life might not disappear.

But for someone to get close to me, to know where I am emotionally and I stupidly give in, just for them to have been using me the whole time? It's fucking sick.

And it has me wondering:

Who else could do the same?

essence

. . .

"OKAY, when you said we'd be matching costumes, I had no clue that meant Faith was involved."

I laugh at Aaron's sentence as I fix Faith's afro puff. Securing a green ribbon around the base of the puff, I tighten it before perfecting the knot. As I gaze into the bathroom mirror in front of us, I see a radiant smile light up Faith's face.

A small yellow, glittery card stock tiara sits on the counter-top, something I'd handmade a couple of days ago for this costume. It's glued to a black headband, easy to blend in with Faith's natural hair.

"There you go," I say, finishing up her baby hairs. They're small and frame her face, pairing well with the overall result. A cheerful expression paints Faith's face as I place the tiara head-band onto her head.

"I'm really pretty," she says, and with a smile, I nod.

"You are."

Faith brushes out the smaller wrinkles on the upper part of her dress before stepping down from her stool. Now in the connected bathroom alone, I glance at myself in the mirror.

My hair's pulled back into a sleek ponytail, and I have on a creme-shade dress, similar to the one Tiana wore in *"The Princess in The Frog*", the scene where she imagines her restaurant. A white fur shawl sits across my shoulders, and I close off the outfit with a pair of white heels.

"Are you two ready?" Aaron yells, and once again, I laugh at his clear excitement. "Just wait a second!" I call. Turning away from the mirror, I watch as Faith pulls out her Tiana doll and holds it up at me, her eyes glowing.

"We're matching," she says, and I smile before nodding. "We are," I respond, and she places the doll back into its spot at the tea table.

Nibbling on my lip, I look toward the door and then back at Faith. With a smile on her face, she nods before reaching for my hand. Hesitantly, I grasp it, her small hand engulfed in mine. "You ready?" I whisper, and her eyes light up as she nods.

I then open the door a crack, just enough for her to peek through.

"Daddy, are you ready?" Faith asks.

A light bit of laughter comes from Aaron before he responds.

"Yup. Show my little princess."

She then widens the door, and I view as Aaron's face expresses adoration as Faith stands in the doorway. I stand a couple of feet away from her, taking a picture of the adorable moment before tossing it onto Faith's mattress.

"Oh my god," Aaron stutters. I smile at his reaction as Faith stands in the middle of us, dressed as a younger Tiana. Her two afro puffs, light green dress, black flats, and tiara bring the outfit together.

She then walks up to him and hugs his legs, and Aaron returns the interaction by crouching and hugging her.

"Essence dressed me as Princess Tiana!" she exclaims. Aaron laughs at her excitement. "I can see that, baby," he responds, kissing her forehead.

Faith moves to the side, allowing Aaron to gather a look at my costume. "Essence is Tiana, too," she announces. With a smile held back, I observe as Aaron's gaze moves from Faith to me, his eyes pausing on mine.

"Um, yeah," I stutter. My hand reaches to push back a strand of hair when I find myself disappointed to push away nothing.

"When she was singing '*Almost There.*'"

Aaron nods at my explanation before standing. "Hey, princess, I bought us some pumpkin buckets for trick or treating. They're in the kitchen on the counter," Aaron begins, and Faith smiles.

"Get them, okay? Ess and I will be in the kitchen in a second," he adds, and it doesn't take her long to race into the other room. I smile as she paces away, wandering toward Aaron.

Now standing beside him, I lean against the wall.

"You're a handsome Naveen," I comment.

"Thank you," he responds, covering his mouth as he attempts to hide a smile.

"You're a pretty Tiana."

His words evoke a smile from me, and I sense a slight warmth in my face as well. He laughs at my reaction for a moment before silence falls between us. I fiddle with the chain straps of the dress as Aaron's gaze fixates on mine.

Nibbling on my lip, we stand a bit longer. As we stand there, the awkward silence hangs in the air, but there's a certain sensation I seem to experience that I can't overlook. A distinct emotion that I can only articulate as resurfacing. And I can't help but sense a flutter in my stomach, wondering if he feels the same thing.

The same way.

My eyes then shift their focus toward the kitchen, observing as Faith dances around. I can't help but laugh at the sight, causing Aaron to glance over as well.

A smile displays on his face as he notices.

Stepping away from the wall, I stand upright. "Well, we shouldn't hold Faith back from free candy, now should we?"

As I walk toward the kitchen, Aaron follows.

"No," he chuckles, keeping an eye on Faith. She stands beside the fridge, an orange pumpkin bucket in hand as she offers the green one to Aaron. He chuckles and watches Faith as she stands beside the fridge, holding an orange pumpkin bucket in hand and offering the green one to Aaron.

"We shouldn't."

aaron

. . .

STREETLIGHTS ALIGN THE QUIET NEIGHBORHOOD, casting a warm glow throughout the street.

Laughter and chatter fill the air as groups of people dressed in different costumes stay scattered across the sidewalk. Teenagers mess with each other, while younger kids bounce around and smile with their parents, their small candy baskets scuffling around as they do so.

Essence walks alongside me, while Faith stays ahead, her small puffballs bouncing with each step she takes.

"Who's your favorite princess?" Faith asks Essence, and for a moment, Ess seems to think before giving her a response.

"If you asked me that when I was younger, I would've called out Belle," she pauses, and a smile comes across her face before continuing.

"But now that I'm older, I'm realizing that I resonate a lot more with Tiana."

A smile tugs at the corners of her lips, matching the excitement in her voice. "You know how much I love cooking, right?" Essence asks, and Faith nods.

"Well, Tiana's determination and passion for her dreams

resonated with me. She showed me that with hard work and unwavering dedication, dreams can come true. I want that for myself, too."

As we walk up to a large house, I watch the two walk up the driveway.

"And the restaurant she wanted so bad, she got it. With all the dedication and willingness she gave, she received her dream. That's what I want."

Watching as the two approach the front door, I can't help but smile at the sight as the door opens and they exclaim, 'Trick or treat!'

It's an adorable sight to see, not only from the matching costumes, but the energy that Essence seems to have as she says it. It's almost as if she's loosened up her exterior more than she does. Her smiles are more frequent and her laughter is never-ending.

Maybe it's for Faith, but either way, I like her this way. I want that smile on her face. It's beautiful.

The woman at the door then shuts it, and Essence and Faith head back down when my phone buzzes in my back pocket.

Looking down, a message from Malia pops on screen, causing my smile to falter.

Happy Halloween! Don't worry about drop-off on Thursday, I'll be picking her up.

The sound of heavy footsteps echoes, and I look back up from the screen to find Faith running down the rest of the driveway.

Turning the screen off, I shrug the message off with a laugh as Essence walks down. Faith now tucks to my side, showing off the candy that the homeowner has handed them.

"There's a lot of *Skittles,*" Faith states, and I laugh.

Glancing toward Essence, I raise an eyebrow, to which she

lifts her bucket as well—a pile of the small packets on top. "Must like Skittles," Essence chuckles, and I smile.

"Maybe," I shrug.

Faith the grabs my hand before reaching for Essences'. Her head looks down at my bucket as she does so, a subtle way of her doing a "candy check."

"Daddy, your bucket's empty," Faith states, and I click my tongue.

"I know, baby. I haven't gone to any of the doors with you because I wanted you to have fun," I respond, and she gives me a look. "What?"

"I want *you* to have fun, Daddy," Faith pouts. We now stand in the middle of the sidewalk, Faith's arms crossed as she throws a miniature tantrum over my lack of participation.

I exchange a look with Essence, and she gives me a quick shrug paired with a smile before I sigh.

"How can Daddy have fun?" I ask, and Faith snatches my hand before interlocking it with Essence.

"You and Essence can do the next house," she states, and I smile.

I take a quick glance at Ess, who now bites back a smile as well. Her eyes wander around the neighborhood, trying their hardest not to land on me.

I nudge her ankle with my foot and turn back toward Faith before she looks at me.

"Together?" I ask, and Faith nods.

"Together."

Faith stands at a spot of the driveway that Essence and I can keep an eye on, yet distant enough for us to have our own conversation.

"This is the last house for tonight," Essence says, her tone a bit saddened. I furrow my brow at her sentence, as watching her and Faith's laughter had been the highlight of my night. I'd be out here forever if I could, as long as I was keeping an eye and watching them.

Walking up the house's porch steps, I turn around to watch Faith from where we stand. She smiles before waving.

"It was fun," I state, a smile playing at my lips as Essence rings the doorbell.

She pauses in her tracks just before doing so, and I give her a look as she stands still.

"Ring the bell," I nudge, and I watch as she just shakes her head. "Knock?" I suggest, and once again, Ess shakes her head.

"I did this shit all the time growing up. It's your turn," she states. Admired by her thought, I smile.

"No, Ess, it's cool," I laugh. Rolling her eyes, she turns me around before walking off the porch and monitoring Faith. "I got her. Now turn around and knock on the door."

Holding back a smile, I ring the doorbell before turning back toward Essence and giving her an awkward smile. I reflect one back as well as I hear the hinges creak open.

A black woman with faux locs stands at the door, a confused look on her face as she greets us.

"My daughter wanted me to come up and knock," I say, and Essence points toward Faith as an expression of understanding washes across the woman's face.

"Oh," she laughs. Grabbing an orange bowl, she holds it out for me to reach in.

"Beautiful family. Is she your wife?" she asks, referencing to Essence. Turning around, I notice Essence hadn't seen, or heard, the question. For a moment, I hesitate before speaking.

"Oh, no, she's—," I laugh, unsure of what to say.

I stammer a bit before going mute and nodding, and once I do, a smile appears on the woman's face within seconds. "Beautiful, Beautiful."

I can't help but smile at her compliment.

Even though I know what I'd just agreed to was anything but true, it's something about the thought of it being true that has my mind on edge. What if it were true? And even if it isn't, do I even mind that she thinks it is?

"Thank you," I nod, and once again she smiles.

Nibbling on my lip, I shove my hands into my pockets.

"Goodnight, and Happy Halloween," I mutter.

"Happy Halloween to you, too. I love the matching costumes."

essence

. . .

"IT'S THEIR LOSS."

The words exit Yasmyn's mouth smoothly, and I let out a dim smile. "They missed out on an amazing chef," she comments, and sniffling, I roll my eyes.

This morning, I woke up to an email from the culinary tech I applied to a couple months ago, letting me know I was denied.

I was with Aaron when I'd gotten it, and the minute I read it, I broke down in tears.

I can't believe it.

The very first thing I do regarding my plan, and it failed. I managed to get declined into one of the top schools in New York.

My portfolio must've not been enough, or maybe I didn't do good dishes. I should've done ones people are more familiar with, rather than the generational ones. Some of them have recipes that aren't easy to catch on.

Or maybe I just don't have enough experience.

Fuck.

If it weren't for Christopher and his *stupid* behavior over the years, maybe I would've gotten in.

Or maybe I could've gotten in when I first moved down.

If I never met him.

Looking down at the screen, my eyes scan the display once again, somehow hoping that the words had changed.

They're words I've wanted to read for years, words I've hoped to see for years, yet find myself on the other side of the degree.

I don't know what to do.

I failed, I tried and I failed.

"You need to get your mind off of things. Let's go drink. Loosen up a little, you know? I promise it'll make you feel better," Yasmyn says. She nudges my shoulder in an attempt to get me to loosen up, and it seems to work a bit as the smile I didn't know I'd been holding quickly slips out. Sitting beside me, she grabs the box of Mike & Ikes before pouring a few into her mouth.

"Invite Aaron, too," she adds, and I bite back a smile.

"Fuck you," I say with a laugh, rolling my eyes as well. Yasmyn smiles, a teasing one that I haven't seen since high school.

She knows something I don't, and I've known her enough to recognize she won't tell me what it is.

"Anyways, have you gotten a response from that happy-ass woman?" Yasmyn asks, and I laugh a bit at her struggling reference.

"Carmela?" I fill in for her, and she rolls her eyes before nodding.

"Yeah, her."

Carmela's this wide known food blogger from Central.

She's recorded and listed more recipes than I could name, and I've tried practically all of them. She cooks for high listed celebrities, caters reputable parties, and is known for getting smaller chefs out there more.

Something I need more than anything.

Recently, she posted online about hiring an assistant chef for her program.

There's no schooling required, nor experience.

All that matters is the quality, your ability to cooperate, and willingness to be flexible. Perfect.

"Not yet," I mutter, and Yasmyn scoffs.

"Lame. She's dumb as hell to push your application to the side."

Her attempt to lighten up manages to work, as a smile appears onto my face.

Lying my head onto her shoulder, I attempt to steady my breathing before speaking. "I feel so fucking stupid, Yas," I mutter, and she sits up.

"Essence," she states, and looking up at her, I feel as my eyes begin watering.

"You are not stupid."

"I am."

"How?" Yasmyn pushes, and I sigh.

"I believed Chris when he showed up. I believed that he would help, that he would get me out there. And I believed him when he said he loved me," I say. My voice begins to weaken mid sentence, but clearing my throat quickly stops it.

"Even when it got bad, I stayed."

"That's not your fault, Essie," Yasmyn begins.

Moving me off her shoulder, I sit up as she faces me, her eyes searching mine.

"He took advantage of someone who was looking for who they were. That is not your fault. None of it was your fault," she pauses.

Yasmyn pulls me into a hug before continuing her sentence.

"Stop allowing your mind to tell you that it is. Because I'm telling you right now, Essence: It isn't your fault."

Standing in front of the mirror, I struggle to tie the straps of my dress.

"Aaron!" I call, and he quickly reciprocates.

"Hm?"

"Could you?" I ask, holding the straps up.

"Yeah, of course," he responds, walking over. As Aaron steps closer to me, I can feel the warmth of his breath on my neck. He carefully adjusts the straps, his fingers grazing my skin. I can't help but shiver at his touch. I look up at him through the reflection in the mirror and our eyes meet.

Taking a deep breath, I turn to face him. "Thank you," I say, smiling gratefully. Aaron meets my gaze and returns the smile, his eyes sparkling with admiration.

"You look beautiful," he says, his voice soft and sincere. I picked out a halter dress, "Thanks," I shyly respond.

"Well," he exhales, shaking off the tension between us.

"Are we meeting Yasmyn or picking her up?"

"Picking her up. She'll get wasted tonight, and I know that for sure," I respond, grabbing my purse. My phone buzzes against the counter, and I hesitate a moment before grabbing it.

> Get y'alls asses over here, Ess. I've been waiting for the past hour. I'll type in the address when you get here, just hurry TF up.

After a quick second, another text pops onto the screen.

> Derrion's bullying me.. HURRY TF UP!

The second message causes me to laugh before I put my phone into my purse.

Derrion is Yasmyn's twin brother, as the two share a place down in New Hyde. They've picked at each other for years, the constant sibling rivalry never ending.

I've always been surprised because they agreed to live together.

Looking up, I watch Aaron fix the collar of his shirt. His fingers mess with the fabric, careful to make sure it looks presentable.

"Ready?" I ask, grabbing a shawl.

He turns around from his reflection, a smile appearing on his face at the sight of me.

"What?" I ask, and as it still lingers, he shakes his head.

"Nothing. I'm ready. Are you?" He asks, and without speaking, I nod.

"Where's it at?"

"Yasmyn's gonna type in the address when we pick her up. It's this new place that she heard from a cousin or someone. Not sure where or what it is," I respond, and Aaron chuckles.

We walk toward the doorway when I ignite small talk.

"Anything new with Malia?" I ask, and his body language seems to tense up, causing me to regret asking.

I shouldn't have brought it up. It's too early to even mention Malia. She's prone to start shit, and she's not letting this case with Faith go.

Opening the front door, Aaron and I head down the staircase when he mutters a quick response.

"Nah."

Reaching the ground level, I look up at the starry sky, my eyes examining each constellation I find.

We don't speak until we reach the car.

Getting inside, I connect my phone to the radio.

"We've got about a ten-minute ride," I say, placing my purse onto the floor.

"Okay," he mutters, and I nod.

Licking my lips, I can't help but blame myself for his sudden silence. If only I hadn't mentioned Malia, maybe he wouldn't be closing himself off right now.

Taking a deep breath, I try my best to push all the negative feelings aside.

All I've got in plan for tonight is to have a nice time. Enjoy my night out with my friends, and even though I have nothing specific to celebrate, in my mind, I do.

I'm celebrating an accomplishment I've been waiting for *years* to reach.

The years that I was attached to Christopher—they're over.

Finally.

They're over.

aaron

. . .

ESSENCE MENTIONED something about Yasmyn being a turned-up person, but she could've had a better warning than that.

I watch as Yasmyn and Essence dance in the middle of the floor, a flask in Yasmyn's hand as she takes drunken sips. Turning back toward the bar, I ask for two shots of vodka, enough to at least keep me at least livened up for the night.

To be honest, the club has never been my scene. I mean, sure, I'll go, but I find myself here from my friend, Trae, pushing me out. Says I need to find someone to distract me from all my troubles or whatever.

But with Essence, hell, I'll come any day.

As I wait for my drinks, I look around the club, trying to get into the mood. The music is loud and the lights are flashing, casting a colorful glow on the crowd.

People are dancing and laughing, all having a good time. As I turn back around with my drinks in hand, I glimpse Essence in the room. Her smile is infectious and her energy is magnetic.

The club doesn't seem so bad. Maybe I can let loose and have a little fun. I mean, this *is* a celebration, after all.

"Lemon Lime Margarita, sent from the green dress to your

left," the bartender says, handing me a glass. Looking to my side, I spot the woman who talks with her friend before giving me a brief glance.

She has a darker tone than mine, dark brown hair, and wears a short sequin dress. Her friend beside her has a similar look, but with dyed ginger hair.

Taking a sip, I grab the glass before walking over and sitting on the empty stool beside her. The woman speaks almost immediately, starting with her name, Kami.

"Aaron," I greet. Leaning in a little closer, Kami flashes me a smile.

"Aaron," she repeats. Nibbling on her nail, she bites her lip a bit before continuing.

"I like your name."

"Thanks," I respond.

Taking another sip, I try to come up with something interesting to say. Kami watches me, her eyes locked on mine, waiting for my response.

"So, uh, what's your favorite holiday?" I ask, and her laughter fills the air before she responds.

"Well, that's a new one."

With a nonchalant shrug, I play with the stem of my glass.

Kami's smile widens, and she tucks a strand of hair behind her ear before answering. The way she does it reminds me a bit of Essence, who usually does it whenever nervous.

"Well, then," Kami pauses, her gaze becoming more intense, her eyes flickering between my lips and my eyes. "I guess I'd have to say Valentine's Day."

My eyebrows shoot up in surprise as I repeat, "Valentine's Day?"

Kami nods, her eyes still locked on mine.

"Why?" I ask.

"Because," Kami pauses, her voice softer now, "it's a day dedicated to love, and *love* is a beautiful thing."

She pulls me closer than her hands glide along my arms,

trailing toward my neck. Continuously locking on mine, her eyes make me feel a certain way as she continues.

With her delicate fingers, she traces the contour of my neck, sending tingles of anticipation through my body. The world fades away as the anticipation builds.

And then her lips find mine. They're tender, like a gentle caress against my own.

The warmth of her breath against my skin sends shivers down my spine, awakening every nerve ending in my body.

Kami then pulls back, leaving me wanting more than she darts her eyes toward the restroom. Standing up, she calls for her friend—who now sits on the other side of the bar—before motioning for her to watch her things.

The redhead nods in acknowledgment, her lips forming a slight smile as she engages discussion about the guy beside her.

I stand up as well, and it doesn't take long for Kami's fingers to grasp mine, pulling me directly to the bathrooms. And for a moment, I almost leave.

I *almost* do.

But as I peek a glance at Essence, I watch as the guy she speaks to seems to "discreetly" slip something into her drink.

Something I can only infer that leads to the worst.

essence

. . .

WAKING UP, I face Aaron.

His arm lay draped across my body, and a bag of water sits beside his face. Sitting up, my head throbs as I do so.

The room is hardly lit, and rubbing my eyes, and I reach over on the nightstand for my phone, just to be met with nothing.

Careful not to wake Aaron up, I slide off the mattress before standing, then wander into the kitchen.

My purse sits on the ground beside the front door, my things scrambled across the floor. My phone sits just barely inside the bag, and I curse under my breath as I pick up each thing.

Standing back up, I turn around and become startled by Aaron's sudden presence, causing a couple of items to fall right back out again.

"Shit," I stammer, and a sly grin appears on his face as he crouches to pick each thing up, then hands them back to me.

Absentmindedly, I stumble to put them in place.

"I thought you were asleep," I say, and Aaron shrugs. Walking toward the pantry, he then pulls out yet another plastic baggy before heading toward the fridge and filling it with ice.

He turns around as he does so.

"I was," he mutters.

His back faces me as he closes the bag before placing it on his face. "You okay?" I ask, and he nods. "Yeah. Just a nasty headache."

"You and me both," I exhale, and a chuckle escapes from Aaron before an exasperated groan comes from him as well.

Exhaling, I gather a better grip on the overflowing bag. Aaron's back continues to face me. Nibbling on my bottom lip, I stand for a moment, waiting for any other words from him, before wandering back toward the bedroom.

Staring at my reflection, my head throbs from the lights in the bathroom. I apply the last bit of foundation when Aaron walks in.

He looks toward the mirror, and as he does, I notice a large bruise placed onto his eye.

"Holy fuck," I mutter. Placing the beauty sponge down, I head toward him.

Grazing my hands across his face, he winces before lightly pushing me away.

"What happened? You okay?" I ask, and Aaron shrugs.

"No big deal," he mutters, walking toward his sink. Grabbing his toothbrush, he rinses it under the now-running water before adding toothpaste.

"Do you remember what happened?" I ask once again, but Aaron goes silent.

"Aaron," I state, and he sighs. "Please."

He takes a deep breath before speaking.

"Some guy spiked your drink."

Narrowing my eyes, I watch as he then brushes his teeth. He leans over the sink as he does so, his head weighed down.

"Wait, what?"

"Someone spiked my drink?" I repeat, my voice filled with disbelief. Aaron spits out the foam from his mouth and rinses his toothbrush. He looks up at me, his eyes reflecting a mix of concern and frustration.

"Yeah," he replies, his voice muffled. "I watched him slip something into your glass *mid-conversation*."

He continues brushing for a couple more seconds, allowing my mind to process what he'd said.

That would explain the blacking out at what felt like hardly into the night.

I thought it had been an over drinking that I didn't notice, or that inquiry to try something new, but my drink being *spiked*?

I struggle to form a coherent response.

"Did you…" I stammer, "did you try to stop him?" Aaron nods, his eyes avoiding mine in the reflection of the mirror.

"I did. I walked right over and punched him square in the eye," he says, rinsing off his toothbrush and placing it aside.

He points to his eye, a small smirk tugging at the corner of his lips.

"He got a good hit on me too, though. But after that, I couldn't find Yasmyn anywhere. I figured she must've left earlier or something, but I already decided it was time for us to head home. It didn't take long for you to pass out once we got here."

"Oh," I mutter, and he nods.

Crossing his arms, I watch as Aaron leans against the countertop.

"Has that happened to you before?" he asks, and I think for a moment before speaking.

Unwanted memories of the times Christopher's burning hands grazed across my skin come to mind, yet I push them away.

"Has what happened?" I ask, and Aaron sighs.

"The spiking. Has anyone spiked, or at least *tried* to spike your drink before?"

My mind things back to the many times I've bumped into some creep who's attempted to, but failed.

Any guy who tried to slip something came to find themselves with a face full of pepper spray, and I found myself within some lecture about how my dress was a signal that I was "asking for it."

It was back when I was with Christopher, and he made me bring him everywhere I went.

The only person who ever *successfully* drugged my drink was Chris.

Somehow, I've always thought that was worse.

"No," I stammer, and Aaron raises an eyebrow.

"Are you sure? You know you can tell me anything," he says, his voice becoming soft. My heart skips a beat as my mind recounts the many times I found myself pinned between Christopher and my bed.

His heavy breaths.

The marks left on my skin.

The demands he gave.

I always try to ignore, try to forget. But I can't.

I never can.

Gathering my composure, I give Aaron a reassuring nudge and force a fake smile.

"I know," I say, my words laced with feigned confidence.

"I promise."

aaron

. . .

MY MIND REHASHES everything from the night before.

The way the guy stumbled to lace her drink, and how defensive he'd become when I confronted him. How it didn't seem to take long for it to kick in, and how Essence passed out within seconds of laying in the backseat.

I tried to wake her up, but couldn't. She was breathing, and feeling her breath was the only thing that seemed to bring me ease.

Essence sits tucked on her side of the bed, her laptop pulled close to her.

She's in the fetal position and has her Airpods in as she sits. Wandering onto my side of the bed, I move the pillow wall before sitting closer to her, laying my head on her shoulder after I do so.

Essence pauses her music as she then takes an earbud out and speaks.

"How's your eye?" she asks, and sitting up, I turn a bit before shrugging.

"Still sore. Ice helped with the swelling," I respond, and she nods.

"Your vision? Can you see?"

"Yeah."

Essence then turns to face me before lifting my head, her eyes scanning the recent bruise. "We need to go to the doctor, Aaron," she says, and I scoff.

"The doctor? For a black eye?" I ask, and rolling her eyes, Essence nods.

"That dude could have fucked up your vision."

"Ess, I can see fine," I comment, and she gives me a look before sliding her laptop to the side and getting off of the bed.

"I can!"

"Well, still. It's better to be safe than sorry," Essence mutters, and I laugh. Taking her other earbud out, she places it on the nightstand beside her before stretching, and then shutting her laptop.

"We can go to the doctor's office, then stop someplace to eat after," she recommends. Walking toward the dresser, she digs around for a bit before pulling out a pair of dark green leggings.

"That okay with you?" Essence asks, and I lean back against the headboard.

Standing beside the dresser, she flaps out a few creases in the fabric before looking back at me, her eyes questioning my decision. I laugh a bit at her concern, as I find it a bit adorable.

"Fine," I state with a smile.

"Doctor's, then lunch."

A bright smile illuminates Essence's face at my answer, her reaction expressing excitement. She then shifts through the drawer a bit more, her hands grabbing onto an orange graphic tee.

"Got it," she beams, tossing it onto her arm.

"Give me about 15 minutes."

"Nothing too big, just a simple bruise."

I give a quick look to Essence, who sits on the armchair in the room's corner. Rolling her eyes, I watch as she also bites back a smile. "Maybe swap between an ice pack and warm compress every so often," the nurse states, and I nod.

"I could give you a cover if you'd like," she offers.

I glance at Essence for approval, and she nods. Holding back a smirk, I accept the cover. With a warm smile, the nurse exits the room, leaving me to slip off the exam table and put my shoes back on. I make my way towards Essence, who's now standing by the supply counter.

"I told you everything was alright," I say, unable to contain my satisfaction. Essence rolls her eyes, but there's a hint of relief in her expression.

"Well, it's still a good thing I dragged you to come, isn't it?" she says, a touch of smugness in her voice. I chuckle and nod in agreement.

"Yeah."

The nurse then walks back in, a white eye patch in hand.

"It doesn't have any magical healing powers, but it'll make you look like a cool pirate," she chuckles, and grabbing it from her, I laugh a bit.

"Thank you," I say, and she grins.

"No problem."

As I start to follow Essence towards the door, the nurse suddenly intervenes, gently pulling her aside. Curiosity peaks within me as I watch their interaction.

"Could I have a moment alone with Essence, please?" the nurse requests, her tone both polite and serious.

Essence's eyes wander toward mine, gradually filling with confusion and worry.

"Yeah, yeah," I stammer, and just like that, she nods before leading Essence into the hall, leaving me alone in the room.

· · ·

"What the *fuck*?"

Essence sits in front of me, her pointer finger playing with her rings.

"That's why she pulled me to the side."

I watch as Essence's eyes change, wearing an obscure expression. An expression I can't piece together aside from one word—Fear.

"And he did it more than once."

"Did which? The," I stammer, struggling to speak. I clear my throat, watching as Essence nibbles on her bottom lip. "The rape or the abuse?

She exhales before sitting for a moment, her eyes beginning to water as she does so.

"Both."

❤ ❤ ❤ ❤ ❤

"I'm not kicking her out."

Malia glares at me from over her glasses as she assembles a stack of files.

Faith lies on the couch beside her, and I sit across the coffee table, on a nearby armchair. "Then I'm not revoking the appeal," she retorts, and I give an exasperated laugh.

Rising from my seat, I snatch Faith's backpack from the chair next to me and sling it over my shoulder. I then walk toward where Faith lays, her eyes shut as she sleeps. Picking her up, Malia gives her a quick kiss on the forehead before I hold her close.

"The court date's December 6th," Malia states, flipping through a journal. I can't help but scoff at her audacity, licking my lips in anticipation of the argument to come.

"Malia, I promise you, this is the *last* thing you want to do."

Finally, she lifts her gaze from the journal, a mischievous smirk playing on her lips as she sets her pen down.

"Aaron, it shouldn't be hard to prove your willingness. If you had just kicked her out as I told you to, this could have been avoided," she states with a hint of challenge in her voice.

I can't help but laugh.

"*Fuck you.* I'm raising my daughter," I add, watching as Malia's eyes quickly change from the appearance of annoyance to hate.

My breathing quickens as I prepare myself for the sentence that lingers on my lips.

"And I'll be *damn* sure you won't see her again."

❥ ❥ ❥ ❥ ❥

I take a quick look at Faith from the overhead mirror.

Her head lays against the left side of her car seat as she continues to doze off. The sight causes me to smile before I continue to face forward. Rain slicks the streets, causing not only a wet road, but quite stupid drivers.

Having to come to an abrupt stop due to someone in front of me, I press the car horn before muttering under my breath, quickly stopping as my phone begins ringing through the cupholder. I press accept, finding myself greeted by Essence's uneasy voice.

"Hey, Ess, you okay?" I ask, turning the volume down a bit.

Her breath shakes before she responds.

"I can't breathe, Aaron," she says, and I quickly furrow my brow.

"What? What do you mean? Are you okay?" I feel as my patience with the traffic around me quickly fades, my mind only focused on Essence and what she says.

"I was," she pauses, trying to gather her breath, "I was

making something for dinner later tonight, and I just suddenly couldn't fucking breathe."

I disconnect my phone from the car's speakers before putting it up to my ear, keeping the conversation and situation away from Faith.

"What were you thinking about?" I ask.

Turning the corner, the landmarks around me signal my apartment is nearby.

"Um," she pauses, almost seeming to think. Her breath slows, not too much, but just enough for me to notice.

"At first it was the recipe. How much seasoning I was trying not to add. And what might piece the dish together."

I nod, having some kind of signal in my silence of my attention.

"But then I started thinking about what happened at the clinic today. How easily she'd noticed, how everything went, and all the questions."

Essence's breath speeds up once again, and I speak affirmably to calm her down. "It's okay. You're okay. You're safe, alright? I want you to know that."

As I speak, I can sense her calm down, her breathing becoming slower and more steady. The panic that had gripped her just moments ago begins to subside.

"You got this, I promise," I continue, my voice filled with unwavering support. "We're gonna get through this together, okay?"

Her response is a simple, yet powerful, "Okay," and I smile.

Turning the corner, I pull into my complex's parking lot.

"I'm pulling in, Ess," I say, and Essence goes silent.

"I'll see you when Faith and I get inside."

How did I not notice?

The signs were there all along, so obvious in hindsight. The way Essence has always flinched when I try to give her a high five, or hand her something when she's not paying attention. It wasn't noticeable, sure, but it still should've been so clear. So clear that she was hurting. And I didn't know.

And Christopher. How can someone even sleep at night, knowing they're hurting someone they're meant to be helping?

The way he would stifle her dreams, treating her like a pawn in his own game, it's sickening. It's like he took pleasure in inflicting pain on her when things didn't go *his* way.

I already didn't like him from the start, but knowing what I know now, I just want to fucking pummel him.

Hurt him until he begs for it to stop.

Hurt him the way he hurt Essence, but worse.

As I shift my attention back to the present, I feel Essence stir beside me, breaking me out of my thoughts. She must have woken up and settled back down. I turn to look at her, her peaceful face just inches away from mine.

She fell asleep not too long into the night, and I rubbed her back a bit until she drifted off.

I feel her small breaths against my face, giving me a feeling I haven't felt in ages.

As her hand rests beside mine, I can't help but intertwine my fingers with hers. Essence moves a bit before relaxing, her fingers wrapping more with mine.

And damn it, it feels so right.

essence

. . .

"ARE YOU OKAY?"

The nurse's words bring me to a halt as I give her a look of confusion.

"Um," I stutter, giving an awkward laugh. "Yeah, of course. Why?"

"This is a safe space."

"I know," I respond, and she nods. Pushing a strand of hair from her visionary view, she lowers her voice before speaking. "Do you experience physical abuse?"

I raise an eyebrow before she gestures toward my upper wrist, which is exposed because of my raised sleeve. There lays a darkened mark, a bruise that never seemed to leave from when Christopher would cling to me tightly.

I cover it with foundation, but I guess this morning I'd forgotten.

"Oh, no, it's nothing like that," I laugh, tossing on a smile. "I sometimes scratch my arm when I feel anxious. Those marks are from previous incidents, nothing serious. I'm working on it," I lie, my voice betraying my certainty.

She nods.

It's clear in her expression that she doesn't believe me, and just like that, I regret mentioning the doctor's office.

"Well, if it's okay with you, could I get a couple of minutes to check that mark out?"

Nibbling on my lip, I give a wavering nod, and she paints on a comforting smile. "It shouldn't take long, okay? Just a quick check-up here and there."

My eyes wander toward the exam room's window, where I spot Aaron pacing back and forth, a habit he does whenever he's nervous. My mind races with thoughts, unsure of how to respond to the offer.

If Aaron gets blamed, what happens then? What if they don't believe me when I say it's from Chris?

But then again, my mind replays the many times I've felt that same grip.

The grip that I can only explain as fear.

The grip that came from only *one* person—*Christopher*.

Looking back at the nurse's eyes, I give her a strengthened nod.

"Okay."

essence

. . .

I'VE CHECKED my email for what feels like the *thousandth* time today.

Even with the amount of times I've opened and closed the app, I've yet to find an answer from the application.

Maybe my skills aren't enough. Maybe she *wants* someone with experience, even though she says otherwise.

I mean, I've worked nowhere near food—professionally, at least—aside from two settings—The vegan place I waited and hosted at back during high school, and my abuela's restaurant down in Missouri.

Between fourteen and seventeen, I'd go down every summer and help bus tables, every so often helping in the kitchen where I could.

The summer before senior year was the last time I'd done that.

College stressed me out, and when I met Chris, he convinced me to drop out of the culinary specialty to work with him.

I regret that more than ever now.

As Faith runs into the bedroom with me, she holds a Cinderella doll in her left hand and smiles.

"I'm having a princess tea party. Do you want to join?" she

asks, and looking up from my laptop, I smile. Closing it shut, I grab the remote before putting the TV on pause.

"Yeah, of course," I respond, and she cheers before wandering back into her room, with me following behind.

A *Barbie* episode plays on her iPad, and it sits propped onto a pillow across from her small table. Dolls sit in separate chairs around the surface, small teacups in front of them.

A bowl of Cheez-Its sits in the center of the table, and the sight causes me to smile.

Faith sits in her seat before moving a doll out of the way, allowing a spot for me. She then hands me a silver tiara, which I then place on my head.

"You can be any princess, but Ariel, Rapunzel, and Cinderella are mine," Faith states, and I nod. "Okay, then," I chuckle. "I guess I'm Tiana."

A teapot sits in the center of the table beside the bowl. "I put water in the teapot instead of tea. I wanted orange juice, but I can't reach it in the fridge so I just got water," Faith informs, and laughing a bit, I nod.

"Hey, Tia." A familiar voice sounds from behind me, and I turn around to find Aaron standing in the doorway, a lit smile on his face. "Hi, Daddy!" Faith exclaims, rushing over to hug him.

"Essie and I are about to have a tea party. Can you play?" Walking into the room, I watch as Aaron's eyes linger on me for a moment before he responds.

"Not right now, princess."

"Aw, Daddy," Faith whines.

"I've got something to fill out right now. But I promise we'll do something tonight to make up for it, okay?"

Faith nods, and Aaron tosses a quick smile before turning around and walking off.

"Why does daddy call you Tia?" Faith asks, pouring water into my teacup. I hold back a smile as I answer.

"It's from when you and I dressed as Tiana for Halloween," I pause, taking a sip. Faith gives me a stern look before I poke my pinky finger out, causing her facial expression to fade.

I bite back a laugh as I swallow.

"I don't know why he still calls me Tia, though," I add, taking a Cheez-It. "Oh," Faith responds. She then lectures Ariel, who sits beside her, about manners before continuing to speak to me.

"Sorry about Ariel. She doesn't know how to be polite," Faith says, and with a smile, I nod at the sight.

"But you look like Princess Tiana to me," she adds, and my smile becomes larger.

"A lot."

Walking into the kitchen, I spot Aaron sitting at the table, papers scattered around him once again.

"Okay, what's all this?" I ask, wavering my hands over the many documents. He gathers them all into an organized pile before shoving them into a manila folder.

"Nothing, just filling somethin' out. How was the tea party?" he responds, throwing me off topic with the sudden question.

"It was nice. Cinderella had some drama with Rapunzel," I laugh, and Aaron rolls his eyes with a smile.

"Rapunzel stole Cinderella's shoes that Prince Charming gave her, so she took Pascal as payback," I add on, the silly scenario earning a laugh from him. "Anyway, how was work?"

"It was alright. Got a bonus," Aaron sighs, shifting positions. His hands reach for the folder before hesitating, instead just moving it aside.

"You got a response yet?"

"Aaron, you asked me this yesterday," I groan, sitting next to him.

"I know, just checking in. Wouldn't hurt to get a quick update, would it?" he asks sarcastically, and I roll my eyes.

"I haven't picked up my phone since last night. Lord knows

what's in my notifications," I mutter, watching his fingers fly across the keyboard.

"I'm sorry for what happened Thursday," I say, and Aaron sighs.

"Essence, stop saying sorry. You have nothing to be sorry for. None of anything that happened to you was your fault, and you need to quit telling yourself it was," he comments, and I nibble on the inner lining of my lips. Turning to me, his hand shuts the laptop before looking into my eyes.

"*Stop* telling yourself it was," he repeats.

"Because it *wasn't*, and it *isn't*."

❤ ❤ ❤ ❤ ❤

My phone buzzes against the mattress, and I grab it before being surprised by the name attached:

Mama.

"Hi, Mami!" I say, answering. Standing up, I walk around the bedroom, searching for things to do.

"Hola Bébé, Yasmyn me mando un mensaje en Facebook sobre tu trabajo nuevo!"

Of course.

"Yes, I got it, mama," I respond, now holding my phone against my ear with my shoulder. I've found some clothes in my dresser that need to be folded.

"Why didn't you text me?"

"Because I know how you and Daddy can get," I say, rolling my eyes.

"Essence, honey, tu papa y yo reaccionamos en esta manera por que te queremos mucho." I stifle a laugh a bit before responding.

"Okay, Mami," I say with a smile, and I can sense hers through the phone.

"Como estan las cosas por alla?" she asks.

I nibble on my cheek, as the conversations and questioning I'd found myself in at the clinic appear in my mind, yet again.

"Everything's good," I say, hoping I hadn't spoken too late. Knowing how she can get, she'll try her hardest to pry.

I hear a harsh exhale from the speaker.

"Estamos muy orgullosos de ti!"

I smile at her excitement. "Thank you, Mami," I say, tossing a folded t-shirt to the side.

"Oh, yo me acuerdo cuando tu me ayudavas en la cocina. You always had that stool that you stood on," Mom comments, the memory popping into my mind.

"You looked so adorable," she adds, and I smile once again. Finishing the wad of clothes, I walk toward the same dresser drawer before placing them inside.

"And look at you now. Working your way to open your own business," she coos.

We sit on the phone for a moment, and as usual, I feel comforted. Comforted by the way she always listens, by the way she talks, the way she fawns over sentiments, and the way she's always there for me when I need her.

"Mami," I call, breaking the silence.

"Yes, Mija?" she responds, attention perked.

"I think I have a case for you."

aaron

. . .

MAEKO SITS in front of me, her hands messing with the strands of ripped fabric from her jeans.

Her leg bounces up and down as she does so.

"So, what'd you want to tell me?" I ask, and Mae licks her lips before fixing her posture.

"Well," she stutters, popping her knuckles.

It's like we're in high school again, her nerves getting the best of her when she has bad news. Either that or an explanation of some shit that happened.

The TV plays a muted episode of *Shameless*, where an argument between the two characters Frank and Fiona display on screen. Essence had been watching it before Mae got here, and when Maeko did, Ess wandered into the bedroom.

Mae clears her throat before continuing to speak. "I've kind of liked you for a while, and I was wondering if you wanted to maybe go out for dinner sometime?"

Her words catch me off guard, causing my eyebrow to shoot up in surprise.

"Wait, you *like* like me?" I repeat, needing confirmation.

Mae then nods silently, her eyes filled with a mix of hope and uncertainty. "I mean, if you don't feel the same way, I understand 100%—"

"No, it's fine. It's okay, Mae," I interrupt with a chuckle.

Her eyes gleam at mine, waiting for a response to her question.

"Yeah," I nod, watching as a smile forms on Maeko's face.

"Really?" she asks excitedly, and yet again, I nod.

"Yeah. I'd love to go out for dinner," I add. Mae's bodily expressions make it clear of her excitement, despite her attempts to hide it.

"Okay, okay," she stammers, her voice filled with a mix of excitement and nervousness. Her fingers find their way to her lips as she seems to think.

"Would tonight be okay? I'm kind of jam-packed for the rest of the week," Maeko asks with a laugh, and with a smile, I nod.

She lets out a small sigh of relief and starts picking at her jeans.

"Okay, cool. Well, um," Maeko speaks, her voice gaining confidence as she stands up.

"I've got to head to work, but I'll text you everything else, okay?"

"Alright," I respond, standing as well.

Walking toward the front door, I open it for Mae as I then watch her exit, her eyes lingering on mine. "See you tonight," she says, breaking the silence with a slight smile.

"See you."

❥ ❥ ❥ ❥ ❥

The sound of sizzling oil fills the air as Essence pours batter into the hot pan.

Faith stands along the side, watching as Essence tosses the dough sticks around.

"Hey," I say, and Faith turns around before speaking.

"Hi! Essence and I made churros!" Faith exclaims, pointing toward the pan. Essence looks up, tossing me a smile.

"Faith wanted something sweet, so I pulled out a recipe my mom used when I was a kid," she says, and I smile.

"I see," I respond, leaning over the pan. A quick bead of oil pops out, causing me to jump as Faith giggles, and Essence laughs a bit, too.

"You guys have just been in here, making sugar sticks while I've been in the room?" I ask, sitting at the table. Essence thinks for a bit before responding.

"Um, yeah, pretty much," she shrugs, and I chuckle.

"Faith, get the sugar ready. This batch is ready to come out," Essence notes, and Faith nods. Stepping onto her stool, she grabs a sugar-filled plate before stepping down and placing it beside Ess. She then moves back toward her stool and moves it closer to the plate.

Essence then places 3 plain churros into the bowl, Faith's hand moving toward a nearby fork as she rolls it around.

"Get it covered," Ess points, and Faith nods. Essence then places an empty plate beside Faith, and Faith places the now-sugared churro onto it. Standing up, I reach to grab one, but Essence quickly smacks it.

"What was that for?"

"Wait until they're all done," she says, pointing are finger at me. A smirk sits on her face, and I cross my arms at her request.

"Not even one?" I tease, and she licks the sugar from her lips before laughing.

"Nope, not even one."

It takes about 10 more minutes for the full batch to be done.

"I think we might've gotten carried away," Essence says, and I laugh. A plate of 30 churros sits on the counter, Faith's small hand grabbing one before she takes a bite. Her face expresses clear satisfaction, and I grab one myself.

"Oh my god, Ess," I groan.

"What? Need more cinnamon? Is it too doughy?" she says, seeming to panic.

"These are so good," I comment, taking another bite.

"You and Faith did *amazing*," I muffledly add on, watching as Faith's face scrunches up with joy.

"I wish I made the cajeta de Celaya, but we kinda made this out of the blue," Essence says, adding laughter to the end of her sentence.

"What's cajeta de Celaya?" Faith asks, struggling to pronounce it.

"It's a thicker kind of caramel you can use with dulces, like churros. It kind of reminds me of chocolate," Ess answers, and Faith nods before grabbing another.

"Can we make these again?" Faith then asks, looking up at me. Cinnamon sits encrusted in her face, and I laugh before walking toward the paper towels and grabbing one.

"Of course, baby," I respond, wetting it up. Walking back over, I wipe Faith's face before tossing the damp towel into the trash.

"We can make them again next week," I add, and I watch as Essence's face enlightens with happiness.

My phone buzzes in my pocket, and I wipe the sugar off my hands. The screen displays a text from Mae, letting me know of the location of the restaurant.

"Whatchu smiling at?" Essence asks, leaning against the table's surface. I type up a reply to Mae before shutting my phone off and speaking.

"Oh, Mae planned a night out. Grabbing dinner and maybe checking out a new arcade," I respond, and Ess nods. She takes a bite from her churro before talking.

"So what time are you leaving?" she asks, and I think for a moment.

"I mean dinner's at 8, and it's 5:40 right now, so maybe around 7:30-ish?" I respond, and once again, Ess nods.

"Got it."

I take the last bite of my churro before wiping my hands again. "Yeah, so I should get ready now," I chuckle, and with a smile, Ess nods.

"Duh. Wouldn't want to head out *sugar*-coated, would you?" she jokes, and playfully, I scoff.

"Ha, ha," I chuckle, and Essence smiles.

Sitting up, she wipes Faith's face with her thumb before she grabs another churro.

"No, I would not."

Giving me a smile, Essence takes a bite from the coated dough before talking.

"Let me see you before you go." A smile appears on my face as I wander toward the bedroom. Turned to face her, stumble back a bit, causing her to laugh.

"Why?" I ask, and with a smile, Essence shrugs.

"I can't see you dressed nice?"

As I iron my black button up, Faith wanders into the bedroom.

As she tucks her head underneath my elbow, I see her small afro reflecting in the body mirror I have in front of me. Essence and her constant outfit checks prompted me to place the mirror there.

"Baby," I say with a chuckle, and placing the iron down, I look down at her as she looks up at me.

"You can't be right there when I'm doing this, I've told you before," I say, and Faith pouts for a moment before walking to the side.

She's wearing a light blue t-shirt paired with black pants, some cargos Essence bought for her a couple of weeks ago.

"Is Essence going to stay with us for Christmas?" Faith asks, her little eyes looking up at me.

I lift the shirt up to check for any wrinkles, and after realizing there are none, I respond to Faith's question.

"Maybe. I hope she does. Why?" Slipping my shirt off, I glide my right arm into the sleeve of the button up.

"Because," Faith says.

"Because why, princess?"

"Because she's fun and cool. She's really good at doing my hair, too," she adds, and I can't help but smile.

"Oh, really?" I ask, looking in the mirror. I fix a couple creases in the first before rolling up my sleeves and popping the collar.

"Yup!"

Faith now plays with a pair of Essence's heels, which causes me to laugh a bit. "Well, baby," I say, pulling her close. I plant a kiss on her forehead before continuing to speak.

"Daddy would like Essence to stay, too."

I fix the sleeves of my coat as I toss it on, my hands adjusting its appearance.

Essence wanders into the room, holding a carton of ice cream as she takes a bite from the spoon. I spritz a bit of cologne before she walks over, and I watch as her eyes seem to glow at the sight of me.

"You look," she pauses, gathering her words.

I chuckle a bit at her reaction before fixing my watch.

"Nice?" I say, finishing her sentence, and rolling her eyes. Essence shakes her head.

"No. No, I mean, you *do* look nice, but I mean—"

I laugh at Essence's nervous stammering for a moment before taking one last look at my reflection. My phone then buzzes against the mattress when I walk over, spotting a text from Maeko saying that she's ready for me to pick her up.

"What time do you think you'll be back?" Essence asks, looking up at me from her fiddling fingers. Slipping my phone into my back pocket, I shrug and reply, "Sure. I'd probably say around midnight, knowing how Mae can be."

Essence nods, her eyes showing a hint of jealousy that catches my attention. I decide to hold my tongue and just give her a slight smirk in response. "That way I can tell you how *horribly* the night went," I tease. She rolls her eyes and swats at me with a mock scowl.

"Don't flatter yourself. I just want to make sure you survive the night," she retorts, trying to hide the concern in her voice.

"Yeah, *sure.*"

❤ ❤ ❤ ❤ ❤

Maeko takes a sip from her wineglass before placing it down, then pushes a slip of hair away from her face. "How's the case going?" Mae asks, and taking a bite from my salmon, I think of a response.

"It's alright, I guess. Malia's being a real pain about the whole thing, even went and lawyered up," I inform her, frustration clear in my voice.

Mae lets out an exasperated sigh, shaking her head in disbelief. "I don't get why she didn't just come to you first to talk things out," she remarks, drawing nods of agreement from me.

"That's what I told her! If she was worried about Faith, she could've just come to me. I'm not exactly running a covert operation here," I add, waving my fork for emphasis. Mae nods in agreement, her expression mirroring my annoyance.

"And besides, Essence is just crashing with us until she gets back on her feet."

Mae's body seems to tense at the mention of Ess. Not enough for me to want to mention it, but enough for me to notice.

"So, how's the job hunt going?" I inquire, trying to shift the conversation to lighter topics. Mae rolls her eyes in response, a sarcastic grin playing on her lips.

"Oh, you know, *smooth* sailing," she replies with a hint of mock enthusiasm, eliciting a chuckle from me.

"What's going on?"

"Offices are fully booked with interviews. Clinics are over-staffed, and hospitals are too busy to respond to emails right now."

As she takes a harsh bite of her potatoes, I can't help but smirk at her frustration. "I mean, Thanksgiving is one of the busiest times of the year, from what I've heard," I comment, trying to offer some perspective. Maeko rolls her eyes again.

"Yeah, I guess."

"Just give it time, Mae. I promise you'll get a position. I know you."

Maeko's eyes meet mine, a hint of gratitude flickering in her gaze before she shyly brushes her bangs back and focuses on her plate.

There's a fleeting moment of connection between us, almost flirtatious, before I stammer. "And hey, you're an amazing assistant. They'd be lucky to have you," I compliment, causing her to stifle a laugh.

"Oh, really now?" she retorts, a hint of amusement in her voice.

"Yup," I smile, watching as she places her elbow against the table's surface before leaning into her palm.

"And how am I?" she says, raising an eyebrow, and I grin.

"You remember that one time Junior year?"

"Oh, god," she groans, and I laugh.

"When I slipped and broke my ankle."

"Yeah, yeah, I remember. You *slipped*," Mae says with a laugh.

"It's cause you were being a dumbass and slid across the gym floor."

"Jaxson bet me fifty bucks!" I exclaim, and crossing her arms, Mae rolls her eyes with a smile.

"You idiot, someone waxed it."

. . .

"I'll pay."

I scoff at Maeko's statement before grabbing the bill anyway. Opening the envelope, I quickly clutch my wallet before slipping out my card and placing it inside. The waitress doesn't take long to walk back over and collect it afterwards.

"Ess got into culinary tech," I say with a smile. Looking up from her purse, Mae forces one as well before speaking.

"She did?" she asks, and I nod. "I didn't know she was into cooking like that. I mean, I saw she catered often for launch parties and stuff on her Instagram, but I had no clue she'd want a genuine career out of it."

The server walks back over, handing the bill holder to me as I grab it and reach for my card. "Yeah. Been working on it for a while," I add. Standing up, I push my chair in as Mae does the same, giving me a look as she does so.

Maeko's the definition of "independent," and I realized that not too long after we'd met. Never wants a guy to do much for her, such as paying for dinner, yet when you do, she can't help but smile brightly. I know she silently appreciates it—even if she refuses to admit it.

"Well, that's cool."

Grabbing my coat, I slip it on before glancing at Mae, whose hand reaches out for mine. I smile a bit at the sight before holding on, then guiding us toward the exit.

Mae's heels echo through the parking garage.

Her hand still sits in mine as I let go to unlock the car. Opening her door, she rolls her eyes before getting inside, where I watch as an excited expression paints across her face, and I can't help but smile when I notice.

Now sitting in the drivers' seat, I put the car into ignition and begin to back up. Maeko connects her phone to the Bluetooth, and it doesn't take long before R&B begins playing lightly through the speakers.

"You should come over to my house for a bit," I offer.

Mae looks up from her phone before turning it off and slipping it into the cupholder. It sits face down as her eyes now peer at me. A nervous smile plays at her lips as she attempts to keep it cool.

"I should?"

"Yup," I say with a smile. "I want you to try these churros they made."

"They?" Mae stutters, and now pulling out of the compacted garage, I nod. The streetlamps along the street illuminate the busy road ahead with bare reflections of their images gliding against the sunroof.

"Yeah. Essence and Faith. They made them earlier today," I smile, my mind replaying the interaction through my mind. The smile that'd sat across Faith's face, and how happy Essence had been while they were making them.

Maeko sighs a bit roughly before reaching for her phone, beginning to type across the screen. Reaching for the volume knob, I turn the volume down to a faint amount before asking, "You good?"

"Yeah," she says lightly, yet her bodily expressions reflect that she's anything but good. "Promise?" I poke, and without looking up from the screen, Mae nods.

I then place my hand back onto the wheel, the music volume still hardly audible, and we drive silently.

❤ ❤ ❤ ❤ ❤

Pulling into Mae's driveway, I bring the car to a stop.

She fumbles with the seat belt, then reaches for the door handle. Before she can step out, I clear my throat to get her attention.

"You alright?" I ask, and silently, Maeko nods. "You sure?

You know you can tell me anything, Mae," I add, and thinking for a moment, she leans back into her seat. She then shuts the door, preventing the chilly air from getting inside as she speaks.

"You've only talked about Essence since we got in here."

I try to respond, but find myself interrupted by the raise of her hand.

"No, I mean like since we got in the *car*. No comment on the date at all. Nothing on the food, on the bookstore trip, or how I feel. If I want to do it another time; nothing."

"Oh," I say, and biting her bottom lip, Mae nods.

"Yeah. Just *her*."

Licking my lips, I bring myself to think of an explanation, but find myself unable to. "Aaron, if you like Essence, just *tell* me. It'll save me a shitload of heartbreak later."

"I—" I begin, and Mae raises a brow at my pause.

"Well?"

Once again, I'm unable to defend myself. Maeko nods before opening the door again.

"*Cool.*"

"No, Mae, I enjoyed the night, I just—"

Getting out of the car, she stands beside the open door before closing off the conversation.

"Night, Aaron. Text you tomorrow."

essence

. . .

"ESA MUJER no poder tomar el niña."

Mami takes a sip from her coffee cup before continuing to speak. Her fingers tap against the table's surface.

People's chattering voices fill the air, paired with the scent of ground coffee beans and pastries. Jazz plays through the speakers, and my left foot taps along to the beat. We've been sitting here for almost two hours, discussing the case on Malia.

I'd given Mama all the information she needed.

Now all I need is a confirmation.

"She shouldn't acquire full. You said there was a custodial deal already?"

Silently, I nod.

"Tres meses quedar, correcta?" she asks, and I nod once again. "She can't gain full. Unless he's aggressive."

"Mami, Aaron's not. He's not," I respond, and she inhales deeply before taking another sip.

"Please, Mami," I plead. Taking a hard swallow, I can't help but silently pray. Pray that she accepts. That if she does, we win.

I can feel the tension in the air as I wait for her response, hoping that she will agree. I take a deep breath, trying to remain calm and composed, but my heart is racing with anticipation. After what feels like an eternity, she nods slowly, a small smile playing on her lips.

"Parecer que un fácil caso. I'll take it."

❤ ❤ ❤ ❤ ❤

"Mami, this is Aaron."

Aaron reaches out to shake Mami's hand, and for a moment, she hesitates before doing so. That singular gesture seems to be enough to ease her, because a quick smile fades onto her face as they release.

"Aaron, this is mi mama," I add, and giving me a look, Aaron smiles.

"Nice to meet you, Mrs. Miller," he greets. Mami exchanges a knowing look with me, and I already know of the conversation we're bound to have later.

A conversation asking if he and I are more than it seems— and if I'd ever thought about it.

"Nice to meet you too, Aaron," she says with a smile.

"So I've cleaned out the bedroom. Freshly washed sheets, vacuumed floor, disinfected furniture and bathroom," Aaron lists, and a grin grows across Mami's face as he goes on.

"Essence will be on the air mattress, and I'll sleep on the couch."

"Your mom's a lawyer?"

Grabbing a manila folder, Aaron stacks a few files before sliding them aside. I laugh a bit at his tone before unfolding my comforter. "Yeah. She wins practically every case she gets," I say, and Aaron nods.

"Where's she flying in from?"

"Chicago," I respond. Laying onto the air mattress, I tuck my body underneath the blanket before propping myself up.

My eyes on Aaron, I watch as he tosses the folder onto the coffee table before walking over and laying beside me.

"You're from *Chicago*?" he asks, and with a smile, I nod.

"Born and raised."

"Wow," he mutters, and placing his hand underneath his head, Aaron continues. "I've never thought of leaving here even for a trip, yet you completely moved cities," he says, lightly chuckling as he does so.

"Wait, so you've never left here?" I ask, and he shakes his head no. I give a playful scoff before laying my head onto my pillow, then turning to face Aaron. "You're pathetic," I tease, and he chuckles.

"I mean, sure, I think about taking a break and heading somewhere every so often. But everything I'm familiar with is down here. I've only been here, and I know everything here. All the good spots."

I smile at his response a bit before laying onto his shoulder, when he then pulls me close. I feel his breath against my forehead now, causing butterflies to emerge from my stomach.

Aaron and I lay silent for a moment, my mind whirling with thoughts.

Thoughts I can't help but smile at, but shove aside.

"You look exactly like your mom."

Opening my eyes, I realize I'd almost dozed off. Aaron then gazes down at me, a faint smile playing on his lips at the sight of my tired expression.

"I used to hear that a lot growing up," I mumble. Shifting slightly, I nestle closer into Aaron's chest, feeling his warmth enveloping me as my eyelids gradually grow heavy.

"Ess?" he calls softly, but I'm already on the edge of sleep and don't respond. A soft chuckle escapes his lips as he seems to notice my drowsy state, finding amusement in my lack of attention.

"I'm here for you, Essence," Aaron pauses, taking a breath as he tries to gather his words.

"No matter what, Ess, I promise."

❥ ❥❥ ❥❥

The cool air of the sterile room sends shivers down my spine as I lay onto the examination bed. Placing my legs into the stirrups, the doctor immediately begins the exam.

"Ms. Miller?"

"Sorry, sorry," I mutter nervously, trying to lighten the tension.

"Could you repeat that? Sorry I wasn't listening."

"It's alright, no need to apologize."

The doctor's calm demeanor puts me slightly at ease.

"How often did these alleged assaults occur?"

Her question cuts through me, forcing memories of Christopher's altercation to float through my mind. The feeling of his hands burning against my skin, his overpowering grip leaving me helpless and trapped.

Every instance replayed in my head, a painful reminder of the control he had over me. I was at his will, no matter how hard I'd tried.

"Um," I hesitated, feeling a sense of dread creeping in.

Doctor Jones then moves her chair back, quickly patting the exam table in signal for me to sit up.

"Every so often," I finally respond, my voice barely above a whisper.

While I know the questions are supposed to provide closure, a sense of validation, but they only reopen old wounds.

"Occasionally. Not all the time."

Jones carefully places the cotton swab into a sterile plastic bag, sealing it shut with a definitive click before turning toward me, issuing me to stand up.

"Can you recall the last time it happened?" she asks, her voice gentle but insistent. Unwelcome memories flood back, rehashes of the dressing room flash through my mind.

"Just an estimate," she adds.

I draw in a deep breath, attempting to steady my nerves before offering a response.

"About four months ago."

Aaron's arm sits draped across my shoulder as we walk, my gaze zoned into the many rows of cars we pass.

"How was the consultation?" he asks.

Looking up from the crunchy gravel, I think for a moment before responding, "They're bringing him into the station Saturday for questioning."

"They are?" Aaron says, his tone surprised.

We approach the car before he unlocks the doors, yet we continue to stand still beside the trunk. "Yeah. Enough evidence to report it as an assault," I add, my tone bland.

I take a nervous swallow as I part from Aaron's side, and as he walks along the driver's side of the car, he gives me a worrying look. "You okay?" he asks, and without speaking, I nod.

My hands grasp onto the door handle before I open it.

"Just a bit," I pause, trying to form my thoughts.

The words sit scarcely on my tongue, unable to escape as I think.

"Scared."

"Scared?" Aaron repeats, and I nod.

Placing his arm onto the roof of the car, he stands for a moment, one leg propped on the inside.

"Of what?" He asks.

"Of shit becoming harsh on *me*."

"Why would that happen?"

"Because, Aaron," I respond lightly, and Aaron raises an eyebrow.

"Because?"

"Because that's the way this shit works. Nothing ever traces back to people like Chris. You hear me, Aaron? *Ever*."

aaron

. . .

"MA DECIDED to have Thanksgiving early this year," my younger sister, Aanya, informs. Looking over her glasses, she gives me a knowing look.

Her words carry a hint of mischief, with a familiar twinkle in her eye. "You know she's been on your case about getting a girlfriend," she adds, a mischievous smile playing on her lips.

I let out an exasperated sigh, flopping back on the couch as I throw a decorative pillow in her direction. Aanya catches it, returning the playful gesture with a swift toss back at me, a grin spreading across her face.

As she settles back onto the couch, Aanya then busies herself with her phone, her fingers tapping away at the screen.

"You gonna do anything about it?" she asks, a hint of amusement in her voice. I roll my eyes before giving her a response.

"About the girlfriend thing?"

Aanya shoots me a knowing look before nodding, her attention still fixed on the screen. "No shit," she scoffs, and I can't help but laugh.

"Well, I *tried* something with Mae," I admit, causing 'Nya to sit up, her curiosity very piqued.

"How was it?"

I can't help but laugh at her reaction before reaching for my phone on the coffee table and getting up. "Not great. Turns out, I went on and on about Essence."

A gasp escapes Aanya in response to my revelation.

"What?"

I chuckle at her surprise. She then gives me that same look from before, the look that signals her silent scheming, a look that she has ingrained in her since childhood.

"Oh, *no*," I sigh, anticipating trouble as I see Aanya rise from her seat, her phone falling onto the cushion.

"I'm not getting into this with you," I protest with a smile, heading towards the kitchen only to be hit in the back by a pillow. I spin around to face Aanya, irritation clear in my expression when she smiles.

"I have an idea."

❤ ❤ ❤ ❤ ❤

"My mom wants to make something for de Acción de Gracias."

Essence looks up from her phone before shoving it aside at the sight of me. A smile appears on her face as she slides over to the side. As I sit on the couch beside her, she lays her head down on my shoulder.

"For what?" I ask, and Ess chuckles before translating.

"Thanksgiving."

"Oh really?" I say with a grin, and Essence nods.

"Yup. Probably cookies or something," she adds.

"My mom's wanting to do it early this year," I respond, and Ess chuckles.

"Early? Like when?" Essence asks, and I recall the date for a moment before speaking.

"Around next Thursday."

Essence raises her eyebrow at my statement, which causes me

to laugh. "The actual holiday isn't even that far from then," she laughs, and I nod.

"I mean, sure, but she wanted to get everyone all together before my cousins leave," I add.

A couple of my family members flew in last week for one of cousin's college tours. Wanted to check out NYU, and they don't leave until next Saturday.

Mama found out and realized dinner could be early with them, so here we are, planning a Thanksgiving dinner a couple of days ahead.

With a gentle sway, she moves closer to me, resting her head on my chest.

I smile at the slight movement before tucking a few strands of hair behind her ear, causing her attention to revert from the screen toward me.

As our eyes meet, I sense a mix of emotions flickering across her face. Her gaze lingers on me, almost searching for something in my expression. I notice her fingers fidgeting with her phone case, a clear sign of nervousness.

Despite the tension in the air, a small smile tugs at the corners of her lips. Essence leans in, pulling me closer, and our lips meet.

The touch of her fingers on the back of my neck send a shiver down my spine, igniting a spark of desire within me. Pulling her closer, I savor the warmth of her embrace as our bodies press together.

She now sits in my lap, her arms wrapped around my neck as she leans back, and a rather satisfied smile sits on her face as she pushes a stray strand of hair.

As Essence's lips lingered on mine, I couldn't help but feel a surge of desire run through me. Her touch was electrifying, sending shivers down my spine. For a moment, it seems like it may turn into more.

Her hand grazes down my arm, but as quickly as it began, the moment dissipates, leaving behind a lingering sense of longing.

As she stands up, Essence tosses me a sly smirk before walking away from the couch and heading into the kitchen. Opening the fridge, she grabs a small cup of yogurt.

"Mami wants to hang out with us today," she pauses. Grabbing a spoon, she opens the plastic lid before licking it and placing it aside.

Looking up from the small cup, she gives me a small smile before placing the spoon inside.

"So get ready. We leave in a few minutes."

essence

. . .

MUSIC PLAYS OVER THE SPEAKERS.

Mami nestles into the salon chair, her presence commanding attention as she engages in conversation with the stylist. Aaron and I sit nearby, Faith perched in his lap, engrossed in a game on my phone. She plays that one popular app online, *Roblox*.

Her laughter rings out, breaking the soft hum of chatter in the salon. Catching her gaze, her bright expression meets mine as she smiles before glancing back down.

Aaron's eyes roam around the room before settling on me, his eyes holding memories of a shared intimacy from just a few hours ago.

The fire he ignited within me, the feel of his lips against mine, the playful banter that sparked between us—it was all unforgettable. When I teased him for a moment, I noticed how he looked when he realized I had.

His eyes expressed pleading, begging for me to kiss him again.

I can't help but feel a rush of desire, longing to feel his lips on mine once again, despite the public setting.

But the buzz of Mami's rapid-fire conversation brings me

crashing back to reality, the momentary escape fading as quickly as it had arrived.

"Hacer tú conocer cómo a bailar?"

Looking away from Aaron, I notice a slight smirk form on his face before he looks down at his phone.

"Qué?" I ask, and Mami sighs.

"*Dance*. Does he?"

Her repeated sentence and paired hand motions cause me to laugh a bit before I nod.

"Which way?" she adds, and I shrug. Giving a quick look at Aaron, he continues to stare away onto the screen, but I know he's silently trying to listen. Trying to decipher what he can from Mami and I.

"He has rhythm."

"Cómo buena?" Mami responds, and I can't help but laugh.

"Mami," I groan, and she rolls her eyes.

"Soy seria! Cómo buena es su ritmo?"

Licking my lips, I fail to hold back a smile before giving her a response. "He has good rhythm, Mami. Muy Buena," I say, and she smiles.

The hairdresser then turns her chair toward the mirror, allowing Mami to fluff up her hair a bit. She smiles brightly before motioning for the sheet to be slipped off.

Standing up, she then grabs her purse before tousling her hair a bit more and walking toward the front desk.

I then nudge Aaron and he snaps his head up.

Faith does the same before hopping off of his lap, then looking back down onto the phone screen. "What was that about?" he asks. We both stand up, and I laugh a bit at his wonder.

"Not much," I shrug, and he gives me a sarcastic look.

"I heard 'Buena,'" Aaron seems to smile a bit at himself before finishing his sentence.

"And I'm pretty sure that means good," he adds, and I laugh.

We now walk toward Mami, who chatters away in Spanish with the front desk lady.

Her bangles bump into each other with every hand movement she makes, causing me to smile.

"She was talking about dinner with your mom," I lie, and he nods. I mean, sure, the questioning about dancing isn't much to lie about, but Mami asking if Aaron could dance is like the *biggest* signal of us cooking, especially since I started my habit of doing so while in the kitchen from her.

It was something I've always done growing up—blasting old school salsa while cooking up a storm. The earliest I remember was when I was around 6, and I'd just learnt how to make my Abuela's family-known Empanadas.

Mami wandered around the kitchen, helping around with a few measurements and things. I'd always enjoyed cooking with her, but that day signaled the *true* beginning of my culinary dreams.

The start of *everything*.

We've been out all day.

I haven't gotten the chance to sit down aside from when we're in the car, and even then, it's only for shortened amounts of time. From hopping in and out of the car to browsing the aisles of different stores, there was a constant sense of movement and rush. And now, here we were, in a quaint family-owned shop that Mami had stumbled upon online.

She was on a mission to find a specific set of spices, and nothing was going to deter her from accomplishing that goal. Despite already visiting Kroger and Target earlier in the day, this small shop had piqued her interest, and she was determined to explore every nook and cranny in search of her desired items.

"Mija!" Mami's voice echos through the shelves, pulling my attention away from the array of fresh produce in front of me.

Aaron then chuckles, and checking to be sure Faith hadn't been looking, I flip him off.

With a resigned sigh, I abandon the bottle of wine I had been contemplating and made my way over to where Mami stood. Sure enough, she filled an entire cart with an assortment of spices, herbs, wines, snacks, and more. I couldn't help but shake my head in disbelief.

"You don't need all of this, Mami," I said, attempting to reach for the overloaded cart.

But she evades my grasp, insisting, "Si, I do."

"No."

"Essence, you don't know what I need," she adds with a sigh, and chuckling a bit, I cross my arms.

"Mija, what are you in the taste for tonight?" she asks, and I shrug.

"Essence."

"Mami, everything you make is good," I add, and with a smile, she nods.

"Lo sé," she grins, and I chuckle.

She then continues to browse the aisle of canned goods, her hands grasping onto a few items from time to time. Just as I walk away, Mami then clears her throat, the signal of her gathering my attention.

Turning back around, I raise an eyebrow.

"Yes?"

"Who is he to you?" she asks.

"Mami," I groan, and walking over, she hits me on the shoulder.

"I'm serious, Mija. Who is he? Is he a friend?" she asks once again.

As we make our way towards the counter, the familiar scent of spices and freshly baked goods fills the air of the small neighborhood grocery store. Colorful packages and cans line the aisles.

Mami and I unpack the small basket and place each item onto

the heightened surface. "Well?" she asks, and just before I can answer, Faith runs over and hugs my legs. Aaron's presence appears not too long after.

Mami gives me a look as I toss on a smirk and shrug.

The question she asked just moments ago now rings in my mind, leaving me to do nothing but continue questioning. Because really, who *is* Aaron?

Are we friends or are we something *more*?

essence

. . .

THE ROOM IS BRIGHTLY LIT, and it's paired by the strengthened scent of fresh sterilization.

A cup of lukewarm hot chocolate sits in front of me, along with a plate of stale oatmeal cookies. My lawyer, two officers, and a detective sit in here with me, and the two officers standing alongside the door as they chatter.

Printed copies of captured images, zoomed in, sit scattered across the surface as well, paired with an open laptop positioned in front of the detective.

They're pictures of me from Instagram, posts of which I'd failed to cover some bruises and scrapes. I would notice after posting, but no one else did. Not even Christopher. I prayed for someone to one day notice, and now that I'm here—I'm only speechless.

I'm sure I've been sitting here for the past three hours, yet it feels as I've been doing so for years. I fiddle with my rings for a moment before the detective, Joyce Payne, scrolls along the laptop before pressing something. She then turns the screen over to me.

There plays a video of Christopher and I conversing back with the director, Kiana. The quality is grainy, and the coloration is in nothing but black and white. You can just barely hear us speaking, but a few words throughout the conversation monitor through.

"So we've got seven shots we need to get. We're gonna get this dye onto your head, then you can get dressed. That alright?"

My breathing shallows as I recollect what happened not too long after. Christopher was always full of big talk, but when it came down to it, he occasionally followed through.

He was more of a barker than a biter, tossing in the intermittent snipe for good measure. The few other times he'd followed through, I can hardly remember it from how incoherent I had been.

He *always* made sure I couldn't remember.

Whether it had been a pill in my drink or the push of my limits, he made sure I could hardly recall.

Yet, I still remember the way his grip felt on my skin, the burning sensation that seemed to sear right through me. I remember how long I'd been in the shower those nights.

How hard I scrubbed. No matter how hard I tried, feeling of dirtiness he left behind, it never went away.

Watching the video now, it's like reliving a nightmare in fast forward.

Eliana slows down the footage, and I watch myself stumbling out, pushing my hair back and avoiding Christopher's gaze at all costs.

"Alright. Head on toward the hairdresser's area and she'll get you settled."

His voice exclaimed, and everyone agreed before the video then stopped, leaving it with a paused image of my stance toward the backdrop. Eliana then swivels the laptop back toward her, causing me to snap back from my remembering gaze.

"Essence," my lawyer, Rylee Barnes, calls out my name, breaking the silence in the room. I shift my gaze from my array of rings to meet her eyes, her expression a mix of concern and curiosity.

I give a nonchalant hum in response, trying to mask the turmoil of emotions swirling inside me.

My heart beats against my chest.

"Can you tell me what happened in that dressing room?"

❤ ❤ ❤ ❤ ❤

"Geez, turn your notifications off, Mija," Mami says.

The car's been silent ever since I'd gotten out of that suffocating room.

Aaron didn't speak, and neither did Mami. No questions about what we talked about, no mention of any updates—nothing.

I fiddle with the radio a bit before shifting in my seat, watching the passing people as we stop at a red light. I pop a quick glance at Aaron in the backseat from the rearview mirror. He averts his gaze downward at his phone screen.

He then looks up, causing me to snap back as he clears his throat before speaking.

"What's the plan for tonight?"

Mami, who has been lost in her own thoughts, replies with a puzzled, "Que?"

I stifle a laugh.

"I meant, do we have any plans for tonight? Or maybe dinner?" Aaron explains, and she nods.

She responds to him in Spanish, her words blurring together

from the speed at which she talks. Looking at the mirror, I take a peek at Aaron's face.

It holds a confused expression, and I can't help but laugh at it before nudging Mama's side.

"English, Mami," I insist, and she sighs.

"I'm planning on making dinner," she repeats.

"Do you need any help?" Aaron asks. I watch as Mami raises her eyebrow before glancing at him in the rearview. A dim smile appears on her face before she shakes her head.

"No," she responds, and turning toward my window, I bite back a smile as she continues on her sentence.

"How'd it go?"

There's the *grand* question.

We've been sitting in silence ever since the question about Aaron helping with dinner, and I've done nothing but pray that no one mentions the consultation.

As I sit up from the window, Mami gives me a quick glance from the corner of her eye, a clear sign of her wondering just the same.

"Um," I stutter. I nibble on my bottom lip for a moment before forming words.

"It was okay. They got some evidence, pictures from my Instagram."

"There were signs? On your page?"

I look at Aaron through the rearview once again, and his eyes burn into mine as he waits for my response.

"Yeah."

He pulls out his phone from his back pocket.

Mami sighs for a moment before turning the corner and putting the car into park. Looking around, I notice she'd pulled into the parking lot of an Office Depot.

Friskly, she unbuckles her seatbelt. "I'll be back, Mija. Lock the door," she instructs, and giving a dimmed smile, I nod.

The car door then shuts behind Mami as she exits, leaving Aaron and I alone—in silence.

essence

. . .

THE KITCHEN'S ABNORMALLY BUSY.

The sink is filled with dishes, the counter displays bottles of seasonings, and the table holds platters of food. Mami scrambles across the kitchen, her apron stained with flour, yolk, and other wipable ingredients.

Her hair's pinned up in a messy bun, and her glasses sit perched on her nose. Meanwhile, Aaron stands along the side, confused at his unmentioned assignment. Sitting on a nearby bar stool, I can't help but laugh a bit at the sight of his confusion.

"Mami," I laugh, and looking up from her cookbook, she glances at me. Raising an eyebrow, I revert my gaze toward Aaron, causing her to dry her dampened hands against the apron's fabric.

"Shit," she stammers, and I chuckle a bit more.

"Wrap up the food, Mijo," she instructs, and Aaron nods. Mami then turns her gaze towards me, conveying a silent message that I, too, should help with the task.

With a resigned sigh, I slide off the stool and make my way over to Aaron, who is now clutching a roll of aluminum foil.

"You get your cooking from your mom?"

Looking up from the tray of stuffing, I give Aaron a smirk. "Yeah, I guess you could say that," I respond, and he nods.

Licking my lips, I wrap up the silver tray before creasing the foil around the corners. "What time is dinner?" I ask. Aaron drops the roll of aluminum as he also covers his tray.

"Lord knows with my mom," he chuckles, and I smile. "But she set it for around 6. Now, with it being the *true* set time, that's something I'm not sure about."

The four trays of food now sit covered, the shiny foil reflecting from the overhead lights. Aaron and I now stand, watching as Mami paces through the small kitchen. I feel like I'm 12 once again, standing along the sideline as Mama cooks. I'd keep a notepad in hand for some recipes, ones I wanted to recreate, in case I came up with additional details I wanted to memorize.

The oven clock displays the time as it reads 3:45. We've been standing around, watching the delicate process of cooking, for almost two hours now—and that's not even how long Mami has been in here.

My phone buzzes in my back pocket, and pulling it out, a notification from Instagram sits displayed on my screen. Pressing it, it loads up a DM from Yasmyn, a post from a celebrity gossip page about Christopher and I's upcoming court case.

"*New York Producer Christopher Evans to Face Court Hearing Amidst Sexual Assault Allegations*," I read, and quickly, Aaron grabs my phone.

He scrolls across the screen for a moment before muttering under his breath, "What the fuck?"

"What? What're they saying?" I ask, and Aaron shuts the screen off before tucking it into his pocket.

"Bullshit. What they're saying is bullshit," he responds. His tone is bitter, and his face expresses nothing but frustration.

"Just ignore them, okay? Ignore all the press. They know nothing," Aaron states, his tone firm. "Don't touch your phone for the rest of the night, alright? Let's just worry about dinner. You showering first?"

I nibble on my lip for a moment before pushing a strand of my hair back. "Hop in. That way, if your mom finishes the food while you're in there, I can help her bring it over to my mom's place."

❤ ❤ ❤ ❤ ❤

"You want me to *pretend* to be your girlfriend?"

Aaron's eyebrow sits raised on his face as he waits for my response. I'd just gotten out of the shower when he laid down the news of a fake relationship.

"My mom's been pressing me for the past *four* years about bringing someone to dinner, and if I just brought you as a friend, it'd turn the small jabs at dinner into passive-aggressive texts every morning," he explains with a hint of desperation in his voice, and I can't help but chuckle at the predicament.

Standing in front of the mirror, towel wrapped around me, I work on my hair as Aaron leans against the counter, his gaze fixed on mine through the reflection.

"Just for tonight. Tonight and tonight only, you'd be my girlfriend."

I think for a moment as I inhale, a smile playing on my lips as he continues to wait. Grabbing a nearby hand towel, I wipe the hair lotion from my hands.

My heart thuds against my chest, signaling the hidden excitement at his offer.

"Sure," I say, biting back a smile.

Aaron's eyes almost light with excitement at my response.

"I'll be your girlfriend for the night," I add, and he grins.

"Thank you so much," Aaron exclaims, pulling me close for a hug.

For a moment, he holds me a little longer than a *friend* would.

Pulling back, Aaron's eyes lock onto mine as we now face each other. His hands rest in his pockets. "I mean it—thank you."

I smile at him.

"No problem. Besides, as long as your mom likes me, I'll be fine," I add, and he chuckles.

"Oh, I promise, Ess," he pauses, walking toward the doorway.

"She'll love you."

Shutting the door behind him, Aaron leaves me in the cluttered bathroom, alone, with my thoughts.

It's just one night, after all.

Who knows, maybe it could be fun *pretending* to be in a relationship for a few hours.

Right?

aaron

. . .

MAMA TOSSES me the hundredth smile for the night.

Essence and her mother walk around the kitchen, chaotically moving around platters and dishes to make opportunistic room for others. They speak in Spanish as they do so, a bit of laughter emerging from their conversation from time to time.

Mom nudges my hand as I place down the stack of paper plates.

"How long have you guys been together?" she asks, her eyebrow raised. I bite back a small bit of laughter at her peak of interest. She then fixes the cup of forks before reverting her attention towards me.

"Almost a year," I lie, and a bright smile appears across her face.

"So, since?"

"Since last December."

Every sentence does nothing but cause Mama's smile to grow larger. Leaning against the table, she crosses her arms. "And you didn't bring her to the Fourth because?" she asks, and with a smile, I roll my eyes.

"Ma, we were hardly together long enough for that," I chuckle, and she rolls her eyes back.

"A quick audio call of a hello would've been nice."

"Mama, you get to meet both her *and* her mom tonight," I groan, and she clicks her tongue.

"Oh hush, Aaron," Mama shrugs, and I laugh. "Go make sure the living room's clean. The littles are eating in there this year."

Placing the small stack of plates onto the table, I toss the plastic bag into the nearby bin.

"Yes, ma'am."

❤ ❤ ❤ ❤ ❤

Essence smooths the fabric of her dress.

Her thumb grazes across the skin of her fingers but comes to a pause as she realizes she'd forgotten her rings at home. Without hesitation, I grasp her hand and hold it tightly, rubbing my thumb along her fingers to calm her down.

It seems to work as her once-tightened grip loosens against my palm.

Family members of mine sit scattered around the living room, the kids sitting on the ground watching a movie. Mama sits on the couch across from us, laughing with Mrs. Miller, while Aanya sits on the ground as well.

Music plays from the kitchen, some familiar melodies from when I was younger. Grandma and Grandpa stand in the kitchen as well, fixing up the last details of the displayed look.

Nudging Essence's shoulder, I raise an eyebrow before speaking.

"You okay?" I ask, and she nods.

"Yeah, yeah. I don't know why I'm so nervous," she says, a nervous chuckle sprinkled throughout her sentence.

She lowers her voice before continuing, "I mean, this is all for tonight. I'm just your girlfriend for the *night*, but still."

I squeeze her hand for a moment before smiling. "It's something that just has me," Essence pauses. "Nervous."

"Is it me?" I ask, and her eyes meet mine.

"What?"

"Is it me? Am *I* making you nervous?"

She stammers for a moment before responding.

"No."

"Are you sure?" I say slyly, and hiding a smile, Essence rolls her eyes.

"I'm sure. You're not making me nervous."

"Do I *ever* make you nervous?" I ask, and Essence freezes. Her smile now threatens to come out, and I can't help but smile myself at the sight. Her fingers mess with mine, searching for a way to express her horribly hidden excitement.

"Well?" I add, and roughly, she sighs. "Do I?"

"Aaron, I'm not answering your silly—"

Essence's statement is cut short by her mother calling everyone to eat.

Standing up, Essence's fingers slip from mine. She now stands in front of me, facing forward as she tries to keep herself from turning toward me.

Leaning over her ear, I whisper—

"Saved by the bell."

aaron

. . .

MRS. MILLER and I have been sitting outside this courtroom for hours.

Malia and her lawyer sit across from us, their eyes peering over and giving us dirty looks. Mrs. Miller shuffles through her briefcase before pulling out a manila folder. "There isn't enough proof regarding negligence on your part of Faith's custody, Aaron," she states, and I nod.

"Unless there's clear evidence of abuse or absence, they don't grant full custody to the grandparents. Given that Sierra's out of the picture, it was granted to you and Malia as a split," she adds, and once again, I nod, trying to absorb all the legal jargon.

"Not a question."

"Sorry," I murmur, and she chuckles.

"Your bills are all paid, Faith is well-fed and in school, the media doesn't paint you as a neglectful parent, and you've got witnesses to vouch for you."

"Who?" I interrupt, and Mrs. Miller gives me a look.

"Got any friends who babysit?" she asks, and I nod. "There you go. Plus, there's Essence, who doesn't show any signs of abuse either. And I'm not just saying that because she's my daughter," she says, and I bite back a smile at the mention of her.

Mrs. Miller then glances toward Malia, who now gives a rather more defeated look than she's given the past few months. Maybe the realization is setting in.

"Is she sure she wants to bring this to court?" Mrs. Miller asks, and after giving a rough sigh, I nod.

"She wouldn't budge. Insisted on full custody, no matter how hard I tried to reason with her," I explain, frustration clear in my tone. Mrs. Miller lets out a disapproving scoff, unimpressed.

"Well, then, with the lack of evidence, reasoning, and presentation," Mrs. Miller begins to say, but the courtroom doors swing open and cut off her words. The security guards signal for us to rise as Malia takes a deep breath and enters the room, heading towards the plaintiff's side. I steal a last glance at her, a mix of worry and determination in my gaze.

"You should have full custody by the time we walk out those doors."

❤ ❤ ❤ ❤ ❤

The fluorescent lights hum overhead, casting a sterile glow on the polished wood of the courtroom. Across the aisle, Malia sits ramrod straight, a picture of composure in her tailored suit. Her lawyer, Sierra, questions me with things that only feel unnecessary to ask. Things that don't feel needed to press the case across. Yet when I exchange a glance with Mrs. Miller, she only gives me a look asking me to calm down.

"Mr. Anderson," Sierra snaps, her voice dripping with condescension, "You admit to the sudden appearance of online influence, Essence Miller?"

The draining question causes me to bite back a sigh before responding.

"Yes," I say, my jaw clenching. God, how long could Malia

hold on to such a small thing? "Essence is a friend of mine. She was in a tough situation, so I helped her out."

"And how long had you known Ms. Miller at the time?" I bite hard on my bottom lip as I glance at Selene, who ushers for me to respond.

"A couple of months."

Sierra nods for a moment before continuing.

"And how dangerous is this? Letting a woman you know live in the house, I mean. What happens if Essence weren't the woman you think she is?"

Her words bring me nothing but frustration, yet I'm urged to swallow them down.

"I've made sure she isn't a threat to Faith. Essence is a good person, your honor. She helps around the house when I'm unable to, makes sure I'm on top of things when I'm not, and she makes *both* of us happy—"

"Both of you? Or just you?"

Sierra's interruption causes me to become nothing but irritated, but I try my hardest to hold it in. Mrs. Miller, conscious of my clear frustration, then leans forward and whispers, "Don't rise to the bait."

These questions, comments, references. They're all so stupid. Ridiculous.

"What kind of question is that?" I ask, my voice tight. "Why would I have someone in my house that doesn't make my daughter happy?"

The judge, a stern woman with a silver bob, taps her gavel. "Mr. Mayers, please answer the question."

Taking a deep breath, I force myself to calm down. This isn't about winning the never-ending argument, it's about Faith. "Both of us. Essence makes *both* of us happy."

"Has the child explicitly expressed this sentiment?" she inquires, her words laced with skepticism.

"Yes, ma'am," I respond.

I glance at Malia, her expression as blank and unreadable as it had been when she first brought the claim up. Does she not remember when she first met Essence? How happy Faith had been when she'd seen her walk through the door? The drawing she made of the three of us roller skating?

A flicker of doubt sparks in my gut.

Maybe it is reckless.

Inviting a person I hardly know into my home, knowing my custody situation, maybe it *was* reckless. Maybe I shouldn't have been so quick to offer my place for her to stay. Essence *had* been drunk, after all. Maybe she has alcohol problems that could only arise from there.

But then again, why would she lie about everything? Why would she lie about her situation, about her life? About Christopher, her financial situation, and her social media presence. Her feelings—even the ones she refuses to confront.

Why would she *lie*?

"Your Honor," I state, my voice steady this time, "I believe in providing my daughter with a safe childhood. I wouldn't do anything to put her life in jeopardy."

Silence stretches through the courtroom, but then the judge speaks. "We'll continue this discussion after a short recess."

As the bailiff calls for a break, I meet Malia's gaze for a moment. A flicker of something, maybe the doubt that I'd noticed earlier, maybe something else entirely, passes through her eyes.

But just like that, just as soon as it'd arrived—it'd gone away.

The air in the courtroom crackles with tension.

Across the aisle, Malia fiddles with the silver bracelets that align her wrists. Her gaze let go of the tense glance she'd held so far, as Faith now stands on the witness stand.

My gaze darts between her and Malia, and I give Faith a

quick smile to give her ease. Her bright eyes were wide and nervous, flicking between me and the judge.

"Faith, honey," the judge began, her voice gentle, "your grandmother tells us you don't feel safe with daddy. Is that true?"

Faith gazes at me, her eyes begging me to hold her, and I want that more than ever. To hold her to me, and kiss her forehead. I'd do anything to get her away from this situation, keep her away from this pressure that no child should experience.

Faith hesitates, undurety clear in her expression.

"Nana says that Essence is only there to take Daddy from me. Like, to hurt me," she mumbles, audible. My breathing slows, almost stops, as I glance over toward Malia.

Her eyes avoid mine, as her nails now grip the armrest of the leather chair she sits in.

The judge leaned forward, her gaze softening further. "Has Essence ever hurt you, Faith? Like, ever?"

Silence stretched, thick and heavy. Faith's eyes darted to Malia, a simple expression for what to say next.

My breath hitched.

"No," Faith whispered, shaking her head. A hesitant smile peeks through her anxiety. "We always cook together, and she does my hair all the time. We also have dance parties whenever we cook!"

A ripple of suppressed laughter ran through the courtroom. Even the judge cracks a smile.

The judge continues, "Faith, your Nana also says that Daddy doesn't have a good home for you. Is that true?"

Faith's eyebrow furrowed in confusion. "But Daddy has a big TV and a cool computer," she said, her voice gaining confidence. "And we're gonna get a dog soon. A Yorkie named Cookie."

Another wave of chuckles rolls through the room. Shooting a look over at Malia, I watch as her once strong stoic look dissipates into one that looks worried. Her lawyer whispers into her ear for a moment before she speaks, words I'm unable to read her lips from.

"Faith," the judge then pressed, "does Nana ever tell you think that aren't quite true?"

Faith hesitates, then pushes through to speak. "Sometimes. She says that Daddy's going to leave me so he can have Essence, but I know that's not true, right Daddy?"

My heart aches for her, and my mind wants nothing more but to scream at Malia. For all the pain, all the frustration, and all the lies. Especially to Faith.

The judge takes a deep breath. "Faith, baby," she said, "sometimes grown-ups don't always tell the truth. But the most important thing is that you feel safe and loved. Do you feel safe and loved with your Daddy?"

Faith's eyes glow again, but this time with an unfamiliar emotion. A smile blooms on her face.

"Yes, your honor," she says, her voice clear and strong. "I love staying at Daddy's house."

The judge's smile widens.

The oak gavel echoes off the high courtroom ceiling. The judge's voice follows—

"…full custody to Mr. Mayers."

essence

. . .

I FOLD a tan long-sleeved shirt before tucking it inside the suitcase.

As I close the zipper, I keep it shut before sliding the luggage off the bed. Just then, Mami walks in from the bathroom, her overfilled hygiene bag in hand as she waddles over. "You need help?" I ask with a chuckle, but she quickly shakes her head.

"No," she mumbles.

Dumping each item onto the mattress, Mami organizes them into categories as best as she can for the small baggy she'd brought along. "Mami," I chuckle, watching as she places each item inside, determined to fit everything in.

With the last item snuggly in place, she manages to zip it shut before looking up at me, a mix of accomplishment and exhaustion on her face.

"What?" she asks, catching my amused expression. I just shake my head with a smile and grab another suitcase, pushing the two bags towards the door.

"What time is your flight?" I ask, and with her back turned to me, she shrugs.

Sighing, I roll my eyes and make my way out of the bedroom and into the kitchen. There, I find Aaron engrossed in his phone until he notices my presence. "You headed out?" he asks, to which I raise an eyebrow and gesture towards the bedroom, opting for silence.

A chuckle escapes Aaron as he straightens up from the counter and reaches for a suitcase. "Aaron, I've got this. You don't have to help," I stutter, but he grabs it anyway.

"I know I don't need to, but I want to, Ess," he says with a smile, walking towards the front door and holding it open for me. Unable to suppress a smile, I grab my coat from the rack and slip it on before stepping outside, with Aaron following behind.

"Are you not going to grab a jacket or something?" I ask, and Aaron shrugs.

"It's just below 25."

"And?" he retorts, and I roll my eyes before making my way down the staircase.

"What?" Aaron calls after me, his footsteps wandering not too far behind.

I can already feel the chill nipping at my skin, but Aaron just strolls along without a care in the world, like he's impervious to the weather.

It's both annoying and kind of impressive, I have to admit.

Pausing at the bottom of the staircase, I wait for Aaron to catch up. He then reaches me with a grin, unfazed by the dropping temperature.

"These are the last couple of bags?" he asks, his voice chipper. I chuckle at his question, shaking my head in disbelief.

"You're something else, man," I reply, and just before I turn in the other direction, he smiles.

"*Yes*, these are the last couple of bags."

"Mi vuelo es a la una," Mami says.

Looking up from my phone screen, I nod. I snap a picture of Mami packing before typing a semi-solid caption and uploading it to my story. I then shove my phone into my back pocket.

"Okay. Tu empacar a botana?" I ask, and placing her tote bag onto her shoulder, Mami smacks her tongue at me as a response before giving me a look, a bodily behavior that only causes me to smile.

"Por supuesto," she mutters, and I chuckle.

I rise from my seat and trail behind Mami as she saunters into the kitchen, with Aaron stationed at the same spot by the doorway where he had been standing since we finished loading the car an hour earlier.

Aaron looks up from his phone as I clear my throat, tucking it into his pocket upon recognizing my mother and me.

"You all set?" he asks, his voice betraying a hint of nervousness. Grabbing my coat, I give him a nod of confirmation.

"Oh, okay," he smiles. Sitting up from where he leaned, Aaron reaches out to Mami for a hug, which she accepts.

"It was nice meeting you, Mrs. Miller," Aaron says, and with a smile, Mami nods.

"It was nice meeting you too, Mijo. And the little princesa, as well. She's adorable," she adds, and Aaron grins.

Slipping on her coat, Mami hands me her purse. "I left the recipe for those tamales you liked, Aaron."

I glance up to the spot as Aaron nibbles on his lip, a clear signal of him holding back a smile. Mami might've ruined a surprise just now, and I can't help but smile at the possibility.

"There are no direct measurements," Mami states, a mischievous glint in her eye.

Aaron's eyebrows shoot up in disbelief. "None?" he questions, puzzled.

Mami chuckles, shaking her head. "None. I never use measurements. Ever. It's all about what you're doing. Identify and believe in what you're doing, confiar en tú mismo."

Aaron then exchanges a glance with me, concern in his eye before I nod.

"It's all in your corazón, Mijo. If the dish is coming from your heart, trust it."

As Mami's eyes then meet mine, she gives me a bright smile

before the words sink in as I realize—she's not just talking about the recipe.

❤ ❤❤❤❤

Mami takes a bite from her pancake before covering her mouth to speak.

"You said your flight leaves at one?" I ask, and taking the last sip from her cup, Mami nods. Grabbing my phone, I check the time. 11:30 AM.

We'd gotten here around 11, and I plan to make sure Mami's at her terminal by at least 12:30. With her plane leaving at one, I don't want her late to the seating at all—especially with the possibility of early boarding.

"We have to head to the seats soon," I say, and she waves me off. "*Aye*, Mija, calm down. Loosen up a bit. The plane doesn't leave until one," she says, and I roll my eyes.

"The terminal is across the airport."

"And?" she asks, her eyebrow raised.

"And it's better to get over there now to avoid having to rush through the crowd and make it right before departure," I respond, and she sighs.

Grabbing her napkin, Mami wipes her mouth before waving the waitress over and requesting the bill.

She then digs in her purse, pulling out her wallet before placing it onto the table's surface. Raising her eyebrows, Mami gives me a look before speaking.

"Feliz ahora?" she asks, her tone rather sarcastic, before I roll my eyes.

"Mami, let me pay the bill."

"No," she insists. She beats me to handing over the card as the waitress walks over, giving a rather bright smile as she walks off.

. . .

Mami and I walk alongside each other, the cart of suitcases being pushed in front of us.

The crowd has thinned out since just an hour ago, but I know it's only minutes before everyone gathers again. Mami slips her glasses onto her forehead as we approach her terminal, her eyes scanning the area for any available seating.

It doesn't take her long before spotting an area, though, and it's beside the windows, which I'm pretty appreciative of.

I unlock my phone to shoot Aaron a quick text before Mami speaks.

"Have they told you the set trial date yet?"

I don't press send when I look up from my screen. Looking at Mami, she combs her hair back, waiting for my response. Even though I knew the looming question was only bound to come, I still tried my hardest to push any thought of it behind.

Especially if it was from her.

But now that it's looming in the air, I have no choice but to face reality.

Clearing my throat, I shut my phone off before slipping it into my pocket, regardless of the unsent message. "No, not yet," I respond, and Mami nods.

"They *should* tell you at the next consultation."

Nibbling on the inner lining of my cheek, I nod.

"Okay," I mumble. We sit for a moment now as she snacks on a bag of peanuts. I can feel the hesitation of her unsaid words lingering in the air, sentences and statements that I know would only break my heart the moment they exit her lips.

Leaning against the armrest of the chair, I reach to check my phone when Mami speaks again.

"Why didn't you tell me, Mija?"

Something about her sentence, about her words and tone, only seem to send tears to my eyes. The way she sounds so hurt by my lack of communication. Looking at Mami, our glances meet when I notice her eyes watering.

It's something about seeing her cry that chips away at my heart the way nothing else ever could.

The way she sounds hopeless, hurt, distressed.

How close her tears are from falling, yet she holds them back, wiping her eyes every other second to prevent them from spilling.

"Essence," she calls, snapping me back to reality.

"Why didn't you tell me?"

I nibble on my bottom lip before speaking.

"It was never that big of a deal, Mami. Everything happened behind the scenes, it was okay, I was okay," I respond, and Mami shakes her head.

"No. Nothing was okay, Essence. Christopher did things to you that no one should experience."

My mind replays the dinner from just weeks ago, paired with a few previous ones. The way his hand seemed to burn every single time. Or the way his grip tightened every time he wanted me to respond a certain way.

"It was my fault."

The very moment those words exit my mouth, Mami's demeanor changes.

"Baby," she mutters, pulling me close. "Baby," she repeats. My head now lies on her chest, her fingers grazing through my hair.

"It was never your fault. Ever. Don't say that it was. It wasn't your fault for trying to get into a better place, it wasn't your fault for trying to stay safe, and it certainly wasn't your fault for his response to you leaving. You left for your own good, Mija. You did everything you knew was good for you at that moment, and I'm proud of you for that."

I wipe my face to realize I'd been crying, and I sit up before Mami digs in her purse for tissues. Mami hands me a sleeve, and I grab a piece before carefully wiping my face, making sure not to smudge any of the makeup that hasn't already been rinsed off.

"I'm here for you, Essence. I promise I am, and I always will be," Mami adds, and grimly, I smile. As leans in for another hug, the woman at the front of the terminal taps on the microphone before speaking.

"Plane 782 departure for Chicago, Illinois, boarding now."

Licking my lips, I feel my eyes swell with tears yet again before Mami stands up, causing me to do the same. Pulling me in for another hug, I hear her sniffle in my ear as she holds me for a moment, hesitate on whether to let me go.

Once she does, she gives me a kiss on the forehead before smiling.

"You know, Mija," she pauses, grabbing her tote bag. In signal that she has my attention, I raise my eyebrow.

"That boy you stay with seems to lighten up a bit whenever he sees you."

I laugh at Mami's comment before rolling my eyes. As I bend down to pick up a suitcase that had slipped off the cart, Mami's words linger in the air.

"I'm serious, Essence. No one smiles that much for just *anyone*."

I pause, nibbling on my bottom lip as I contemplate her words, a subtle smile tugging at the corners of my lips.

"And I wouldn't be surprised if I were to say the same about you," she adds, attempting to delve deeper into a topic that I'm not yet ready to dip into.

"Mami!" I exclaim, a mix of embarrassment and amusement coloring my tone, but she laughs in response.

"I'm just saying!" she says between laughs, and once again, I roll my eyes.

She begins walking toward the plane's boarding area as I speak. "Tell Papi I said hi, okay? I love you," I say, and she smiles.

"Te quiero, Mija."

aaron

. . .

ESSENCE STUMBLES as she glides onto the ice.

Faith laughs at her slight tumble, her small hands gripped onto the kiddy guide. "Hold my hand," I offer, but Essence shrugs me off.

"I can do it myself," she murmurs, her face directly down at her feet.

I scoff at her stubbornness for a moment before scuffling toward Faith. She holds tightly onto the small plastic bars, her eyes glued to her feet in an attempt to prevent herself from falling.

"Daddy," she calls, and placing my hand onto her back, I skate beside her.

"Yes, princess?" I respond, and Faith struggles to stop for a moment before slowly turning toward Essence, who continues to linger around the entrance of the rink, her hands tight on the railing.

"Is Essence going to come skate with us?" Faith asks, and a dim smile appears onto my face. We hadn't even gotten that far, yet Essences' lack of presence is enough to gather Faith's attention.

"Yeah, just give her a second," I exhale, trying to hold back a bit of laughter. Continuing to watch Ess, she stumbles just about every other second, wobbles as she manages to stand upward, places her hands back onto the railing, the the cycle repeats.

Over the past twenty minutes, she's gotten just about nowhere.

"Ess!" I call, and Essence looks up. Somehow, she manages to stand still.

"You okay?" I ask, and with a nervous smile, she nods. Turning Faith around, she laughs at the feeling as I begin pushing her toward Essence.

Her hands continue to grip the railing, and her eyes stay glued to the ground, just as much as Faith's had.

Making sure Faith stays along my side, I tap Ess's shoulder before raising an eyebrow—a silent request to help out. For a moment, she hesitates before shaking her head, but I ignore her stupid denial.

Because I know Essence. She knows damn well she needs help, yet she refuses to get it.

"Relax, Ess," I say, my breath leaving a clear vapor in the air. "Think of it like gliding, not walking on the moon."

Essence tugs at her scarf for a moment before tossing me an playful glare.

"Easy for you to say, Mr. Natural on ice," she remarks, and I can't help but chuckle. "Or maybe you're just a secret skating aficionado."

"Oh, really?" I counter, a faint smirk playing on my lips. Essence stammers for a moment before managing to speak.

"Yeah."

A smile appears onto my face as I let out my gloved hand. "Hold my hand. It'll help out with stability."

Ess then hesitates before cautiously slipping her hand into mine. "There you go," I smile, my tone much lighter, as if I'm instructing Faith on the skating lesson. "Now just lean forward a little, kinda like when we went roller skating," I add.

Quickly glancing over at Faith, a smile appears onto my face as she silently cheers.

Essence's body quivers slightly as she struggles to find her balance, but she manages to stand upright, a gleam of excitement shining in her eyes as she looks up at me.

"See? You're a natural!" I tease playfully, provoking a mock hit from her that nearly sends her toppling over. I quickly reach out to steady her, and as she lets out a burst of laughter, a genuine sound that has been absent for months, a sense of relief washes over me.

Because *God*, it sounds amazing.

❤ ❤ ❤ ❤ ❤

Faith dips her chicken tender in a glob of ketchup.

Looking up from my phone, I slide it aside before asking, "What do you guys want for Christmas?" Faith's eyes glow at my statement, and Essence's do too for a moment before dimming back down.

"You don't have to get me anything," she mutters under her breath.

Essence then takes a sip from her Iced Tea. Faith seems to finish her thoughts before giving me a response, "I want a new tea set."

Fixing my position, I smile at her. "Really?" Faith nods excitedly before nibbling on a french fry.

"Yup. A flower tea set." Essence smiles as well at Faith's statements before nudging her shoulder, exuding a bright demeanor.

"And you?"

Essence looks up at me before pointing toward herself, her eyebrows raised in a seemingly sarcastic concern.

"Me?" she humors, and rolling my eyes, I nod.

"Yeah. What do *you* want for Christmas?"

She nibbles on her bottom lip before biting down on it, almost as if it'd been in a way to hold back her response. "Nothing. You don't have to get me anything," she murmurs, and I scoff.

"*Bullshit.*"

"Daddy!" Faith exclaims, and digging in my pocket, I pull out my wallet before grasping a crisp dollar bill. Sliding it over to Faith, she smiles brightly before shoving it into her pants pocket.

"What do you want?"

"Aaron, you don't have to get me anything. I've got a load of brands who send me stuff every year. That's always more than enough," Essence responds. She then takes the last bite from her burger before wiping her mouth and sliding the now-empty plate aside.

"Holidays, Birthdays, Events," she lists, taking a quick moment as she takes another sip from her glass.

"Being an affiliate sponsor has me covered every time."

"But don't you ever want something a bit more," I pause, trying to think of the proper word. "Personal?"

Essence shrugs at my question before placing her elbow on the table and leaning into her palm. "I mean, they send things accustomed to me."

"No, I mean more meaningful. Something with value. Don't you want things more like that?"

Once again, Ess shrugs. "I don't mind either."

I sigh before giving her a playful look. "What?"

"You're not making this gift thing any easier, you know," I comment with a playful tone, and Essence laughs.

"Isn't gift-giving supposed to be a *surprise*?" she asks, her eyebrow raised in false curiosity.

"Yeah, and?"

"If I told you what I wanted then it wouldn't be very much of a surprise."

"Oh, so you *do* want something?" I tease, and with a smile, Essence rolls her eyes.

"Aaron," she laughs, and I raise my eyebrow.

"Essence," I say, and she scoffs.

"So you want something?" I repeat, and Essence sits silently.

As the waitress approaches with the check in hand, the conversation momentarily pauses. Both Essence and I reach for the bill, our hands meeting on the smooth surface of the table.

I manage to grab hold of it first, a smug expression crossing my face. Opening the check holder, I glance at the total before swiftly retrieving my card from my wallet.

"Ess, answer my question," I prompt, my tone tinged with amusement. Essence leans back, a thoughtful look on her face as she contemplates her response.

"Yes, I want something. But, but, *but*," she pauses, holding up a finger for emphasis.

"That's for you to figure out."

❤ ❤❤❤ ❤

Christmas music plays on a cycle throughout the mall.

It's packed out here, with families and couples rushing to get gifts. Faith's hand grasps tightly to mine, and Essence wanders ahead, somehow managing to stay within my view of the crowd. Finding a clothing store, Essence waves us inside.

It's more calm in here. Women stand around, sifting through the racks, as their husbands or sons sit in the lounge area. Essence messes with her hair a bit before pulling it up into a ponytail, her eyes glued on a tabletop mirror that sits directly in front of the entrance.

She then fixes a few blotches in her makeup before turning toward Faith and I.

"You ever shopped in the mall during the holiday season?"

she asks. Letting out a heavy sigh, I shake my head no. Honestly, I avoid the mall during the holiday season.

Ess raises her eyebrow before leaning against the table, where her hand rests on a stack of light blue children's sweaters.

"I try to avoid the crowds as much as possible," I explain, my voice laced with a hint of weariness. Essence, with her infectious grin, rolls her eyes in jest before flashing me a teasing smile.

"Boring. You don't have much fun around this time of year, do you, Scrooge?" she remarks playfully. I respond with a sarcastic scoff, to which she only grins wider, her eyes dancing mischievously.

"I do have fun," I retort, but Essence raises her brow skeptically, silently questioning my assertion.

"Yes, I do," I emphasize. She then sits up from the table she leaned on once before, her arms crossed along her chest as she does so.

Her eyes lock onto mine momentarily, sending unspoken words I can't quite describe. "Prove it," Essence challenges, and I fight back a nervous laugh.

"How?" I respond, and moving to the side, Essence shrugs. She then turns away from me and toward the many racks of clothes.

"You tell me."

I've been sitting on this couch for an hour and a half now.

Faith wanted to wander around the store with Essence, leaving me to lounge alone on the sidelines. Checking the time, I press the power button before standing up and slipping my phone into my back pocket.

My eyes scan the area as I spot Essence sifting through a rack of sweaters. Beside her stands Faith, who holds a stack of kids' sweaters and dresses. The sight causes me to smile for a moment before I walk over.

"Ess," I call, and quickly Essence looks up.

"Yeah?" she responds, pulling out a hanger. A black turtleneck sits on it, and Ess holds it up to her body before turning toward Faith, who gives her an excited grin and thumbs up.

Essence then turns toward me, her eyebrow raised as she silently requests for my thoughts.

"Well?" she asks, and quickly, I realize I'd been staring. My breath quickens for a moment before I stammer to give a response.

"It looks—" I pause, and nervously, Essence nibbles on her lip. My mind tries to think of words. Words that aren't repetitive.

Words that describe what I feel.

"I'd need to see you in it," I manage to say, and Essence smiles. "Are there dressing rooms?" she asks, glancing around. Faith walks a small distance before pointing in a certain direc-tion, to which Ess walks over and finds a dressing room hidden in plain sight.

"Give me like, a minute, alright?"

As Essence disappears into the dressing room, I can feel a wave of nervousness wash over me. I shouldn't feel this clammy over a sweater. A black sweater that she planned to pull out and hold anyway.

But the way she went to me.

The way she asked me if it looked nice, and how nervous she'd gotten when she waited for my response. It was cute, and it expressed more than she probably even meant.

Faith shows me the variety of sweaters that she and Ess chose. From brightly displayed colors to muted tones, they were all shades that fit her tone, and I'm sure Essence is more than excited to see her dressed in them soon.

"You and Essence picked some pretty ones, Princess," I say cheerfully, causing a bright smile to appear on Faith's face.

"Thank you!" she exclaims, and I give a smile back before standing.

"Aaron!"

Essence's sudden voice perks my attention as I turn around

to find nothing. "Ess? Where are you?" I ask, and laughter erupts from the dressing room as I hear the sound of a door's latch.

"Come in the doorway."

"It's the dressing room, Ess," I respond, and she scoffs.

"Aaron, do you want to see me in the turtleneck or not?" she sarcastically asks, and unable to hide a smile, I sigh.

"Okay, okay," I stammer. Walking into the doorway, I find myself greeted by Ess's presence as she stands directly in front of me.

A bright smile sits on her face as she gives a quick pose, flipping her hair behind her shoulder. She wears nothing but the turtleneck, which just barely reaches the middle of her thighs.

"The pants don't go with it," she chuckles nervously, and I bite back a smile.

My mind races with thoughts, paired with scenarios.

Scenarios of her lips on mine, her fingers grazing across my neck, and her heavy breath against my skin.

"Aaron," Essence's voice snaps me back to reality.

"How's it look?" she asks.

"It looks amazing. Black suits you," I respond, and she smiles brightly before gradually walking back toward the dressing stall.

"You were saying something before this," she states.

"I was?" I respond, and with a laugh, she nods.

"Yeah."

"Oh. Oh! I wanted to let you know that I'm gonna wander around a bit. Is it okay if Faith stays with you?" I ask, and it doesn't take long before excitement spreads across her face.

"Absolutely."

essence

. . .

THE AIR'S cold and bitter.

After a multitude of visits to the station, I have yet to get used to the looming feeling that casts throughout the room every time I enter. Between the stale cookies and frigid temperature, they're not very good at trying to divert the feeling, either.

My lawyer, paired with Detective Carter and an officer, sits in front of me.

Quantifiable evidence and the negative rape kit lay sprawled across the table. Carter scribbles on his notepad before Rylee clears her throat and speaks.

"I've gathered outside statements regarding the case and pairing this with all the evidence. We're more than likely to have a good trial."

Silently, I nod.

"But just to be sure, could you please restate what happened the most recent night of assault?" she adds, and I feel my heart sink. Letting out a rough sigh, my eyes water a bit before I stammer, but Rylee interrupts.

"I understand the discomfort this may cause, but this is for the sake of accuracy regarding the case. Sexual Assault cases are often the most looked into for the sake of both parties."

Biting my bottom lip, I hold back my tears before nodding once again, wiping my face as one slips out.

"Um," I stutter. The officer, Detective, and Rylee *all* stare at me, waiting for my statement as I sit in silence.

I take a moment, but as I glance down at the papers, I inhale and remind myself—We're almost there.

The fluorescent lights of the office buzz overhead, the harsh tone mimicking the nervous tremor in my hand I seemed to pick up since I walked in here.

Glancing around, photographs of all types decorate the walls everywhere. From family pictures to leading suspects in other cases, they garnish the room, giving a strange sense of comfort as I sit.

I've been here for about an hour, just sitting here.

After additional questioning, Rylee instructed I meet her here, at her office, to talk further. Ever since I've gotten in here, my eyes found themselves glued at the right corner of the floor.

Across the desk, Rylee shuffles through papers, her hands rushing to gather documents into a Manila folder before handing it to me. Her movements snap me back to reality.

"We have a trial date."

Blinking back at her, I feel a sudden rush of emotions well up inside me.

"What?" I stammer, and a faint grin plays at her lips.

"There's been a development in the case."

I bite down on my inner cheek to hold myself back from letting out a tired smile.

"With the solid evidence we have, and the valuable information Christopher provided during questioning, it's making progress," Rylee continues, her words sinking in.

Every ounce of pain, every scar, every bit of strength I summoned—all of it is finally paying off.

"When is it?" I ask.

Rylee sits back in her seat, pausing for a moment before answering, "January 16."

❤ ❤ ❤ ❤ ❤

Closing the car door behind me, I don't even put the car into the ignition before I pull out my phone and begin calling Aaron.

It doesn't take many rings for him to answer, and the moment he does, his voice gives me a sense of comfort that only extends the smile I have.

"Essence?" Aaron calls, his voice worried.

"Everything okay?"

My mind replays the consultation from just hours ago.

"Yeah, yeah. Why?" I ask. Aaron's voice softens, filled with genuine concern.

"Just checking up on you. But what's up?"

I can't help but smile as I lean back in my seat, thoughts of the court's upcoming trial date swirling in my mind.

"Hey, are you there?" Aaron's voice interrupts my thoughts, and I blurt out the news, "They've set a trial date."

The line goes quiet, and I can hear the grin on his face.

"Really?" He says, his voice excited.

"Yeah."

As I wipe my eyes, feeling the sniffles coming on, I give a light chuckle before speaking up.

"Thank you, Aaron," I say, feeling a wave of gratitude washing over me.

"For what?" He asks, confused.

"You did everything," he continues, his voice filled with admiration. "You were the one with the energy to keep going, the strength to push through when things got tough, and the persistence to see it throughout to the end."

I pause for a moment, reflecting on his words before responding, "Yeah, but I wouldn't have made it through without you. And for that, thank you."

For a moment, the words almost exit my mouth.

Those *three* words.

Even though I'd been just seconds away from saying them, I bit them back.

Because if I say them now, I don't know where we'll be later.

aaron

. . .

FAITH ZIPS UP her coat before grabbing her sled from the trunk.

It's embezzled with a cartoon unicorn, along with a few rhinestones glued upon its horn.

I bought it a couple of weeks ago, for this matter. Well, that, and the sake of getting Faith to stop whining about her not owning "a pretty sled."

Essence sits in the passenger's seat of the car, her eyes glued onto the overhead mirror as she applies additional mascara.

"Ess, I don't understand the point of that if you're just gonna be pummeled into the ground by snow anyway," I comment, and I hear a faint scoff.

"Who said I'm being pummeled?" She snarks, and I grin.

"Me. I said it."

"Oh, so we're shoving out there now, huh?" Essence says with a smile, and I shrug.

Closing the mirror, Ess steps out of the car, shutting the door behind her. She then waltzes over toward Faith and me, and grabs her sled from the trunk.

It's light pink and circular shaped, something simple and easy that she picked at the last minute.

My sled also sits in my hand, and as I close the trunk's door, I glance around the area for us to begin the fun.

Families stand scattered everywhere.

Teens stand in clusters—doing tricks I can only imagine ending in pure chaos—while kids run around.

We walk, my eyes still scanning the place for us to be. With a smile, I respond to Faith's statement, "I want a small hill."

"I know, baby. I just have to find one."

Essence walks alongside me, her arm wrapped around mine as we walk.

Faith's small hand sits tucked within my left hand, the only free one I have. Her chilly fingers graze across my skin, my mind flashing with the thought that I should've searched longer for her gloves.

Within seconds, my eyes catch the view of a semi-clear area.

Meaning, we'd have it all to ourselves.

Faith slips down the hill, her laughter following as she slides.

I watch as she comes to a stop, and when she does, she turns around, picks up her sled, and smiles.

"I like this one!"

Exchanging a glance with Essence, I toss my sled onto the ground. Sitting on it, I fix my scarf a bit and fix my position.

"Push me," I declare, and Ess seems to hesitate.

"I don't wanna push you too hard," she stammers, and I chuckle. "You're not going to, Ess. Just push me."

She inhales, then exhales, and within seconds, I'm sliding down.

As I speed down, the cool breeze hits my skin. I let out a laugh as I slow down, then coming to a stop.

Standing up, I turn around and look up at the hill.

Essence and Faith stand alongside each other, their hands tucked into their coat pockets as they wait for me.

"Oh, come on, you guys are boring!" I yell.

I hear a faint scoff come from Essence before she tosses her sled into the ground.

"I'm not *boring*," she calls, and I give her a look.

Climbing up the hill, it doesn't take me long to reach the top when I stand behind Ess, who now sits in her light pink circle.

"You're not?" I ask, and with a smile, she shakes her head.

"Prove it, then."

Rolling her eyes, Ess sits crisscross onto the sled, almost seeming to gather herself as she waits for me to push.

"Count down first, okay?" She asks, and turning toward Faith, she gives me a mischievous grin.

"Aaron!" Essence exclaims, noticing the silence.

"Okay, okay," I say. "I'll count down."

"Good. Start from ten."

"I am not starting from ten. You're just being a wuss—"

"Aaron, start from ten," Essence interrupts.

"Five. I'll start from five," I offer, and with a sigh, Ess nods. "Fine. Five."

"Four," I count, and just as I reach two, Faith comes in and pushes Ess, who slips down the hill before coming to an abrupt stop.

"Aaron!" she yells, laughing.

"What? It wasn't me!" I respond, and standing, Essence crosses her arms.

"I don't believe you," she huffs, and I grin. Grabbing her sled, she walks up the hill.

"I swear it was Faith," I offer, and she raises her brow.

Glancing at Faith, she gives an innocent smile before shrugging, which causes Ess to laugh and me to scoff in defense.

"Oh, come on. She looked at me and planned it," I say with a chuckle, and Essence shrugs. "I don't know. I'm not sure if I believe you," she responds, dropping her sled to the ground.

I lick my lips with a smile, regretting it as the chilly air reminds me of what time of year it is.

"I think you did it on purpose. And for that," she pauses, walking close.

Her breath creates tiny clouds in the frosty air, and her eyes seem to delve into mine, making time slow down. I can feel the mischievous challenge in her gaze, and a smile creeps onto my face.

As I glance down at her lips, Essence leans in closer, but before anything can happen, we're interrupted by Faith's voice calling out for us to give her a push down the hill.

"I want Essence to go with me too, so we can race," she says, and just as quickly as the moment happened, it ended.

"Oh, you think you can beat me?" Essence retorts, and with confidence, Faith nods.

Grabbing her sled, Ess plops it down onto the ground and sits down.

"Aaron, push us," Essence demands, and walking over, I smile.

"Let's find out who'll win."

❤ ❤ ❤ ❤ ❤

"So what made them urge the case?" I ask, and taking a bite from her egg roll, Essence shrugs.

"Rylee just mentioned that they saw something that caught their attention. Something that needed to be approached," she responds, and I nod.

Taking a sip from my drink, I lean back on the couch, and Essence does the same. Grabbing the remote, she puts our show on pause when she lays down on my shoulder.

"I mean everything I said, you know," she says, and I nod.

"I don't know what I would do without you."

Pulling her head close, I plant a kiss on her forehead before placing my hand onto her thigh.

Ess tenses up for a moment, but looking up at me, she relaxes.

We sit for a moment before Ess speaks.

"I went through hell, Aaron."

Looking at her, I pull Ess closely.

"Absolute hell. Every day was something with him," she adds.

"And people think it's okay. Everyone else who went through it too, they think it's okay. That it's just a part of the process, but it's not. I know it's not."

Her voice cracks as she continues speaking.

Sometimes I wish I could take all of Essence's pain and endure it for her.

All the feelings and emotions that hurt her, all the thoughts that go through her mind, all the things that she's experienced— I wish I could take it *all* for her.

Essence sniffles a bit.

"But that's why I have to do it, you know? For me *and* them."

Giving her a faint smile, I nod.

"I'm proud of you."

Essence grins before tucking her head closer into my neck.

"And I say it all the time, but I'm fucking proud of you, Ess. You have no clue."

It goes quiet once again.

I now massage Ess's scalp, something I did a while ago. It was mostly to comfort her whenever she would have nightmares about Christopher, especially at the beginning of everything.

That was when they were bad.

But over time, it became something I do with her just out of comfort. Something I do to make her feel safe.

Feel at home.

"Aaron," Ess mumbles, and I give a sound in reply.

"Carmela recommended this culinary academy."

I feel a smile play on my lips as I nod. "Oh, really?" I say, and she nods.

"Yeah. Said it'd be nice for someone like me. You know, since I'm just now getting out there."

"Why don't you apply?" I ask, and Ess shrugs.

"I don't know. I mean, I could," she pauses, "But it's out of state."

I feel my face scrunch up at her sentence.

"Out of state?" I repeat, and Essence looks up at me as she nods.

"It's back home. In Chicago."

essence

. . .

THE SCENT of sweet batter floats throughout the room.

Aaron stands alongside Faith as they stir the bowl, careful not to spill anything over the rim.

My hands fumble with a bowl of strawberries as I go back and forth to rinse them in the sink.

"How long will it take for the pancakes to be ready?" Faith asks, and I hear Aaron chuckle a bit before walking toward me and grabbing a paper towel.

"A couple of minutes," he responds.

I look up from the bowl of rinsed strawberries and glance at Aaron, whose eyes wander on mine for a moment before darting back toward Faith.

"How many minutes?"

A smirk rises on my face as I grab a cutting board.

Placing it onto the counter, I pour the bowl of fruit and lay out the loose strawberries, now beginning to cut them.

"I'd say give it about twenty minutes," I offer with a raised brow. Faith lets go of the mixing spoon before giving a hesitant smile, and once she does, I can't help but smile as well.

"After I cut these up, I want you to pour them into the batter, then mix it again," I assign, and Faith nods.

Aaron leans against the counter in front of me, away from the island where Faith and I stand.

A sly grin sits on his face before he reaches into his pocket and grabs his phone.

"What're you smiling at?" I ask.

Biting back a smile, I wait for his response.

"Nothin'," Aaron shrugs, and I scoff.

Sliding a pile of sliced strawberries to the side, I watch as Faith grabs them and tosses them into the pancake batter.

"I was thinking," Aaron pauses, his tone almost as if he's thinking of what to say next.

"Since it's Christmas Eve, maybe we could head out someplace before settling down for the night."

"Like where?" I ask. Slipping his phone to the side, Aaron crosses his arms.

"Well, one of my friends offered to meet us at a museum. They have little events going on."

Just as the words exit Aaron's mouth, Faith looks up from the bowl of batter.

"I wanna go!" She exclaims, and I smile.

"It starts at around noon. You feeling it?" Aaron asks, his eyebrow raised.

Finishing up the last few strawberries, I place the knife down and think for a moment before nodding.

Aaron grins at my gesture before sitting up and walking toward Faith as she holds the bowl out for him.

Grabbing it from her, Aaron places it beside the stovetop.

"Then that's the plan."

❦❦❦

I tussle with my hair a bit before shutting the overhead mirror.

Grabbing my purse, I then exit the car and shut the door

behind me, watching as Faith reaches her hand out for mine. With a smile, I grasp it, which causes Aaron to grin a bit before speaking.

"So my friend's name is Kyrie," he begins, and I nod. Faith gasps with anticipation before interrupting.

"Is Kayla going to be here?" She asks, and looking down at Faith, Aaron gives her a smile as he nods.

Her excitement is now clear as we near the building.

People sit in groups on the front benches, talking and laughing.

Aaron reaches for the door's handle, then allowing Faith and I to enter the building first as he opens it.

Looking around, I can't help but feel in awe.

Everything looks so beautiful.

Artwork's aligned across the walls, along with beautiful sculptures that seem to carry story.

History persevered in display cases, and their stories lay plastered against the cases' glass.

Faith seems almost just as in amazement as I am, as her eyes wander around the room.

Aaron nudges my shoulder for a moment before seeming to direct his eyes in a nearby area where a man and his daughter sit.

They play hot hands, a game that seems to get her excited and energized.

Nearing the two, the man looks up at Aaron, causing a smile to arise on his face. He mumbles to the little girl before standing.

"Aaron! What's up, man?" He exclaims, starting that hug that men seem to do every time they see each other.

Letting go of my hand, Faith then hugs the little girl, her beaded braids clacking with each movement she makes.

Aaron taps my shoulder before introducing me to his friend.

"Hey, Ky. Essence, this is Kyrie. Kyrie, this is Essence."

I give Kyrie a tight-lipped smile before he speaks. "I know

you. My girlfriend sends me your posts all the time," he chuckles. I stand silently before realizing what he said.

"Oh, sorry, my bad," I stutter. "Yeah. I post here and there," I shrug.

I glance over at Faith and the other girl for a moment before talking again.

"So what's the plan for today?"

Aaron gives Kyrie a look, a silent statement that seems to repeat the very question I just asked.

"There's this holiday scavenger hunt goin' on," Kyrie begins, and I nod. "I figured why not get the girls out here and do it together, you know?" He adds, and with a light smile, I nod again.

"I love a good challenge," I say with a grin. My eyes meet Aaron's, and for a moment, they express something more than words could.

Kyrie chuckles, snapping me back to reality as I turn toward him.

"Well, then. Let's get started."

We haven't even started the hunt for an hour before it's gotten difficult.

Standing in the showing for the history of the Tyrannosaurus rex, I glance around the room for one more moment before looking back down at the crumpled sheet of paper.

It lists the items we're looking for, all things related to winter, and we've been searching for this 'Elf on The Shelf' for a while.

Faith and her friend stand a couple of feet away from me as they mess with an interactive object, searching as well.

Aaron helps the girls out, while Kyrie stands on the sidelines, whispering into his phone.

Grumbling to myself, I sit up straight and shove the paper into my pocket before walking over toward Aaron.

"We've been looking for this damn thing for the past hour," I sigh, and he chuckles.

"We can skip it, you know," he offers, and I give him a look.

"Tell that to the two besties."

Aaron laughs at my sentence before walking toward a bench and sitting on it.

Without hesitation, I follow him and do the same.

Crossing my legs, I sit back in the seat.

"What movies are we watching tonight?" Aaron asks, and I smile.

The thought that Aaron may have had that question on his mind for the past couple of minutes makes me feel some type of way, and a way that I can't describe other than it makes me happy.

"Just a couple of classics," I respond, and he raises a brow.

"Like?"

"'This Christmas,' 'Home Alone,' 'The Nightmare Before Christmas,'" I list, watching as he tries to hold back a smile.

He fails at it, and once he realizes he had, he begins speaking, but finds himself interrupted by Kyrie.

"Hey, I'm gonna take the girls and bring them to the cafe."

Aaron nods before tossing Kyrie a thumbs up.

"Alright," he mumbles, and just before Kyrie turns around, he seems to toss us a smile—a mischievous smile—before walking off.

I glance at Aaron, watching as he forces a laugh before continuing to speak to me.

"I'm pretty excited for tomorrow."

I raise an eyebrow at his sentence, sitting up as I now turn toward him, a subtle action that I hope he hadn't noticed.

"Why?" I ask, and he shrugs.

"I mean, sure, I'm always excited to see Faith's face whenever she opens what I get her. It makes me smile, and it's the best part of the entire day," he pauses, and I smile.

Aaron's effort to keep Faith happy is beautiful to see.

How hard he pushes to be sure she has everything. Everything she wants, everything she needs, everything good for her.

It's amazing to witness.

"But other than that, Christmas has never been anything I look forward to."

Aaron's words bring me back with surprise. Gasping with shock, I playfully place my hand onto my chest and speak.

"Never?" I say, and giving me a look, Aaron rolls his eyes before nodding.

"Not for a while."

"Why?" I ask, and he shrugs.

"Come on, Aaron, you're the most boring person I know," I tease, and he chuckles.

"I don't know, I'm just not a big fan of holidays."

Huffing, I cross my arms and turn in the opposite direction. I think turn back toward him. "Next thing I know, you'll be complaining about birthdays," I mumble, and with the following silence, I already knew.

"Aaron!" I exclaim, and he laughs.

"Essence!" He mocks.

"They're just," he pauses, "Overrated."

"For all the time that I've known you, every single time a celebrating event occurs, it's listed as, 'overrated'.'"

"Because it is!"

I roll my eyes in a scoff.

"When is your birthday?" I ask, and Aaron licks his lips before answering.

"I want nothing big, Essence," he sighs, and I roll my eyes.

"Just answer the question," I say, and he chuckles.

"June 17," he answers, and I nod.

"Noted."

The empty plate that once held our serving of gingerbread cookies sits on the coffee table.

Popcorn's scattered everywhere, along with a couple bits of candy.

Aaron, Faith, and I sit on the couch, as the TV rolls the credits to the movie, *'Best Man Holiday.'*

Faith dozed off a while ago, leaving Aaron and I bickering about what to watch next.

I ended up picking, and even though I know he wouldn't dare admit it; Aaron liked the movie.

Taking the last sip of my hot chocolate, I place the mug onto the table before standing. Aaron stands as well, careful not to wake the sleeping Faith who lays on his shoulder.

"I'mma go put her to bed," he says, and without speaking, I nod.

Watching as he makes his way to Faith's bedroom, I can't help but smile.

A couple of moments with him being gone, and I clean up the pieces of trash that sprawl across the living room.

Beginning to wash the dishes, I listen as Aaron walks over, his footsteps just barely audible against the tiling.

He stops walking, and I feel his presence behind me.

My breath quickens.

I can feel my heart pounding through my chest. The words get caught up in my throat, but I ignore it.

His presence is palpable, sending a shiver down my spine.

I can sense his hand on my waist, and for a fleeting moment, I allow myself to lean into it, relishing feeling closeness and comfort it brings. But then, just as quickly as it came, the warmth dissipates, replaced by a wave of conflicting emotions.

As I stand here in the moment of vulnerability, the memories of Christopher's touch flood my mind once again.

The way he would pull me close, hold me tight, and never let me go until he finished, no matter what I said.

It was a cycle I found myself trapped in, yearning for something different, something real.

The sound of Aaron's voice pulls me back to reality.

"You're okay," he says, and I close my eyes.

Tears form at the rim of my eyes as I breathe, the weight of Aaron's hand lifting with each breath I take.

"In through your nose, out through your mouth," Aaron says, and I follow.

In through your nose, out through your mouth.

In through your nose, out through your mouth.

I feel myself calm down when I turn around.

My gaze meets Aaron's, and in that moment of silence, his eyes seem to delve deep into mine, searching for any hint of emotion. His scrutiny is almost unnerving, as if he is trying to unravel the tangled web of thoughts and feelings that live within me.

As his gaze settles, I'm pulled toward him almost instinctively.

The touch of his lips against mine ignites a long-forgotten spark within me, sending a surge of ecstasy through my veins. It's a feeling that I've kept buried inside, promising never to let it resurface.

Yet, as I pull away, a sudden realization dawns upon me—

This feeling, I know exactly what it is.

I know it all too well.

aaron

. . .

THE MATTRESS WOBBLES as the sound of Faith's voice disorients within my hearing.

Opening my eyes, Faith stands in front of me, her small body towering over mine. A bright smile sits on her face, as her bonnet sits warped on her head.

"Daddy," she sings, her voice faint.

Leaning closer to me, her morning breath kicks in when I push her away.

"Don't get in my face if you haven't brushed your teeth, Faith," I groan, and sitting back, she smiles.

"Okay. But it's Christmas, so you and Essence have to wake up."

Looking out the window, the sun brightens up the neighborhood.

Of course, Christmas is the only day kids wake up on time. All other days—that's out of the story.

Sitting up, I notice Essence lying on her side of the bed, a pillow laid onto her back—as if she'd placed a pillow wall between us in the middle of the night.

As I move the pillow off of her, I listen to her soft and faint breaths, and notice her hair pulled back in a low ponytail, showing that her bonnet must've fallen off again.

I smile at the sight before slipping off of the bed and grabbing a t-shirt from the drawer in my nightstand.

"What about Essence?" Faith asks, stepping off the mattress.

Walking toward my side of the dresser, I dig around in the drawer a bit before pulling out a small blue box—a ring box.

It lays unwrapped in my hand, as the brand's label—Tiffany's—sits upward. Faith walks over, then pushes my arm downward, allowing her to see.

"Is that for Essence?" she asks, looking at me, and I nod.

"I didn't wrap it."

"Why not?" Faith asks, and with a smile, I shrug before walking toward my closet. Feeling along the side of the closet, it doesn't take long before I grasp a hold of the small gift bag I tucked away some time before.

Pulling the bag out, I shake it as I give Faith a response. "Because I have more things for her. They're in here."

I didn't put everything in one place because I wasn't sure if I'd lose it. That, and if Essence were to find the bag, she couldn't find the most important gift. It's not an engagement ring or anything, but it's something I thought she'd like. Something that reminded me of her when I saw it, and when I did, I bought it.

Regardless of the price.

Faith tries to grab the bag, but I quickly take it away, raising an eyebrow as she folds her arms and pouts. "I'm giving it to her later tonight," I say, and Faith sighs.

"Daddy!" she groans, and I shush her.

The sound of shuffling blankets emerges from the bed, and turning around, I watch as Essence tosses around for a moment, a couple of moans and groans coming from her before she goes silent.

"Can we wake her up now?" Faith complains, and placing the box into the bag, I shake my head.

"No. Not yet."

"Daddy, but it's Christmas! We're supposed to wake up early. I wanna open my gifts."

Standing up, I smile at Faith's impatience before ushering her toward the door. "I know it's Christmas, baby," I begin. Faith now stands outside the doorway, her tired eyes giving me a look of annoyance.

"Give me a couple of minutes to get ready and we'll get started on some breakfast, okay?"

Faith groans a bit and slouches before nodding, her dramatics coming into play. "Meet you in the kitchen. Cereal and milk are on your shelves if you want anything."

I walk from the bathroom when I hear Essence's voice.

"Aaron?"

Her voice is tired and hoarse, a tone that I've only grown to hear over the past couple of months. "Yeah?" I respond. Grabbing my phone from the bathroom counter, I check the time before walking into the bedroom.

Looking up from her phone, Essence gives me a strained smile before turning the screen off. "Mornin', sleepyhead," I say with a smile, and Ess rolls her eyes.

"Morning."

Sitting up, she stretches against the headboard before standing up, walking toward the dresser as she digs around in her drawer.

Pulling out a pair of shorts, Essence slips them on before turning toward me.

We stand for a moment as I walk toward the door, my hand on the knob while I speak. "Faith and I are making breakfast, so when you're finished getting ready, just walk into the living room and we should have everything set by then," I say, and I watch as Ess bites back a smile.

"Okay," she murmurs, and I give her a muted grin before opening the door and walking out.

"Aaron," I hear Essence call. Opening the door a crack, I peek my head through. "Yeah?"

"Thank you."

I nibble on the lining of my cheek to prevent a smile from spilling out. "For what?" I ask, and fiddling with the bottom of her shirt, Essence's eyes meet mine.

"For," she pauses, almost as if holding back her sentence. She then shakes her head, a silent gesture of her saying, "Never mind."

"Just thank you."

Essence places her plate into the sink as Faith jumps up from her seat to do the same.

She then wanders toward Ess before grabbing her hand and pulling her toward the couch. "It's time to open gifts now!" Faith exclaims, and as Essence exchanges a glance with me, I can't help but smile.

Giving into Faith's excitement, Essence wanders behind her as I stand. Wandering into the bedroom, I grab their two Christmas cards and a couple of smaller gifts.

Faith's voice then calls for me from the other room.

"Daddy! Where are you?"

I laugh at her impatience before hurrying back into the living room. Making my way to the couch, I give them their cards and settle down next to Essence. She greets me with a cheery grin and eagerly opens her envelope.

"Merry Christmas," I say with a smile, watching as they read their cards.

As Faith finds a 10 dollar bill, her face radiates with joy, while Essence chuckles before turning her attention back to me.

She glances at my lips for a moment before saying anything.

"You've got 'Ho Ho Ho's'?" She reads, and I laugh at the sentence before raising a brow.

"Funny, isn't it?" I ask, a hidden laugh laced in my words.

Essence nibbles on her bottom lip before nodding. Then, she glances back at the card and reads the brief message I wrote. Even though it's something sweet, at the time I was writing it, I *wanted* something more. Something memorable, something better, something significant.

Something romantic.

As I anticipate her reaction, memories of last night fill my mind. For the first time, Essence's eyes spoke volumes. They conveyed something deep, something profound, and she let them.

She didn't divert her gaze or create a distraction. She didn't nervously chuckle or avert her eyes. Instead, she let her eyes speak, and what they communicated surpassed any words she had uttered before.

Feeling arms wrapping around me snaps me back to reality.

Essence hugs me, her face tucked into my shoulder as she whispers. They're words I can't comprehend.

Pulling away, a bright smile sits on her face.

"Merry Christmas, Aaron," she says, and I smile.

"Merry Christmas to you too, Ess," I respond, and just as the words exit my mouth, Faith walks over, a gift box in her hand as she holds it up in the air.

"Can I open my presents now?" She asks, and I glance at Ess, who holds back a laugh.

Looking back at Faith, I smile before nodding.

"Yes, you can, Princess."

I bite down on my inner cheek before speaking.

"I'm taking you out to dinner tonight."

Before I have time to think, the words slip out of my mouth, instantly causing surprise to appear on Essence's face.

"Dinner?" she repeats, and I nod.

I feel as her hand, that was once tense, now sits in mine.

My mind reels with thoughts, unsure of how she's taking

this. Maybe she's taking it as just a simple dinner. A night out on the town, a Christmas dinner that's meant to get her mind off of things.

Yet, a small part of me hopes she takes it more than that.

Essence clears her throat before asking, "Where?"

I give her a shrug in response, something that causes her to roll her eyes with a smile. "Don't worry about it," I say.

I glance down at our hands, which now sit within one another.

Glancing back at Essence, I feel my breath quicken and I hold back a smile.

"Be ready to go at 8."

"What about Faith?" Ess asks, and I turn toward the living room, where the TV now plays an episode of *Barbie.*

"I've got everything covered, Ess," I respond. "Just wear that dress you love, okay?" I add, and she nods.

"Tonight is about you."

❤ ❤ ❤ ❤ ❤

The sound of Essence's laugh brings a smile onto my face every time I hear it.

I can't even hide it anymore.

I have feelings for Ess, and I can't do anything about it.

Ess takes a sip from her wine glass before speaking. "The Roux sent over some pamphlets today," she says, and I raise an eyebrow.

"Oh?" I ask, and with a smile, Essence nods.

"Yup. Just a bunch of information," she pauses, taking a bite from her breadstick. "As if I already didn't know a shitload about it."

Her sentence causes me to chuckle a bit before speaking. "You thought about applying?" I ask, and she shrugs.

"A little. I just don't know about it, Aaron. What if this is a mistake? All the money I'd be putting into it—what if it's not worth it?"

I furrow my brow at her sentence before taking a sip of water. I swallow, then speak.

"No. Not happening. You are *not* doing this to yourself again," I begin, and Essence looks at me in confusion. "You're doubting yourself."

"How is it doubting if we don't know, Aaron?" she responds, and I sigh.

"Essence, you have a talent, and you're pushing it aside just because you have this uncertainty."

She quickly scans my face before taking another bite of her food.

"Do it. You have to. For you, Ess," I add.

My hand fiddles with the gift bag.

It sits beside me, and has been for the entire dinner. Inside it has a few journals, candles, a cookbook, and, of course—the ring.

God, despite not being a proposal, my heart seems to think otherwise.

Essence takes the last sip from her cup before beginning to stand, but one glance at me and she sits back down.

"I thought we were leaving," she questions, her voice almost in a whisper.

"I have something for you," I declare, and she raises an eyebrow.

"What is it?" Essence asks, and I give her a look.

"If I tell you, it wouldn't be much of a surprise now, would it?" I say, and a smile spreads across her face as she eases her shoulders.

Slipping her coat off of her arms, she lets it sit on the back of her chair.

My eyes glance over at her left hand, where she fiddles with the ring she's wearing. I can't help but smile, knowing of the gift that I have for her.

I carefully hand her the bag, making sure it doesn't hit anything. Essence's face glows as she grabs it.

"Merry Christmas, Ess," I say, and she smiles.

Essence begins searching inside the bag, removing each item one by one. "Aw! A cookbook!" she exclaims, a bright smile across her face.

As she flips through the pages, she suddenly notices.

"Wait," she pauses. Stopping at a spot in the book, I watch as her eyes scan the page. "Are these the recipes we made so far?" Essence asks, looking up from the book.

Leaning back in my chair, I shrug.

A light sniffle comes from Ess as she continues to flip through the pages. "Goddamn it," she mutters to herself. After that, she dries her eyes, closes the book, and places it on the table.

"I love this, Aaron. Thank you," she says, and I smile.

"There's one more thing, Ess," I point, and she licks her lips before looking back into the bag and moving things around. As she does so, her movements come to a stop. The pause in her actions ignite me to already know.

"Aaron," she states, slowly looking at me. Nibbling on my lip, I raise an eyebrow.

"Tell me you're kidding," Essence begins. She reaches into the bag, takes out the small box, and opens it, letting out a gasp. Looking up from the ring, her eyes meet mine, begging for answers.

I then stand up, walking over and taking the box as I signal for her to grab the ring.

"Just so you know, I'm *not* proposing," I tease, and Essence chuckles uncertainly, clearly thinking that was the intention.

"But I am giving you something that I want you to look at every time you miss me."

Grabbing the ring, I slide it onto her finger. Essence looks down at it, then back at me.

"Aaron, this is too much. You didn't have to," she whispers, her voice filled with a mixture of astonishment and gratitude. I shake my head, a small smile tugging at my lips.

"Essence, I *wanted* to."

"But why?" she asks, her eyes searching mine.

For a moment, I stand, trying to gather my words.

"Because you're worth every bit of it, Ess. You deserve the world, and I want to give it to you," I say earnestly.

Her eyes glisten with unshed tears.

Thoughts surge through my mind. Her gaze, her laughter, her touch—they combine to create an undeniable feeling. I want to tell her everything. I want to tell her how her smile brightens my day, how her laughter is contagious, how her strength throughout the past few months is something that I have nothing but respect toward her for.

Damn it, I can't hide it anymore.

I want to tell her I love her.

essence

. . .

YASMYN HANDS me a glass of wine, to which I give her a look before taking a sip from it.

"What? You told me to get you a drink!" She laughs, and with a smile, I roll my eyes.

"Yeah, a *drink. Beverage.* Like water, soda, juice. You know, things that don't give me a midday hangover," I state, and with a playful scoff, Yasmyn rolls her eyes.

Sitting beside me, she holds her glass as she lays her head on my shoulder.

"What's 'The Roux'?" She asks, reading off of my laptop screen as she does so.

"It's this," I pause, thinking of what to say.

Even though I've looked at it for months now, I can't seem to describe exactly what it is.

It's a culinary school, sure, but it's one of America's top competitive places to be. Like an Ivy League for chefs. It's got the best education, top-notch instructors, the best quality appliances. It's everything a beginning chef could ask for. That, and it's the best place to start if you're thinking long term.

I watch as Yasmyn sits up and scrolls through the page, clicking a few things along the way as she does so.

"Culinary school?" She asks, completing my sentence, and I nod.

"Yeah. I've been looking at it," I say, and she nods.

As Yasmyn takes a sip from her glass, she casually scrolls through the "About Us" page, her brow furrowed in concentration. Her eyes scan the screen for a couple of seconds, then revert toward me.

"In Chicago?" she asks, her voice a clear indication of her shock.

Taking a large inhale, I nod slowly.

"Ess, that's back home," she adds.

"I know, I know," I groan, grabbing the laptop from her.

I haven't been back home in years. Yeah, I've seen family members and attended important familial events, but that's because they've always come to me. Plane tickets, hotel rooms, and even a couple of things for them to do around the city would always be fully paid for by Christopher.

It was nice to see them covered for, so I dealt with more than I should've.

Nibbling on my bottom lip, I look down at the map that displays across the screen. There lays the pinpoint, 16981 West Randolph, Chicago. Only a few minutes from my childhood home, where I would stay for a bit while I search for places to live.

"I just... I don't know," I hesitate, my gaze wandering aimlessly around the screen.

Yasmyn finishes the last bit of her wine before placing the glass down onto the coffee table, then grabbing the laptop from me. A couple of clicks, a bit of typing, and she turns the screen to me. The page for admission glows across the screen, and she hands it back over before I can protest.

"Apply," Yasmyn demands, her voice tinged with excitement. I furrow my brows, puzzled by her sudden insistence.

"What?" I ask, a hint of uncertainty creeping into my tone.

Yasmyn chuckles, her eyes sparkling with mischief as she nods in confirmation.

"But what about everything I have? It's all here."

Yasmyn's gaze softens, a knowing look in her eyes. Speaking, her voice is gentle, yet insistent, "What about everything you *will* have if you go, Ess?"

Glancing down at the screen in front of me, a mix of apprehension and anticipation stirs within me.

"You need to let go of your past. You persevered. You didn't give up, Ess, you did it. You can finally be you," Yasmyn pauses, allowing her words to sink in. She reaches for her phone, briefly checking for messages before resuming.

"So be *you*."

♥ ♥ ♥ ♥ ♥

Being Yasmyn's best friend for years has its perks—like knowing what to expect when she mentions a night out on the town.

I sent in the application to the school a couple of hours ago, and out of nature, Yasmyn demanded we celebrate.

As Yasmyn gets ready for our night out, she meticulously attends to every detail, ensuring that her baby hairs are perfectly laid down and her makeup is flawless. "Am I good?" she asks, seeking my approval.

I give a nod and a smile, watching as she then reapplies her mascara and lip combo—both things she'll never leave the house without.

"Tonight, I want you to focus on you," Yasmyn begins, and looking up from my compact mirror, I glance at her and smile.

My mind thinks back to Christmas night.

It's been a couple of days ago from now, yet it feels like yesterday. Everything he said is still fresh in my mind, along with everything I felt.

My heart pounded with anticipation the whole way through, and the ring didn't help with that, either.

Glancing down at my hand, I smile as my eyes meet contact with the ring.

It's a gold band. I haven't taken it off since, and my mind just replays what he said, over and over.

"Ess."

Yasmyn's gentle nudge brings me back to reality, making me realize I've been staring at the ring for far too long.

"Yeah?" I ask, I ask with a hint of confusion, earning a laugh from her in response. "Nothing," she shrugs.

After I finish up my makeup, I glance at Yasmyn, who's still engrossed in applying lip gloss in front of her mirror. "Are you ready?" I ask, to which she nods without even looking up.

I chuckle a bit at the sight before walking into her bedroom and toward the nightstand, where my phone lies.

Grabbing it, a stack of notifications from all kinds of apps sits on my screen, but the only ones I tend to are from Aaron.

Send a pic of you before you guys head out. Have fun!

As I glance at the message from him asking for an outfit check, a smile creeps onto my face. I grab the opportunity to check myself out in the nearby body mirror, snapping a quick picture as well.

After getting the perfect shot, I send it over to him and take a moment to admire myself in the reflection.

It's a strange feeling, but for the first time in years, I catch a glimpse of the person I used to be.

The girl who wanted nothing more than for her dreams to be accomplished, her voice to be heard, and her vision to be applied. I let her down when I came here, because the moment I did, I pushed her away.

But she's back, and this time, I won't let her go.

I snap one last picture, this time it being for my Instagram, before pairing it with the simple caption, *"Me, myself, and I."*

For the first time, I finally feel a sense of familiarity with my image.

Just as I finish posting the picture, Yasmyn emerges from the bathroom, breaking me out of my thoughts. "You ready?" she asks, drawing my attention away from the screen. I can't help but roll my eyes and give her a playful nod.

"I literally just asked you that," I joke, to which Yas responds with a nonchalant shrug.

"You're all set, though, right?" she says with a grin, and I nod in agreement.

"Exactly."

"Whatever," I sigh, and she chuckles.

Grabbing my clutch, I shove my phone inside before grabbing my coat and slipping it on.

"Did Aaron text you?" Yasmyn asks, and I feel a grin slowly grow across my face, which causes Yas to smile as well.

We walk toward the garage as we speak, and Yasmyn says something that signals for us to pause.

"You wanna know something?" She asks, and I raise my brows, waiting for her to speak. "I think you love him."

Love? I scoff at the idea, dismissing it almost instantly. But beneath the nonchalant exterior, a part of me hesitates.

Do I?

No, I can't.

"I'm serious, Essence. Look at me," she urges, and with a sigh, I finally meet her gaze. A smile dances on her lips as she continues,

"What you feel is love. Those butterflies and the nervous energy you get whenever you're around him? That's love, plain and simple."

aaron

. . .

"RESOLUTIONS ARE LAME."

Essence's eyes peer over her phone before she shuts the screen off and speaks, something that causes a smile to grow across my face the moment she does so.

"There's something seriously wrong with you," she states, and I let out a soft chuckle. Scoffing at my response, Essence grabs a nearby pillow and hits me with it as I toss out a reply.

"I'm not laughing!" I exclaim, and she gives me another look.

"Okay, okay," I say, catching my breath. "Maybe I am," I utter, and sitting up, Essence leans back against the headboard and rolls her eyes.

"I've never met a more boring person than you," she groans, and I chuckle.

"I'm not boring," I retort, and she scoffs.

"All your statements about *classic* holidays prove your ass otherwise."

I chuckle a bit before sitting next to her, and Essence lays her head down on my shoulder.

"Resolutions give you the opportunity to try something new," she says, and I nod.

"Yeah, I get that part."

"Okay, so what's so lame about it?" She asks, and I shrug, careful not to bump Ess too much.

"Ugh," she groans, and I laugh again.

"I'm fixing you while I'm here, you know," she teases, and playfully, I scoff.

"Oh, really, now?" I ask, and closing her eyes, her voice goes soft as she gives me a quick, "Yup."

"What's one thing you wanna do?" Ess asks, and I shrug again. "Aaron, be serious for once."

"I am," I respond, and she sighs.

"Okay, fine. Something I wanna do?" I repeat, and looking up at me, Essence nods.

I think for a moment before speaking, ideas popping into my mind that I want to say, but don't.

Instead, I go with something simple.

"I do want to go out more."

Seeing Essence's face filled with disappointment, a feeling I've never witnessed so strongly, I can't help but laugh.

"Everyone says that, Aaron," she says, and shrugging, I roll my eyes.

"*Well*, I'm gonna do it," I respond, and she smiles.

"Pick something different."

"*Ask* me something different."

Essence sighs at my statement, and I suppress a chuckle.

"Okay. What's something you want to take seriously?"

Yet again, there goes another question that I can't answer.

"Essence, what am I supposed to answer to that?" I ask, and sitting up, Ess chuckles.

"Uh, something you wanna take seriously, *duh*."

A smile pops onto my face at her statement before she grabs her phone. She scrolls through Instagram, occasionally responding to comments as she does.

"Let me hear *your* resolutions," I say, which catches her off guard.

"Mine?" Essence asks, and I nod.

Licking her lips, she shuts the phone screen off again and thinks.

"I wanna be more outgoing," she starts, and I give her a look.

"What?" she laughs, and I narrow my eyes.

"You're already outgoing if you were to ask me, Ess," I shrug, and she laughs.

"Not really," she mutters, and draping my arm across her shoulder, I hold her for a moment. Ess then looks up at me, her eyes meeting mine, before she continues to speak.

"I also wanna build my brand."

"Your brand?" I ask, and she nods.

"If I make it into the culinary place, that's where it all starts. I'm known for my fashion and style, but if I start this new thing with food, that'd be the *real* beginning."

I chuckle at Essence's vision, then gently kiss her forehead, making her momentarily freeze before breaking into a wide smile.

God, that smile.

"What else do you want to do?" I ask, and she nibbles on her bottom lip as she thinks.

"I need to workout more," she responds.

"We should workout together," I offer, and turning to face me, Essence's eyes almost seem to glow.

"Really?" she exclaims, and without speaking, I nod.

A smile aligns her face at my sentence before pulling me in for a hug, something that catches me by surprise.

"What was that for?" I ask, and looking up at me, Essence gives me another smile, but this time, it's more sly.

"I got you to say a resolution."

Pouring the last bag of ice into the cooler, I shut it before pushing it to the side.

Maeko comes in carrying a box of beer bottles, almost as if they're nothing. She then places it beside the cooler, pops it open, and begins putting each bottle into the ice.

"Is Essence coming tonight?" Mae asks. Her tone differs from usual. I'd label it as jealousy, but something about it causes me to decide otherwise.

Grabbing my phone from my back pocket, I check the time.

9:40 PM

"Yeah, why?" I respond, and without speaking, Mae shrugs.

She hesitates before falling silent, battling her own thoughts.

Music from the living room plays on the speakers, and she Maeko finishes placing the bottles of beer into the cooler. She shuts the lid and stands.

Her eyes meet mine, then move around the room as she speaks.

"You like Essence."

Mae's sentence sounds more like a demand than a statement or observation, leading to a scoff from me. "How would you know?" I chuckle, and a light grin tugs at her lips.

Maeko approaches the counter, discards the empty box beside the trash bin, and starts fiddling with the aluminum foil on top of the side dishes for the party.

"I know you, Aaron," she says.

Mae's hands search around for things to do, a habit that she does whenever she's nervous.

It wasn't until she asked me out that I realized I had never paid attention to this habit, and that night I couldn't stop thinking about Essence.

"What's that supposed to mean?" I ask, and sitting on a nearby dining chair, I cross my arms.

Mae chuckles a bit, which sounds more sarcastic instead of genuine.

"I'm just saying that you've done more for Essence than you have for anyone else," she pauses. Letting out a large sigh, Mae leans against the counter, then continues to speak.

"If she comes to the party tonight, you should say something to her."

"Mae, I'm not even good with shit like that," I respond, and Maeko lets out a sigh similar to disappointment. Moving closer to me, her eyes stay locked onto mine.

"I've seen the way you look at Essence, Aaron," she mutters, and I give Mae a look of confusion.

She licks her lips and lets out a sigh, much as if she were preparing herself for the sentence she's about to say.

"It's different from when you looked at Kiara. Something inside of you clicks when you see her," she adds.

I glance toward a corner as I think of Ess.

Thoughts of when I first met her pop into mind. The way I met her, and she didn't hesitate to help me out. How her smile was bright and inviting. How whenever I'm around her, I can't help but let myself loose.

I feel vulnerable around her. My heart is unguarded with her.

Returning to reality, I turn around and see Mae standing in front of me, hands on her hips, wearing an "I told you so" expression.

"You like her, Aaron," she begins, and refusing to identify with the words said, I shake my head.

Behind her eyes lies a concealed expression, something unresolved and left unsaid.

Something unrequited.

Maeko's gaze meets mine, followed by an awkward chuckle and a failed attempt to divert my attention by kicking my chair.

With a broken voice, she proceeds to speak after clearing her throat.

"You like her."

aaron

. . .

ESSENCE FITS IN EVERYWHERE she goes.

That's what I love about her.

She's like a chameleon, adapting to every room she enters.

It's as if the world opens its arms, welcoming her.

Even in the most crowded room, she stands out—not because she demands attention, but because she's the person people gravitate toward naturally.

I remember the first time I saw her this way, standing in the middle of a room, speaking to a herd of people—talking about all kinds of things.

The press party was organized specifically for the clothing brand she promoted. Dozens of other influencers, representatives and organizers were there.

It was like watching a magnet at work, pulling everyone into her orbit the very moment she began speaking.

I couldn't take my eyes off her.

Even with the easy-going exterior, there's a bit of her that not everyone sees. A side of her she hides from others. A side of her she would do anything to keep anyone from seeing.

Essence has been through a lot more than she lets on.

While she tries her hardest to keep people from knowing, I know.

I know what goes on behind the scenes; I know what goes on in her head; I know what she tries to hide.

I know *her*.

❤ ❤ ❤ ❤ ❤

Pouring myself another shot, the sound of Essence's voice over the blaring music causes me to look up from the glass.

"Nice to see your face again," she gleams, a bright smile on her face as she leans against her palm.

I let out a slight chuckle before placing the bottle of tequila to the side. "Hey," I say, and Ess smiles.

We sit in silence, Essence's hand fiddling with any nearby bottle or cup beside her. For a moment, my eyes lock onto her, but the moment she looks back up, I glance away.

"It's crazy how much can change in just twelve months, isn't it?"

Her voice is hardly audible over the loud music, and a smile plays at her lips. Grabbing a cup, she takes a sip from it before leaning closer to me, her face just inches apart from mine.

"I mean, think about it. In just under seven months, I moved in with you," she adds, her gaze drifting past me.

Her sentence causes me to smile, but my attention stays peaked from her sudden glance away. "Yeah, you've got a point," I mutter, and Ess looks back at me.

Her eyes meet mine, and even though she's listening to what I'm saying, I can tell she isn't *really* listening.

"You okay?" I ask, concerned, and quickly, Essence tosses on a false smile.

"Yeah, why wouldn't I be?"

I narrow my eyes at her, questioning my belief in her answer.

Her eyes then wander behind me yet again, but then snap back as she sits up.

"Fuck. I just—," she stutters.

Grabbing a nearby cup, Essence pours herself another shot before stammering out another sentence.

"I'm just gonna get some air, okay? I'll be right back."

Before I can even reply, she turns and disappears into the crowd. Watching as she wanders off, a knot tightens in my chest.

For a moment, I stand alone at the counter, watching as nearby people walk by.

Smiles align their faces, and laughter escapes their lips. People talk about their resolutions, the countdown, their plans for the year.

Maeko stands across the room, and just as my eyes meet hers, they give me a look.

A look that gives me a feeling.

Inhaling, I glance toward the door that Essence exited.

Looking outside the window, I can see her along the side, her body slumped over as she sits in the patio chair.

And just like that, I walk toward the front door and head out.

The sound of sniffling arises from Essence as I shut the door behind me.

Sitting in the patio chair beside her, I can hear the music continue to play from the inside, followed by an occasional bustle of laughter from groups that chatter throughout.

Glancing at Ess, I watch as she wipes her face before turning in the other direction, her left leg bouncing nonstop as she does so.

A sniffle breaks the air before I speak.

"You okay?" I ask, and without speaking, Ess nods.

She continues to face the other way, her head down as she looks down at her nails. She picks at them a bit before leaving them alone.

"Ess," I call.

Silence.

Taking a deep breath, I bring my chair closer before calling her again.

"Essence."

"What?" she responds exasperatedly, turning toward me. Her voice is strained and hoarse, and her eyes are puffy, almost as if she'd been crying within the small time she was out here alone.

"Are you okay?" I ask, concern creeping into my voice. Essence remains silent for a moment. Her gaze lost somewhere beyond me.

"Essence?" I say again, this time with a bit more urgency, and she lets out a heavy sigh.

"What happened, Ess?"

"I keep *seeing* him," she replies, her voice hardly above a whisper.

Confused, I move the chair closer, a silent signal that I'm listening.

"What do you mean?"

Essence moves back a strand of hair and stammers a bit. Her eyes glisten with tears, and as they spill over, she wipes her face before speaking.

"I just want to let it all go, Aaron," she pauses. Nibbling on the inner lining of my cheek, I nod.

I see movement in the corner of my eye, so looking down, I notice Essence playing with her ring.

My ring.

Her leg bounces again, a nervous habit that seems to have a life of its own, and another sniffle breaks the silence before she continues.

"The plan was simple. Get out of that place, do what I wanted, just shake off all the baggage and live my life. You know, leave everything behind and start fresh. It sounded so *easy* in my head," she says, her voice trembling.

"I get that," I respond, and she nods.

"But I can't do it," she admits, frustration creeping into her tone.

"I just can't. No matter where I go, it feels like he's right there with me. Every single place I visit, I see Christopher. I can't escape his face, his movements, the way he used to smirk when he thought he was in control. And when I see him, I think back on everything. I think back on what happened that day. I think back on how he hit me, or how he would do anything to get his way."

As she speaks, tears flow down her cheeks.

Essence stammers with every word. Her leg won't stop bouncing, and her eyes stay glued to mine, wide and searching for understanding.

"I saw this dude grab onto a girl's waist," she mutters.

Laying her head onto my shoulder, Essence sighs before sniffling. "She pushed him away, but the interaction just reminded me of all the bullshit from the past few years."

"Like everything replayed in my mind," she explains, and once again, I nod.

I plant a kiss on her head before we go silent.

The muffled audio of the music from inside only seems to become louder, along with the paired sound of nearby crickets.

Another sniffle breaks the stillness before I speak.

"You're strong, you know that, right?" I ask, and Essence looks up at me.

Her face expresses confusion, which causes me to chuckle a bit before Essence scoffs. "No, I'm serious, Ess. You're the strongest woman I know."

Sitting up from me, Essence shifts back a bit before turning to face me, settling into a criss-cross position, her hands flopping into her lap as she speaks.

"You found me drunk in a parking lot a couple of months ago, Aaron. How is that strong?"

I take a moment to gather my thoughts, the right words aligning in my mind as I respond.

"Look at where you are. You got a job under one of the most influential culinary influencers, are building your brand, and figuring out who you are."

Ess licks her lips before rolling her eyes, a smiling playing on her lips as she turns away.

Even though she hides it, I *know* she let smile out.

She can't help it.

Turning back towards me, she shrugs.

"I mean, but *anyone* could do that," she mutters, and I can't help but raise an eyebrow in disbelief.

"Anyone?" I repeat, and letting out a chuckle, Essence nods.

"Well, then. If anyone can do that, then you're doing it better," I shoot back, watching as she bites her bottom lip and looks down at her lap, a mix of shyness and surprise flickering across her face.

She glances down at her lap, nibbling on her bottom lip, a sign of her nerves creeping back in.

Looking back up, Essence's eyes seem to scan the neighborhood.

"The trial's in a couple of days," she mutters, and I can sense the worry underlying her words. My hand moves to the side of her arm, offering a reassuring grip.

"You got this, Ess. You know that, right?" I ask, looking deep into her eyes, searching for that spark of confidence I *know* is buried beneath her uncertainty.

Looking up at me, her eyes convey an expression I can't quite name. An expression I've seen before, yet can't seem to title.

Sitting up a bit, I seem to speak without thinking.

"You'll win this thing. I promise you. Just remember—you're not alone."

Three minutes until midnight.

Three minutes to gather the courage I've been trying to muster up for the last *four hours*.

People gather around the TV as the screen displays a news reporter in front of the ball drop.

The music's now turned down, and those plastic cups are now replaced by champagne and shot glasses. Essence stands beside me, her phone in hand as she snaps a photo of the television screen.

Everything's a blur around me, everything but her.

Essence then types a caption over it before tucking the device away.

"How you feeling?" I ask, trying to keep my voice steady.

She breaks her gaze with the TV screen before looking up at me and smiling, her eyes almost seeming to glow as she does so.

"Jittery," Essence responds anxiously, her voice barely audible amidst the chatter. "What about you? How are you feeling?"

Shrugging, I think of how to respond.

Whether to tell her how I'm feeling, or tell her a random emotion that comes to mind.

"Nervous," I respond, and for a moment, Essence hesitates before giving a secondary question.

"About?"

I nibble on my bottom lip before raising an eyebrow and giving her a look, a subtle way to express my thinking.

"Just about this whole new year," I stutter, and I kick myself for the awkwardness that seems to follow. But she laughs, a soft sound that makes my pulse quicken.

"I get that, though. Feels like everything just flew by."

Grabbing her phone, she checks the screen before once again tucking it into her back pocket. She then looks toward the large TV screen in the center of the room, where the countdown flashes.

Two minutes now.

The crowd across the screen is getting louder, and the surrounding people seem to laugh and cheer more, excitement obvious through the air. It's groups of people bunched in their own crowds standing around us, yet it's just the two of us.

Essence fiddles with her hair a bit as she stands, her eyes glued on the TV screen.

"If I'm being honest, Ess," I begin.

Her eyes revert away from the display, and now rest on mine. A slither of a smile slips through her lips as she waits for me to continue.

"I'm glad we spent the last few months together."

The words tumble out faster than I intend, but I don't regret them. I mean them.

Essence's smile widens, and a warmth in her eyes seems to settle, making me think maybe she's been waiting for me to say something like this.

"Me too," she breathes. Her voice is gentle, yet there's a weight to her words, like she's testing the water, just like I am.

I glance toward the TV.

One minute left, and my heart is pounding.

The anticipation in the room is thick enough to cut with a knife, but all I can concentrate on is Essence.

Her head tilts to the side, a gesture that's both curious and inviting, as her eyes bore into mine with a depth that feels almost searching. It's as if she's trying to read my thoughts, unraveling the tangled mess in my head.

Then she takes a step forward, closing the distance between us in a way that sends a shiver down my spine. I can now feel her steady breath on my lips. Warm and inviting, it mingles with the adrenaline coursing through my veins. Time seems to freeze as I glimpse her finger grazing along my hand, a feather-light touch that sends sparks flying.

I can see the hesitance in her gaze, a flicker of uncertainty that makes my heart race even faster.

One more glance toward the TV, and everyone begins counting down.

"*Ten!*"

The crowd's voice swells, yet I just barely hear it. Each beat of my heart's louder than the other.

"*Nine!*"

There's no more time to waste.

It's now or never.

"Essence," I begin, my voice low, trying to steady the nerves that threaten to choke me.

"*Eight!*"

The room explodes with noise.

"I need to tell you something—"

But just as I open my mouth to speak, her phone buzzes in her hand.

As I pause, our contact breaks, and the words hang in the air while she glances down at the screen.

"*Seven!*"

Her face lights up, eyes widening as she reads the message.

"Aaron," she calls, unable to contain her excitement. "I just… I got in! The Roux accepted me!"

"*Six!*"

My heart sinks, and I feel the confession I was about to make slip away as I force a smile. "Ess, that's amazing," I say, trying to match her enthusiasm.

She looks up at me, her eyes shining with tears of happiness, and in that moment, I know I can't take this from her.

This is *her* moment.

"*Five!*"

Essence now throws her arms around me, pulling me into a tight hug. Holding her close, I swallow back the words that now feel so out of place.

"*Four!*"

She pulls back, smile radiant, and I know I can't say it now. Not when everything she'd worked so hard for just came true.

"Three!"

I swallow hard, trying to push down the disappointment, telling myself that there will be another moment.

Another opportunity.

Another time.

Yet that still doesn't stop the sting of realizing: This isn't it.

"Two!"

The crowd now roars back to focus, the last seconds slipping away faster than I can hold on to them.

"One!"

The room now erupts into cheers as the ball drops, confetti raining down from handheld poppers, a mix of color and sound.

Essence now holds my arm, maneuvering as she turns the side contact into another hug. As everyone around us now celebrates, I can't help but stand here—the words I've been so desperate to say, now buried beneath the weight of a moment.

A moment that just simply wasn't meant to be.

essence

. . .

THE SUN IS UP, but I've been awake for hours, my mind racing in circles around the same thoughts.

Today is the day.

The day I finally face him.

In a couple of hours, I'll be standing in front of a courtroom full of strangers, forced to recount every moment, every violation, every fucking bruise and whisper that Christopher left behind.

Sitting up, I look around the dimly lit room.

I shoot a glance beside me, and Aaron lays quietly, his snores faint beneath the muffled sounds of voices from the TV.

My eyes are heavy from the bare amount of sleep I've gotten.

Rubbing my face, I reach for my phone against the night-stand, desperately yearning for some kind of distraction.

Notifications flood through as I unlock it and load Instagram, the primary of things flurrying through being random comments and DMs from people who are in tune with the upcoming trial for the day.

Unfortunately, they're fans of Christopher, so the notifications are anything but good.

Licking my lips, I let out a sigh before shutting off my phone and tossing it across the mattress.

I've been dreading this very day for months, *months*, and here it is, here in the very first week of the new year. I've been rehearsing everything in my head a thousand times, but now, as I stand here in the quiet of the morning, I feel like I'm unraveling. All of my thoughts seem to be unorganized, my emotions feel wild, and the way I feel inside—I can't seem to describe it even with a singular word.

A groan comes from Aaron, causing me to turn around, watching as he tosses around the blankets before seeming to fall back asleep. The very moment he goes still, I let go of a breath I haven't realized I'd been holding.

Now heading into the bedroom, I press my hands against the counter, my eyes glued on the mirror. My reflection stares back at me, eyes wide and fearful, a far cry from the composed person I'm supposed to be today.

I keep trying to remind myself that this is about justice, that telling my story is the only way to move forward. But my heart won't stop pounding, and the anxiety is like a living thing inside me, clawing at my insides.

I haven't slept.

I haven't eaten.

All I can do is replay the memories, the moments that I've tried so hard to lock away, but today—today will be the day that I will drag everything into the light.

A knock from the doorway snaps me back to reality.

Looking away from my reflection, Aaron stands in the doorway, his tired expression somehow displaying some concern as well.

I breathe deeply before tossing on a fake smile.

"Hey," I say, and I feel as my words almost quiver.

Without saying a word, Aaron walks over and pulls me into a

hug. I bury my face in his chest, letting the warmth of his embrace push away the icy fear that's been gripping me all morning.

We stand for a moment before he speaks.

"How you feeling?" he asks, his tone clear with worry. His eyes convey that he already knows what I'm about to say, already knows what I'm feeling, but I know he wants me to speak.

He wants me to tell him how I feel, to get it off my chest.

But I can't.

Even if I tried, I can't.

Aaron clears his throat before burying his chin into my bonnet.

"You holding up?" he adds, and I shake my head.

"Barely," I respond.

Once again, we stand. Closing my eyes, I try to focus on my breathing, trying to steady the chaos in my mind. I can't afford to fall apart now, not when I'm so close.

"I'm scared," I whisper, my voice trembling.

He holds me tighter, his hand stroking my back. "It's okay to be scared. But you're stronger than you think. And I'll be right there with you, every step of the way."

I pull back from Aaron's chest, just enough to look up at him, my eyes searching for his reassurance. "What if I fall apart? What if I can't do it?"

"You won't fall apart," he says, brushing a strand of hair from my face.

"But even if you do, I want you to know something, Essence," Aaron pauses mid sentence, his eyes locking onto mine.

They almost water up for a moment before they swell back down.

"If you fall apart, I'll be right there to pick up the pieces. And if you can't do it, we'll figure it out together."

Licking my lips, I nod.

As he presses a gentle kiss onto my forehead, I close my eyes for a moment, letting the warmth of his affection wash over me.

Without thinking, the words slip out of my mouth.

"I love you."

♥ ♥ ♥ ♥ ♥

The courtroom is colder than I expected.

Not in temperature, but in the way everything feels so stark, so removed from the reality I've been living for years.

Rylee sits in the chair beside me, her hands shuffling through the manila folder.

Photos lie in unorganized piles along the table, paired along with handwritten dates that match each one. Some are recent, and some go as far as two years back. Either way, they're zoomed in on subtle bruises—ones I thought I'd covered up.

People fill up the room, and scattered chatter echoes throughout as they sit.

Cameras flash at every moment, blinding me for temporary seconds before I lay my head against the surface.

Closing my eyes, I try my hardest to only imagine the joy that must come after.

How freeing it'll feel, knowing that Christopher can't put anyone through the pain he'd once put me through. That he once put many others through.

I'll be the one to break the chain, the chain of silence.

But am I sure I want to?

Feeling a light tap against the table, I look up.

My eyes meet Rylee's.

They're stern, determined, and somehow seem to express worry all at once.

"*I believe in you,*" she mouths, and I give her a straight faced smile before lying back down. Feeling a hand on my shoulder causes me to tense up, but the moment I realize that it's Rylee, I soften.

My mind rehashes everything we've gone over so many times before. Today, we're just going through files, images, and statements—tasks that should be simple, easy, and quick to fly by.

I should be fine, going off the schedule, at least.

The sounds of the room shift; the camera shutters seem to gain speed, creating this consistent rhythm that gathers my attention.

I don't even need to sit up to know that Christopher entered the room.

I can tell, all just from the distinctive observations. Voices rise in pitch, nearby movements become swift and urgent, and throughout the middle of it all, there's Rylee. Her hand, which had once grazed along my shoulder in a comforting gesture, now sits still and unresponsive.

Panic rises within me, a tide that threatens to drown out all rational thought. My mind whirls, replaying snippets of conversations, paired with the fragments of images that I thought I'd kept locked away.

Taking a deep breath, I try to calm down. I can feel the warmth of tears welling in my eyes, blurring the boundaries of my attempt at composure.

Sitting up, I glance across the room. My eyes lock on Christopher's as our gazes meet. A smile appears onto his face, and suddenly, memories flood back.

They're uninvited and relentless, and somehow leave me with the same burn I would feel whenever his hands made their way around some part of my body.

Then, just as quickly as the flashing of the cameras began, they ended, and I look up at the stand to find the judge beginning to sit down.

She pairs her bright red lipstick with her lightened skin, and she pins her hair up into a high bun.

Rylee nudges my shoulder, a silent signal for me to sit up.

As I do so, she does it once again, this time shooting a quick glance at me.

She tries not to speak with her mouth, but her eyes, and they express a silent questioning—wondering if I'm okay.

Honestly, I don't even believe I am.

I let out a heavy breath, despite the struggles that I'd had just moments ago.

Looking back toward the judge, I watch as her eyes scanning the room, her face displaying an expression that marks rather as stone.

My heart pounds within my chest, a sound that only rings in my ears, drowning out the distant sound of shuffling papers and murmurs.

"All rise," the bailiff announces, and we all stand in unison. A tug pulls at my hand, and looking down, I watch as Rylee's hand entwines with mine, tightening for a quick moment, a reminder that everything will be okay.

Taking a deep breath, I exhale, the air seeming to thicken the very moment I let go.

"Please take a seat," the judge says, her voice calm yet commanding.

Her eyes then met my gaze.

"Miss Evelyn Miller," she pauses.

The room falls silent, the tension almost palpable.

The way my name echoed through the chamber, sharp and clear, gives me a feeling of unease. A feeling I can't do anything but push to the side.

Standing up, I can feel the weight of every eye, every lens of the cameras on me—watching, waiting for one misstep.

But more than that, I can feel the weight of what I'm about to say.

My story—our story—is about to be written. Taking a deep breath, I now step forward.

"You may begin."

Looking up at the display ahead, there lies the evidence.

Images of bruises display on the screen. Bruises from when he'd hurt me, time and time again. They all vary in locations, places such as my neck, wrist, upper arms, thighs.

The courtroom lies silent, and I can feel the weight of everyone's eyes on me, waiting for me to speak.

A few cameras flash among the crowd, but they stop just as quickly as they'd began.

The prosecutor's voice then cuts through the tension, his tone sharp and unforgiving as he begins his question. "Ms. Miller, could you tell us how you got these bruises?"

Swallowing hard, I find my throat dry as I struggle to find the words.

I can't breathe, yet alone speak.

They don't know what happened.

And I know they don't know what happened. I know what they *want* to hear, I know what they *expect* me to say, but forcing a lie feels worse than speaking the truth.

"Essence," the judge urges.

Her voice is gentler than the prosecutors, somehow giving me a bit more ease.

My mind whirls, searching for the thoughts I had last night.

Those sentences I said to myself in the mirror, those statements I wrote on the paperwork.

"We need to hear it from you."

Closing my eyes, I feel the sting of tears align the rim of my eyes. They're threatening to overflow as I recall the nights that they ask for, yet I hold them back.

"They—," I stammer.

My eyes wander toward Rylee, who sits, her gaze begging me to continue. Taking a deep breath, I swallow hard.

"They're from Christopher."

aaron

. . .

ESSENCE HASN'T BEEN herself lately.

She hasn't spoken, slept, or eaten anything in days.

The spark in her eyes that once lit up whenever she'd see me is gone, replaced by a dull, vacant stare.

The past few days, I've watched her drift further away each time I glanced at her, trying my hardest to speak to her.

Every time I've said anything, I get nothing. No words, no sound, no signal expressing that she'd heard me.

Just silence and the view of her staring into the distance, drilling a nonexistent hole into the wall.

Sitting up, I grab my phone from the nightstand and scroll through Instagram.

My feed loads a bunch of videos and images, all of the people trying to format what's going on between Christopher and Essence.

People don't believe her.

They think she's making it all up just to gather attention back toward her brand, and although it's not outside of Chris's character to, it still disgusts me to realize that he's not doing a single thing about it.

He's letting them tear her down, letting them talk all this shit about who she is, and what her plan is.

The more I scroll, the more frustrated I get. The more photos I find of her mascara-stained face, puffy eyes, and nervous antics, the more I agitated I feel.

I close my eyes for a moment, then take a deep breath before turning my phone off and slipping it to the side.

Turning toward Essence, I watch as she moves for a bit, to pull the blanket toward her, before settling and going still, going silent.

Everything is so unlike her, and it scares me.

I've tried giving her space, hoping she'd come around, but every time I peek into our room, the sight of her just lying there, eyes fixed on nothing, rips at me.

Every time I turn around in the mornings, I don't find her bright smile anymore.

I don't hear her joyous laughter or the nervous rambling about her upcoming culinary attendance.

I hear nothing, and that—*again*—is what scares me.

❤ ❤ ❤ ❤ ❤

The smell of pancakes wafts through the kitchen.

Placing the platter of pancakes to the side, I grab an egg and crack it onto the pan, its edges beginning to bubble as it heats. I then crack another one, watching as it joins the other.

Behind me, the sound of a cheerful cartoon fills the air, interrupted by the occasional giggle from Faith.

She's curled up on the couch and holding a cup of milk, her attention fixed on the bright colors and playful characters.

It doesn't take long before I hear the soft patter of her feet against the tiled floor, to which I turn around in curiosity, our gazes meeting as a bright smile appears onto her face.

Beginning to stand on her tippy toes, Faith swipes a small nip of a pancake from the stack before tossing it into her mouth. The sight causes me to chuckle a bit before continuing with the scrambled eggs.

"Daddy," she calls, tapping my side.

Looking down at her, I raise my eyebrows to signal myself listening.

"Whose plate is that?"

Her small finger points in the direction of the last counter, which holds three plates. One for each of us; Me, Faith, and Essence.

Looking back down at her, I watch as her little brows furrow, a small action that she does whenever she finds herself deep in thought.

"It's for Essence, baby," I respond, lifting the pan off the stove as I finish cooking the last of the eggs. I then walk over to the plates, scraping a reasonable portion onto each one, trying to maintain some semblance of normalcy.

Faith follows behind me, her footsteps quickening with an eagerness that seems out-of-place today.

"What's wrong with her?" she asks, her voice laced with concern. I turn to give her a questioning look, my heart sinking at the mention of Essence.

"What do you mean?" I ask, hoping to deflect the conversation, but I can see the worry etched on Faith's face.

"Why won't she get up anymore?"

The innocence in her voice is both heartwarming and heartbreaking. The way Faith notices her absence, her struggle, stirs something deep within me, a mix of sadness and helplessness that I can't quite shake off.

I let out a soft sigh as I finish plating our food. "I'm trying to figure that out," I respond, my eyes drifting toward the living room where Essence used to sit, her laughter filling the space.

Turning off the stove, I hand Faith her plate, watching as she takes it and wanders off back toward the TV, her tiny figure disappearing into the glow of the screen. I can't help but replay the moments leading up to Essence's change, the laughter that once filled the air now replaced by a heavy silence.

The question lingers in my mind, gnawing at me: What can I do to bring back that light that once laid in her eyes?

The conversation between Faith and me lingers in my mind as I place a tray down.

It holds the plate of Essence's food, paired with a glass of orange juice. Her eyes follow my movements as I do so, but move back toward the blank area of the wall that she's been staring at for the past few days.

Sitting on the bed, I take a sip from my glass before placing it onto the nightstand. I then grab my phone, hesitating for a moment before placing it back down onto the mattress.

Tapping Essence's side, I speak.

"Hey," I begin. She doesn't speak, doesn't move—nothing. Taking a deep breath, I continue, careful to keep my voice soft.

"I'm worried about you."

For a moment, I think it's going to be like all the other times —me talking to the walls, my words vanishing into the silence. But then she shifts, her head turning just enough for me to see her eyes.

They're not as empty as they've been. It's like there's something there—a small acknowledgement, maybe even a flicker of emotion.

"Yeah?" she says, her voice raspy due to not using it in days.

It's the first word she's spoken to me since the trial, and even though it's small, it feels like a victory.

Moving closer, I sit on the edge of the bed, careful not to push too far too fast.

"Yeah," I reply, relieved and nervous all at once.

I let out a breath that feels as if I have been holding it back for days, grateful that Essence eventually turned around.

"I just…" I pause, thinking of what to say before continuing, "I need to know you're okay. Can you talk to me?"

She stares at me for what seems like an eternity, the silence stretching between us. But then she sighs and looks away, her fingers fidgeting with the edge of the blanket.

"I'm not okay," she whispers, and I watch as the admission seems like the first crack in a damn that's been holding back a flood.

And just like that, the wall that she once had built high around herself crumbles.

"I keep thinking back over and over from times he hurt me," she begins.

Her voice sounds frail, almost weak, and her eyes water. "And I've seen what they're saying about me. I've seen the comments, the stories, the clips, and the podcasts."

She rolls her eyes at the end of her statement, annoyed by the pestering feedback that seems to live. Essence almost adds to another sentence before deciding against it, muttering on, "I don't know."

"I don't think I can keep doing this, Aaron."

"Doing what?" I ask, and staring at the ceiling, Essence shakes her head.

"Facing him. The consequences of facing him. This entire trial itself. I don't think I can do it."

The very moment Essence finishes her sentence, I turn toward her. Tapping her leg, I make sure her eyes meet mine, and when they do, she sits up.

A heavy exhale exits her mouth, and for the first time, I can see the toll that all of this has on her. Her under-eyes have bags, her face looks drained, and her gaze looks cold and empty.

"Essence, I need you to know something," I begin, and fiddling with her ring, she nods.

"You are strong. You are resilient. You are *the person you are*. I don't know a single being who could go through as much as you have and would still be standing."

Essence sniffles a bit before letting out a dimmed smile.

"Essence, you are perfect."

Just as I think she might respond, she interrupts me mid-sentence, leaning in with an urgency that takes me by surprise. Her lips meet mine, soft yet fervent, pulling me into a moment that feels suspended in time.

Essence's hands graze my face, and I feel as she reclines back. Within seconds, she now lays against the mattress, lips still on mine.

As we break apart, I can't help but see the glow returning to her eyes.

The joy that once found its way away from Ess was back to her, and I'm more than excited to realize that.

A smile appears on her face, and she lets out a laugh.

My mind then reels back to days before, the first day of the trial.

How panicked she had been, and how nervous she was. How she was tempted to give up and just be a no-show, let him win.

But she couldn't. I couldn't let her give in. Because that's what he wants her to do. He wants her to give up, to feel like there's nothing she can do about it.

I let her know that's what he believed.

But when I had, I heard her say something I've never heard her say before, not even to close friends like Yasmyn or Zaara.

"You okay?" Essence asks, her face expressing concern.

I still sit propped on top of her, my hands pressed into the mattress.

She wraps her legs around my waist and drapes her arms around my neck.

My eyes search hers for a moment, hoping for some kind of answer.

"Essence," I say faintly, and she raises an eyebrow.

"Did you mean what you said the other day?" I ask, and she grows silent. Essence's eyes dart away from mine, a flicker of uncertainty crossing her face. Her expression reads hesitance, unsure of whatever I might have to say about the interaction.

I can feel my heart pound through my chest, begging for the answer to my question.

"Did you?" I press, feeling the tension hang thick in the air, desperate for clarity. Without uttering a word, Essence nods, her gaze locking onto mine with a mix of vulnerability and resolve.

A smile breaks across my face, and she mirrors it, her relief clear. I lean in, capturing her lips with mine in a gentle kiss that feels electric. Pulling back just enough to speak.

"Say it again," I say, my voice almost a whisper, but she furrows her brow in confusion.

"Say what?" she replies, and I can see the realization dawning on her face, igniting a grin that spreads across my own.

"Say it," I insist, relishing the way her breath catches in her throat.

"Aaron," she stammers, but I'm quick to silence her with another kiss, my heart racing with anticipation.

"Come on, let me hear it."

Licking her lips, Essence lets out a soft chuckle before rolling her eyes in playful exasperation.

She tries her hardest to hold back a smile, but I know her.

Despite her best efforts to maintain a serious demeanor, I can see her resolve crumbling, and soon enough, the corners of her mouth betray her.

With a bit more boldness this time, she states, "I love you," and her voice is filled with sincerity.

"Again," I tease, and I laugh as she rolls her eyes, her playful frustration clear.

"I love you," she mumbles, her cheeks flushed, and I lean down for yet another kiss.

Pulling back, I gaze into her eyes before whispering,

"I love you too, Essence."

aaron

. . .

"YOU GUYS ARE TOGETHER NOW?"

Maeko's question catches me off guard, and I can't help but chuckle in response. As I sink into the familiar comfort of my office chair, I grip my phone against my ear, the slight weight of it grounding me at the moment.

"Good morning to you too, Mae," I reply, my tone laced with playful sarcasm.

I can almost picture her rolling her eyes on the other end of the line, and sure enough, I hear a scoff escape her lips before my laughter bubbles up again.

"Where's this coming from?" I ask, curious. I grab a nearby pen and begin jotting down random notes from a file report. My mind focused on the task at hand, but intrigued by Maeko's sudden line of questioning.

"Check what I just sent you," she mutters, her voice tinged with mischief. Just as she finishes speaking, a notification dings from my phone, prompting me to pull it away from my ear. My pulse quickens as I swipe through to see what she's referring to, and the moment the image loads, I can't help but smile.

On the screen is a photo of me and Essence, posed in front of a mirror.

In the picture, my hands are resting on her waist while we both smile brightly.

Best part of it all? It's posted on her Instagram story, paired with a song by Coco Jones and a caption that reads, *"Hard Launch?"*

A snicker comes from Mae's side of the phone as I place the speaker back up to my ear.

"So?" she begins, and with my smile only growing bigger, I only seem to give in.

"When did this happen? Why didn't I know about this?"

Her raid of questions only causes me to laugh a bit more, gathering the attention of my nearby coworkers. Noticing weary eyes toward me, I quiet down before responding.

"The first trial. She was all nervous and scared; she almost backed out and couldn't breathe," I begin, and I can almost hear the smile grow across Mae's face.

"What?" I ask, and she dismisses me, her eagerness palpable as she insists I continue with the explanation.

"Well, after I calmed her down, she told me she loved me." An audible gasp comes from the phone, and I lean back in my chair, a grin spreading across my face.

"She what?" Mae's disbelief is almost comical.

"She *loves* me, Mae," I add, my voice above a whisper as I ponder the weight of those words.

My jaw tenses as I recall the days leading up to this moment —the anxiety etched on her face as we approached the court-house, her hands trembling, and how even after the trial, she struggled to find the strength to get out of bed.

How I reassured her that no matter what happens, I'll always be there for her.

"Did you say it back?" Mae asks, her voice a mixture of curiosity and excitement. I fall silent, my smile growing larger as I replay the moment in my mind. "Aaron," Maeko calls, and I come back from my thoughts.

"Of course I did," I reply, my voice above a whisper.

An excited squeal comes from the phone, a sound I haven't heard from Mae in years.

"Holy shit, my best friend's in love!" she exclaims, and I laugh. Glancing toward my picture frames, my eyes landing on an image of Essence and Faith standing side by side, bright smiles on their faces.

"I am. I *really* fucking am," I mutter, the weight of my confession settling in, a mix of excitement and anxiety swirling within me..

I can almost hear her grin over the phone when she continues, her voice laced with curiosity. I can almost hear her grin over the phone when she continues, her voice laced with curiosity.

"You thought anything about when she leaves?" she asks, and suddenly the air feels heavier.

"What?" I reply, surprised.

Fuck.

"For Chicago. That culinary school down there. What are you guys gonna do?"

I haven't thought about that.

Essence leaves for Chicago in less than three weeks, and we've just now admitted what we feel for each other.

The idea of her leaving this place—and me—behind, packing her bags, should provide me with some sort of comfort for her. The comfort of knowing that she'll accomplish her dreams. The comfort of knowing that she'll be back home with her family.

There's a comfort that everything she's fought for will be worth it.

But it doesn't. The thought of her being gone *doesn't*.

Sure, we could try to make long-distance work; we could send texts and schedule video calls, but the idea feels hollow when I think of the distance that would separate us.

What if she finds someone else?

What if we drift apart?
Nibbling on my nail, I sit as I think.
What does this mean for us?

❤ ❤ ❤ ❤

The house is almost still when I shut the door behind me.

For a moment, the silence is deafening, but it's soothed when I hear Essence's laugh.

A smile appears on my face as I place my coat onto the hook, walking toward Faith's bedroom—where the laughter occurs.

Peeking my head through the doorway, I feel my eyes light up when I spot the two of them sitting on Faith's bed, talking as Essence paints Faith's nails.

"I remember when I was ten, my older cousin would come to my abuela's restaurant all the time. She made the best tres leches," Essence says, and Faith glances up, a curious smile stretching across her lips as she absorbs every word.

"What is *tres leches*?" Faith asks, trying her hardest to nail the accent that Essence has.

The way she sounds causes Ess to giggle a bit, then helps Faith out with the pronunciation before explaining it to her.

"It's a kind of cake."

Licking my lips, I lean against the doorframe before crossing my arms, continuing to watch the interaction unfold.

"I want to make it! Can we make tres leches?" Faith exclaims, and laughing a bit, Ess laughs.

"We can," Essence replies, laughter bubbling up as she nods, her hands still working on the final touches of Faith's nails.

Just then, I clear my throat, a playful attempt to announce my presence, and Essence's head whips around to meet my gaze, her face lighting up with a bright smile.

She turns back to finish painting Faith's nails, the nail polish bottle clicking shut as she places it to the side, then stands up and walks toward me.

She plants a kiss onto my lips and leans on the other side of the doorframe before speaking.

"How was work?" She asks, and I can tell that's a question she's been wanting to ask for a while. The expression that sits on her face makes that obvious.

The way her brows furrow just, well, that and the way her cheeks fade toward a soft tint of red. It's subtle, just hardly noticeable, yet I always seem to spot it.

I like when her cheeks turn that red.

It's cute.

Faith then stands up and wanders toward me, her hands raised to show me her nails before she speaks.

I take her hand, examining the delicate polish with feigned seriousness before letting it go, unable to suppress a grin. "I see them, baby. Essence did good, didn't she?" I reply, glancing over at Ess, who struggles to hold back a proud smile.

Faith smiles and hugs Ess's leg the most cautious way she can before talking.

"She did!"

Sitting on the mattress, I slip my shoes off and toss them to the side, the soft thud of the soles hitting the floor punctuating the stillness of the room.

Essence sits beside me, her presence both calming and charged with unspoken words.

"You never answered my question," she says, her tone teasing yet laced with an undercurrent of seriousness. I let out a laugh, trying to deflect the gravity of the moment.

"Oh, really?" I reply, raising an eyebrow in mock surprise. Without a word, Ess crosses her arms and gives me a pointed look, an action that makes me chuckle again.

"Work was okay," I admit, as I toss my shoes further to the side and lean back onto the bed, the springs creaking beneath my weight. Ess follows suit, lying beside me for a moment before she shuffles closer, resting her head on my chest.

I massage her scalp, my fingers weaving through her hair, bringing a sense of peace to the room.

A calm silence fills the air, but it soon becomes tense, prompting me to ask the question that has been nagging at me for hours.

"Have you thought about what happens when you leave?"

The question hangs between us, heavy and unyielding. Ess doesn't move at my words; she remains still, the rhythmic rise and fall of her breathing grounding me at the moment.

"Ess?" I prompt.

"I don't want to think about it," she mutters, and an involuntary silence blankets the room. I hesitate, feeling the weight of her words, but my curiosity pushes me to continue.

"But I do. What are we doing? Are we planning visits? Am I coming with you?" I pause, restraining the unwanted question on my tongue, and then I ask, "Are we just going to let this slip away?"

She lets out a deep sigh and looks at me, her face showing a combination of vulnerability and frustration. My hand, which had been resting on her head, slips away as she shifts her position.

"I don't know," she begins, her voice wavering as she gathers her thoughts.

"I don't know. I don't know what we're gonna do, Aaron, and that's what scares me." Her words linger in the air between us, thick with unspoken fears.

"I want to love you, you know," she continues, her eyes glistening with unshed tears.

"I want to kiss you. I want to hug you and hold you."

"And you can," I whisper, trying to convey the certainty I wish I felt.

But her eyes, glistening with unshed tears, reflect the fears we both share.

"But what about when I can't?" she asks, and for the first time, I find myself at a complete loss for words.

"I can come with you. Faith and I can come with you. We'll pack up and I'll book a flight," I stammer, and Essence shakes her head.

My words reveal my fear, unsure of what lies ahead for us.

"What about Faith? She has her friends, her grandmother, her family—everyone's here," Essence responds, and I sniffle.

"I can't take that away from her."

I can hear the tremor in her voice, and the minute that I do, I hold her, a silent signal for her to stop talking.

For the first time, I find myself at a loss for words, the silence stretching between us as I grapple with a reality I wish I could change.

I wish I could go with her.

Drop everything and follow her back to her home, supporting her dreams as she goes on.

But I can't.

A tear drops from her eye when I wipe it off, replacing it with a quick kiss on her forehead.

"You know what we can do?" I ask, and looking back up at me, Essence's eyes meet mine.

"We can embrace the time we have together. Even if it's limited."

I watch as her gaze drops to the floor, the gloomy feeling that now envelops us growing heavier, threatening to overshadow our brief respite from reality.

I take a deep breath, steeling myself against the weight of her melancholy, and decide to shift the narrative.

"So in honor of embracing said time," I begin, letting a moment pass to build anticipation, while my finger finds its way to her chin.

With a delicate touch, I guide her face upward, coaxing her eyes to meet mine once more. I can see the flicker of uncertainty in her gaze, and I search for the right words to break through the fog.

"Will you be my valentine?"

essence

. . .

CLEARING MY THROAT, I glance at Rylee, who gives me a reassuring nod.

The prosecutor's voice is steady, almost gentle, as he asks what I've been waiting for almost the entire trial to hear.

"Ms. Miller, can you describe the nature of your relationship with Mr. Reynolds during your time working together?"

Taking a deep breath, I let the air fill my lungs.

"In the beginning, it was professional—at least, that's what I believed. Christopher was my manager, someone I trusted to guide my career. But as time went on, things changed," I pause, my gaze locking onto Christopher.

His once confident demeanor is now cracking, almost as if the reality of the situation's now weighing on him.

Continuing, I hold my voice steady, "One day Mr. Evans told me he had feelings for me. Feelings he 'didn't expect to have.' It wasn't long before he and I began dating."

People around the court nod, and cameras flash for a moment before stopping.

"And this relationship, was everything done consensual?"

"Yes, sir," I respond, and the prosecutor nods, his eyes encouraging me to keep going.

"How long did this relationship last?" he asks, his tone probing, but not harsh.

I hesitate for a moment, feeling the weight of everyone's attention on me.

"It lasted about a year," I say, my voice even.

"At first, everything seemed fine—good, even. But then things changed. Christopher became more controlling, more possessive. It started with little things—telling me what to wear, who I could talk to—but it escalated."

The prosecutor leans forward.

"Can you describe how it escalated, Ms. Miller?"

I swallow hard, recalling the moments that still haunt me.

"He would get angry if I didn't respond to his texts right away, or if I wanted to spend time with my friends instead of him. There were ties when he'd shown up to the house unannounced, demanding to know where I'd been, who I was with. He'd make me feel guilty for wanting any kind of life outside of him."

My eyes flicker toward Chris, who's staring at the table in front of him, his hands clenched into fists. It's as if he's trying to will himself invisible, but he can't escape this. Not anymore.

"I left the relationship after that. But he didn't let me get away that easily," I add, and quickly, the prosecutor hops onto that statement.

"What do you mean, Ms. Miller?" he asks, tone sharp with urgency.

As I pause and collect myself, memories of the conversation we had only a few months ago flood my mind.

"Christopher would remind me of the contract I had signed with him, I say, my voice steady, yet laced with the memories I feel.

"How I would lose everything—everything I had and earned —if I left."

The prosecutor nods, urging me to elaborate.

"It was a management contract," I continue, feeling the weight of those words.

"When I first signed it, I thought it was just standard—something to protect my career, to ensure he'd help me grow in the industry. But after I tried to leave, he started using it as a weapon. He'd say things like, 'You belong to me, remember? You can't just walk away from this.' He'd threaten to ruin my reputation, to blacklist me from the industry, saying no one else would work with me if I broke the contract."

I pause, feeling the courtroom grow silent as everyone listens.

"He'd say he'd make sure I never worked again, that I'd lose everything—my endorsements, my opportunities—if I didn't stay with him. It wasn't just emotional manipulation; it was financial, professional. He made sure I felt trapped, like I had no way out."

The prosecutor steps closer, his eyes filled with understanding. "And is that why you stayed as long as you did?"

I nod.

"Yes. But I recently stepped out. And the very moment I had, Christopher did what he said he would do. He went to the media and tarnished my name. Any claims people made, he didn't clear up, I had to do it on my own. People sent me threatening DMs and messages, sending many insults such as, 'whore' and 'slut.' They insisted that everything I've come out about was just for the sake of me wanting attention."

The prosecutor takes a deep breath, his eyes closing for a moment before going back to the conversations before.

"Back to the statements in which you claimed he was overbearing. Did these behaviors ever resort to physical violence?"

HIs voice softened, and his sentence trails as he waits for my answer.

My mind rewinds back to those nights—the nights of tight grips I begged to be let go of. The grips I found myself in whenever I said or did something he didn't like.

"Yes. The first time it happened, I was in shock. I couldn't believe it was real. He grabbing my wrist and held me during an argument, and I just…froze. I remember thinking, 'This isn't happening. This can't be happening.' But it did, and it got worse after that."

There's a murmur in the courtroom, the weight of my words sinking in.

Tears prick at the corners of my eyes, but I force them back. I won't let him see me break. Not here, not now.

The prosecutor gives me a moment before continuing.

"Ms. Miller, why did you decide to come forward?"

I take a deep breath, my resolve hardening.

"Because I couldn't live in fear anymore. I couldn't pretend that everything was okay when it wasn't. I cried every night after I left. I was broken and left mentally shattered for weeks. Memories only replayed. Signs and wishes that I had left earlier stained my mind."

A slight tear falls from my cheek, but I wipe it off.

"And the guilt, *God*, the guilt. I know Christopher. I know his behavior, his actions, his wishes. I know his *power*. Even though I was gone, I know how quickly someone can replace me. How easy it is for him to find another victim, and how simple it is to keep them quiet. I couldn't let him do that to anyone anymore. When I thought about the other women—I knew I had to speak up," I pause.

"For them, and for myself."

The prosecutor nods, satisfied.

"Thank you, Ms. Miller. No further questions."

Walking out of the courtroom, Aaron's arms lay outstretched.

Tears form in my eyes, and I run into him, his arms wrapping around me the moment I collide with him.

"I did it, I fucking did it," I stammer, breaking down into tears. I bury my face in his chest, my voice muffled as I speak. Lifting my head, my eyes look up at Aaron.

His hands reach for my face and tears fall down his face as he wipes mine. His eyes then scan my face for a moment, and I watch as his gaze rests when they meet mine.

The camera shutters and flashes around us go silent.

I can't hear the crowd, nor the questions that seem to be yelling at me throughout the room.

It's almost as if we're the only ones in the universe.

In my mind, thoughts and memories swirl. Memories of the past few years, all the pain I've endured and kept hidden from the world. The bruises and the marks, the tears and the screams.

The thoughts that say that I wouldn't have made it this far without Aaron. Without his encouragement, without his words and his hope. I wouldn't have any of this.

If it were up to me, I would've given up a long time ago.

Hell, I probably wouldn't have even made it to that first trial if it weren't for him.

My thoughts and feelings would've gotten to me, and I would be back at wherever I would be living, within seconds.

But Aaron, he helped, he listened, he pushed.

He made sure I had the energy to stay, made sure my heart stayed intact. Whenever it wasn't, he made sure it could be put back together.

Because if there's one thing I've learnt throughout this whole thing, it's that I wasn't alone. I had someone by my side throughout the entire journey, someone who was always willing to give their best, regardless of the circumstances.

Licking my lips, my eyes drift down to Aaron's, and I can feel my heart racing in my chest.

The way he looks at me, with that mix of joy and admiration, sends a thrill through me.

I want to kiss him. I do, I really do.

For a moment, hesitation creeps in.

My mind races with a flurry of doubts—what if the timing isn't right? What if this moment is what shatters the fragile balance we've built? But as I look into his eyes, I quickly push all those thoughts aside. The truth is undeniable: at this moment, there's nothing in the world I love more than him.

Nothing.

The way he makes me laugh, the way he listens to my fears, and the way he pushes me to be the strongest I can be—it all feeds that insatiable hunger in my heart.

Taking a deep breath, I ground myself in the reality of my feelings.

I've told this man I *love* him.

I treat his daughter like my own. I can't imagine my life without him. I can't let the fear of just life hold me back any longer. It's now or never, and I know in my heart that this is the moment I've been waiting for.

Leaning in, his lips meet mine, and the moment they do, I can sense the flashes of nearby cameras go crazy.

A chuckle escapes my lips a bit before he and I part, and when we do, our eyes meet as I speak, my voice expressing more than I ever have.

"I *love* you."

❤ ❤ ❤ ❤ ❤

The judge strikes her gavel against the stand, causing the room to quickly become quiet.

Cameras begin to flash, along with the light scatter of mumbles and whispers that seem to continue.

"The jury has come to a verdict," the judge announces, her voice steady and authoritative. The words send a ripple of tension through the courtroom, and I feel my heart begin to race. This is it—the moment everything has been leading up to.

The jury foreperson, a middle-aged woman with a calm demeanor, stands and unfolds a piece of paper. The room is so silent, you could hear a pin drop. I grip the edge of the table in front of me, my knuckles turning white as I wait for her to speak.

"We, the jury, find the defendant, Christopher Evans…" She pauses, the weight of the moment hanging in the air. My breath catches in my throat as I hold on to that silence, praying that all the pain that I, and many others, have gone through will finally be listened to.

Closing my eyes, I make a silent prayer. A prayer that all of this—*all* of it—will be worth it.

"…guilty on all counts."

The words hit me like a tidal wave, and for a moment, I can't breathe. The room erupts—cameras flashing, people whispering, the sound of someone crying out in relief—but it all fades into the background as the verdict sinks in.

Guilty.

He's guilty.

I feel tears welling up in my eyes, but they're not tears of fear or sadness—they're tears of relief, of vindication. I glance over at Chris, and for the first time since this trial began, I see him for what he really is—a man stripped of his power, no longer able to hide behind his lies.

The judge's gavel strikes again, calling the room to order. "Mr. Evans will be remanded into custody immediately. Sentencing will be scheduled for a later date."

As the bailiffs move to take Chris away, he looks up at me, his eyes filled with a mix of anger and something else—something that looks a lot like fear. But I don't look away. I meet his gaze head-on, letting him see that I'm not afraid of him anymore.

His eyes continue to stay on mine when I decide to speak.

"You broke me. Made everything feel like love, like passion. You fucking broke me, Christopher. And finally, *finally,* I get to break *you*. Fuck you, and *fuck* what you did to me," I begin, my voice breaking.

Tears fall down my cheeks, and for the first time, I don't bother to wipe them.

I let them fall. I let them stain my cheeks. I let them, and why? Because I haven't let them in years.

"Fuck you."

A dirty look appears on his face, and his eyes turn red before he's turned away. As he's led out of the courtroom in handcuffs, I finally allow myself to breathe, the weight of everything lifting off my shoulders. It's over. He's finally going to pay for what he's done.

I feel a hand on my shoulder and turn to see my lawyer, a small, proud smile on her face.

"We did it," I say softly, and without hesitation, she shakes her head.

"No, Essence. *You* did it."

essence

. . .

AARON'S right hand rests on my right thigh as he drives, while his left continues to hold on to the steering wheel.

The placement causes small butterflies to flutter around my stomach, and I nibble on my bottom lip light as I fight back the urge to smile.

Driving through the city, streetlights and light signs reflect against the windshield and sunroof. People chatter around us, and Sinead Harnett's *"Where You Been Hiding,"* plays on the radio.

Grabbing my phone, I open Instagram and take a quick picture of his hand against my skin, then type up a quick caption when a message from Yasmyn pops up onto the screen.

> You guys get there yet?? Send pics!!

I only bite down harder on my lip at her text before shooting her a quick reply and placing my phone back to the side.

Last Tuesday, Aaron asked me to be his valentine.

With me leaving for Chicago just a couple days before valentine's day, he figured that since we can't spend the day itself together, then we could make a day to spend together.

So this morning, we dropped Faith off over at her friend's house. Then, when we got back home, we spent the rest of the day coddled up on the couch, watching movies. Once 5 o'clock hit, Aaron told me to get ready for a date night—with no clarification of where we're headed. He handed me a dress, a pair of heels, and told me to let him know when I'm ready.

So, I did.

"What's the plan for tonight?" I ask, trying my hardest to pry. Aaron seems to snap back from a daze before responding.

"It's a surprise, baby," he mumbles, and I groan.

"Come on, tell me. If you're scared I won't like it, there's nothing I wouldn't love," I nudge, and he chuckles.

"It's not that I'm scared you won't like it," he begins, and leaning against the center console, my eyes glued to him as I raise an eyebrow.

"It's just that I want to surprise you one last time before you go."

Crossing my arms, I lean back in my seat with a playful attitude before sitting back up.

"Please?" I begin.

I give him puppy eyes as I plead, which causes him to laugh a bit before giving me a sarcastic scoff and speaking.

"I just want to know what I dressed all fancy for."

"Fine," he sighs, and I give a small dance of celebration.

"There's this art museum I want to check out with you. It looks nice, and I figured you might like it," he says, and I smile.

I've got a feeling I know exactly what museum he's talking about, and if it's what I'm thinking of, I don't know what I'd do.

"Art museum?" I repeat, and shooting a glance at me, Aaron nods.

A grin appears on his face before he continues, a silent signal that what I'm thinking of is where we're headed.

"Yup. Plus, we've got a solid two-hour showing to catch before heading out for dinner."

As he turns the corner, we near a tall building, where cars seem to be parked everywhere.

I look up at the building's sign, and the exact name I expected sits onto the structure.

It reads 'RaeLynn Modernity,' and it's this new museum that Yasmyn checked out just a couple months ago, for her birthday. She went with her cousins, and when she sent pictures to me, I fell in love.

The displays all have looks that I adore, and meanings that you don't have to look very hard to find. Sure, sometimes that's just art in general, but it's something that I just seem to love the idea of.

Especially since that's what it feels like me and Aaron's love was like—in plain sight.

My eyes gaze out of the window, watching as couples walk along the surrounding sidewalks, hand in hand, and smiles on their faces as they approach the entrance.

"Did you get tickets or are you planning on charming our way in?" I ask, now hesitant, as I look around the crowded lot.

For a moment, Aaron doesn't respond. Instead, he focuses on maneuvering the car into an empty spot.

Now putting the car in park, he then unbuckles his seatbelt before digging into his pocket and pulling out two tickets.

A smile aligns his face as he speaks.

"This answer your question?"

With a smile, I roll my eyes before slipping my purse onto my shoulder.

Aaron then exits, leaving me in the silent car alone as I flip down the sun visor and fix a few flaws in my makeup. Watching as he walks toward my side of the car, I begin to shut the visor.

When it closes, Aaron opens the door, and I can't help but smile as my eyes fall onto his.

He now stands in front of me, his hand out and waiting for mine. I grasp it, then step out of the car and shut the door behind me. His hand continues to hold on to mine, and I can feel my heart pound in my chest.

It only seems to go faster as I steal a glance at the museum's building, still astonished by the way he almost seemed to read my mind about my want to come here. Returning my gaze back to Aaron, our eyes lock and a smile spreads across his face.

"You ready?" He asks, and I bite back my smile before nodding in response. He lets out a light chuckle before we walk.

"Then let's go have some fun."

❤ ❤ ❤ ❤ ❤

"This is a beautiful piece."

Glancing at Aaron, I watch as he continues to examine the canvas that hangs on the wall.

His hands sit in his pockets, and he seems to take a moment before looking up to find my ongoing gaze.

I try to nudge it off by looking around me, but I laugh.

"It is," I stammer, and Aaron smiles.

His hand reaches out for mine, and without hesitation, I grasp it. I once again look at the painting. It's an oil abstract of the ocean, a palette of muted tones such as blue and a couple of grays.

Backing up, I let go of Aaron's hand as I take a quick picture.

Aaron stands in front of it, his head raised up as he continues looking, admiring the piece. Walking back toward Aaron, I show him the screen. "You took a secret picture of me," he teases, and I smile.

"I did," I whisper, and he smiles.

"But you know what I want?" He asks, and cocking my head sideways, I raise an eyebrow.

"I want a picture *with* you."

A smile appears on my face as I nod, and we stand in front of the painting.

With my right thumb on the shutter button, I snap a couple of pictures, trying my best to hold back a laugh as I do so.

Bringing my phone back down, I press the pictures and show him once again, this time causing a smile to pop onto his face.

"Send me those," he points, and licking my lips, I nod before doing so.

Looking up from the screen, my eyes meet Aaron's as his gaze lingers on mine. They then wander around my face for a moment before I smile, then talk to cut the lingering tension.

"What?" I ask, and a laugh sticks within my voice.

Without speaking, Aaron shakes his head.

Glancing around, I search for a nearby bench before spotting one and walking toward it, sitting down as I look around the room.

People around laugh and smile, and a few others talk about the surrounding pieces. Aaron sits beside me, and I feel as his hand lands on mine. Turning to him, I watch as he looks at the piece that now sits in front of us, a sculpture of *Alexander The Great*.

For a moment, I admire him. His features, his mannerisms, his appeal. His clothes, his bodily tone, his habits.

"You okay?"

Aaron's voice snaps me back to reality as I laugh, finding it almost embarrassing that he'd caught me staring. "Yeah," I chuckle. A brief smile dances on Aaron's lips before sitting down.

He shifts his position, now sitting in a way that he faces me, but with a small bit of distance.

We now sit silently, and I can't help but notice a mischievous glimmer in Aaron's eyes. Without warning, his fingers reach out, tugging on the loop of my jeans. He then pulls me closer.

Our faces are now a mere inch apart, and I can feel his warm breath against my lips, daring me to lean closer.

With a mixture of anticipation and nervousness, I close my eyes and our lips meet. I can feel the warmth spreading through my body. Aaron's lips are gentle against mine, creating a blissful sensation that I never want to end.

The world fades away as our connection deepens, and I can't help but lose myself at the moment.

Aaron's hand slides up from my waist to cup the back of my neck, deepening the kiss even further. I can feel the intimacy and trust between us growing with each passing second. It's as if time stands still, and all that matters is the electric chemistry we share. Our bodies pressed together. I can't help but feel a sense of completeness and contentment.

Feelings I only have with him.

That I only want with *him*.

❤ ❤ ❤ ❤ ❤

I watch with amusement as Aaron takes a bite of his salad, pausing to chew before he talks. And though he's speaking, my mind seems to tune out his words. Instead, my focus is on him. His laugh, his smile, his expressions.

And I smile as I do so because I can't help it. The night's been everything I could've ever dreamt of, that and more.

Over the past couple of months, I've grown to feel something toward Aaron. A feeling I haven't experienced in a long time, and one I never thought I would feel again. Yet here I am, overwhelmed by it all over again. The butterflies in my stomach, the anticipation that courses through my veins, the nerves that both exhilarate and terrify me. It's a constant whirlwind of emotions, accompanied by a never-ending stream of laughter.

I unconsciously smile, yearning for any form of physical contact with him. I want to hold his hand, to feel his warmth, to see his smiles. It's constant, and I can't stop it. For once, I'm feeling that one feeling I'd swear I'd never accept again—but this time I don't want to push it away.

"Aaron," I call, and as he looks up from his salad, he raises an eyebrow.

"I want you to know something."

"Yeah?" He asks, and grabbing his fabric napkin, he wipes his mouth.

I think for a moment, unsure of what I'm even about to say.

What if I say it in a way that offends him?

Taking a deep breath, I silence the doubts before saying it anyway.

"I haven't been this happy in years, Aaron. Years."

The sentence floats in the air for a moment when Aaron speaks.

"How happy do I make you?" He asks, and taking a sip from my cup, I think before giving him an answer.

"Very."

"But how much?"

"More than I can even explain, Aaron," I begin.

"The day I met you, I did not know how this would be, how it would turn out. I felt that something would happen, and I distanced myself a bit when I realized it. But what I didn't know was that I'd end up here. Time progressed, and small signals of like turned into signals of love. And I realized I can give my heart to you."

He struggles to hold back a smile when I hold up a finger, a signal that I'm not done.

"Everything about you makes me feel the most comfortable I have ever been. Not just your presence, but your actions, your words, the way you make me feel. The way you laugh, the way you look, your personality, the way you look at me," I continue, and a chuckle lingers at the end of my words as I do so.

"Aaron, *you* made me believe in love again."

essence

. . .

I LEAVE IN LESS than 10 hours.

I am on a plane to Chicago in *less* than 10 hours.

Meaning, I've got about 8 hours to spend with my two favorite people.

I slip out of the bed and head toward the bathroom, where everything feels so bare. All of my things are packed into separate hygiene bags, and the makeup tower Aaron bought me when I first moved in now sits empty, between our sinks.

Grabbing my toothbrush and toothpaste from a toiletry bag, I brush my teeth, my eyes staring at my reflection as I do so.

Everything that's happened to me has led to this moment, *everything*.

Everything brought me right back home, where I needed to be in the first place.

Wandering back into the bedroom, I look around, my eyes only landing on the multitude of boxes and suitcases that lay scattered around the room.

The suitcases hold a decent amount of my clothes, along with some shoes. Opening one, I pull out an outfit before shutting it and heading back into the bathroom.

It's so quiet. So quiet, it's scary.

Maybe I hadn't noticed how quiet it can get until now, when I'm about to leave. It's just me awake, left to my thoughts and my wishes, hoping only for the best of this move.

Beginning to do my hair, I peer at myself in the mirror.

Even with how much I've wanted to reach this point, able to do me and feel free, I can't help but feel like this was such a horrible time to.

I found someone I love. Someone I care about and wouldn't bear to lose, yet here I am, damn near about to.

I promised I would never fall in love again. That I'd never feel the pain of being betrayed again, yet here I am, feeling it all over. When I met Aaron, he showed me what love was again. What it does to you and how it feels.

How fast your heart beats when you see them, and how happy you get when you feel their presence. My love, my baby, Aaron fucking Mayers, is about to watch me go on that plane. He won't see me for another four years, when all of my schooling is complete and I'm ready to rebrand myself in the place I wanted to be when it all began.

Why now?

Why must I reach my goals now? Why not later, when I feel like I'm *more* than ready?

A sniffle escapes from me, and it echoes through the bathroom when I wipe my face.

The sound of suffering then emerges from the bedroom, and when it does, I head toward the doorway, where I now spot Faith, sitting up in the middle of the bed. Her small bonnet sits tilted to the side of her head, and her hand rubs at her eye before she looks up to spot me.

A smile appears on her face when she does, and she climbs out of the bed before wandering toward me. "Morning, Faith," I mumble.

She then hugs my legs, causing a smile to fade onto my face before she lets go.

Looking up at me, her eyes wade into mine as she speaks.

"Can you do my hair?"

I zip up the last suitcase, the last sound slicing through the heavy silence of the apartment. The weight of it all presses down on me as I take one last look at the now-bare room, the walls stripped of the memories we'd hung on them. My heart clenches, knowing this is the last morning we'll spend together like this.

The smell of coffee and something sizzling draws me out of the room, a weak attempt to delay the inevitable. When I step into the kitchen, I find him at the stove, his back turned to me, flipping pancakes like it's any other day. But it's not.

"Morning," he says, his voice thick, glancing over his shoulder. I can see the strain in his movements, the way he forces himself to keep going through the motions.

"Morning," I whisper back, my throat tight.

The clatter of the spatula against the pan echoes louder than usual, filling the void between us.

I lean against the doorway, watching him work, and for a moment, I let myself imagine that I'm not leaving—that this isn't the last time I'll watch him make breakfast, pretending that everything is fine.

But the ache in my chest reminds me of the truth.

"Pancakes?" he asks, turning to face me, a faint, sad smile on his lips. The sight of it nearly breaks me.

"Yeah," I say, though I know I won't be able to eat a bite.

Walking toward the cabinet, I reach inside for a stack of plates, just enough for the three of us. Placing them onto the counter, Aaron then puts two pancakes onto both of ours, and one onto Faith's.

I then grab the syrup, pour it across her pancake, and slice it into a variety of pieces—just the way she likes me to.

Aaron's eyes follow my movements, a quiet dreariness in his gaze. I can *feel* him watching me, but I keep my focus on Faith's plate, determined to give her at least one more piece of normalcy before we face the day.

The silence stretches between us, only punctuated by the sound of our plates hitting the wood table's surface.

Faith then wanders over, her hair now done, before sitting in her chair and beginning to eat.

I sit in my chair and Aaron sits in his, across from me.

"Aren't you glad I taught you the recipe for my pancakes?" I ask, an attempt to lighten up the mood. Aaron then looks up from his plate, and a half-smile appears on his face as he takes a sip from his coffee.

"I know, right? I don't think I'd be able to survive without them," he laughs, but it's tinged with sadness.

"It's all in the wrist," I joke, twirling my fork for emphasis. "But you make them better."

"How?" Aaron asks, and I give him a look.

"You put a lot of care into them, and it's clear whenever I eat them," I smile, and he chuckles a little before taking another bite. Faith grins up at me, her small face bright.

"Can I come visit you at your school, Essence? I want to see you make more churros!" She exclaims, and I smile.

"Of course you can, Faith. I'll make sure I'll add in whatever little twists they get us to, okay? That way, you'll have eaten everything I've made."

She nods, her eyes wide with excitement. But Aaron's expression is more subdued, a shadow of worry lurking behind his smile. We all know today isn't just another day, no matter how hard we try. It's the day I leave, and it's the day we've been dreading the very moment I'd gotten my acceptance.

The conversation fades into comfortable silence as we finish breakfast, each of us lost in our own thoughts. After we clear the plates, Aaron stands up and offers me a hand.

"Ready?" he asks, though we both know the answer is no. Swallowing hard, I nod, and the two of us head back into the bedroom, grabbing my bags and boxes as we get ready to pack up the car.

The drive to the airport is quiet, as the hum of the car's engine is the only sound while the city rolls by outside.

I stare out the window, my mind racing with thoughts of what's coming. The culinary school I've dreamed of for so long, the life I'm returning to back home. But as I glance over at Aaron, his hands grip the steering wheel—causing me to wonder if I'm ready to leave any of this behind.

"So, what are you most excited about?" Aaron asks, breaking the silence.

Turning to him, a smile tugs at my lips.

"The kitchens. They've got the best appliances for cooking, an unbeatable array of spices, everything a chef could ever want. And the classes—they're intense, but I quite cannot wait to dive in. I'm down to try anything and everything there."

He nods, but he still keeps his eyes focused on the road ahead.

"You're gonna be amazing, Ess. I know it."

Faith, who sits in the backseat, pipes up.

"And when you're done with school, you'll come back and cook for us every day, right?"

I chuckle at her question, then turn to look at her. "Uh, duh. Matter a fact, when I get back, I promise you we'll have the biggest feast you can imagine. I'll have new recipes to try out and everything."

She grins, satisfied with my answer, but Aaron's quiet again, his thoughts elsewhere.

Reaching over, I squeeze his hand in an attempt to reassure him, but the knots in my stomach only tighten.

❤ ❤ ❤ ❤ ❤

The airport bustles with energy.

People scatter around, paired with the nonstop sound of people chattering and overhead announcements.

We stand near the gate, with my suitcases and a couple boxes stacked beside me, and the reality of the situation sinks in.

This is happening. I'm leaving.

Faith clings close to my leg, her hands fisted in my jeans, and Aaron stands close by, his expression unreadable.

He looks around, watching as nearby travelers pace around.

Nudging his shoulder, I give him a false smile.

"How you feeling?" He asks, shoving his hands into his pocket. My eyes meet his, and as I try to think of a lie, I shrug.

"I *could* stay, you know," I offer, and letting out a gruff, Aaron shakes his head.

"No. I couldn't deal with myself if you did."

"Why not?" I ask, and for a moment, he goes silent.

"Because I love you, Essence. So much. But that's why you have to go. I have to let you go because I love you. I refuse to hold you back from the dreams you've had so long, hold you back from that you've pushed so hard to accomplish. I'm letting you go because I love you."

His words falter near the end, and as I notice, I pull him close. My face buried in his chest, I cry, and he holds me.

The last boarding call then echoes through the terminal, and I know our time is running out.

"Essence?" Faith calls, and her voice is small, trembling under the weight of what she doesn't want to say.

Lifting my head, I look down at her, wiping my eyes as I do so.

"Yeah?" I say, and crouching down to her level, I brush my thumb across her cheek.

"When will you come back?"

Her eyes widen, brimming with tears that only seem to match my own.

I wish I could tell her the truth.

The truth on how long it even will be before I come back.

But I can't.

It will hurt me too much if I do.

"In no time," I promise, my voice thick with emotion.

"I promise, Faith. I'll be back before you know it."

She nods, but the tears spill over, and pulling her into a tight hug, she buries her face into my shoulder.

"I'll miss you so much," I whisper, my heart breaking at the thought of leaving them behind.

"I'll miss you too, Essie," she sobs, clinging to me with all her strength.

Aaron steps forward now, his hand resting on Faith's shoulder.

He sniffles, then speaks.

"Come on, baby," he whispers. "Let's let Essence get going."

Faith lets go, and I stand to face Aaron. The tears in his eyes match mine, and for a moment, neither of us can speak. The emotions between us are too much, too raw.

"I…" I start, but the words catch in my throat.

I can't say what I want to, even if I sputtered them out.

I can't, because if I did, it would only solidify what's happening. Instead, I just step forward and wrap my arms around him, holding him as tightly as I can. Almost the way I had when I first told him.

He holds me back just as, and when he pulls away, he presses his forehead to mine.

"I love you," he whispers, his voice breaking.

My eyes well even more with tears, my mind realizing what's happening.

"I love you too," I whisper back, my heart aching as the words leave my lips.

We hold on to each other for a moment longer, neither of us wanting to let go.

I wouldn't mind if I missed my flight. I wouldn't mind if I had to stay another day, because I'd have another day with him. But if I stayed another day, I know I wouldn't be able to leave, no matter how hard I try.

The boarding call echoes through the terminal again, and I know I have to go. Stepping back, I give Faith one last hug before grabbing my carry-ons and turning toward the gate.

With one look over my shoulder, I see Aaron and Faith standing there, watching me go, and the tears spill over.

Letting out a heavy breath, I whisper, "I'll be back."

It's more of a promise for *me* than for them.

"I'll be back."

And with that, I walk toward the gate, leaving behind everything I've grown to know, hoping that I can find my way back to my *true* home—Aaron,— someday.

epilogue

. . .

THE HUM of the coffee shop fills the air, a soothing blend of chatter, espresso machines, and the soft clink of mugs being placed on wooden tables. I sit across from my assistant, Remi, with a tablet in her hands as she scrolls through the latest blueprints for the restaurant.

"So, they're thinking mid-July for the opening," she says, her eyes flicking to me for confirmation.

I nod, but I can feel my mind drifting. It's been four years since I've been back in New York, and everything feels both familiar and strange. The city hasn't changed much, but I have.

"That sounds good. Let's stick to that timeline," I reply, my gaze sweeping the room.

People sit at tables all around us, a multitude of both laptops and stacks of paperwork cluttering the surfaces. A couple of people wait in line, all of them standing impatiently as a young girl seems to fumble with her wallet.

Her hair's done in braids, with it about waist length and styled in a top bun.

Grabbing a few coins from her pouch, I watch as she hands them to the barista, who shakes her head before speaking.

The words just barely connect as I try to listen in.

"Not…all…remaining."

Once again, the girl begins messing with her wallet before seeming to give up, and when she does, she turns toward a nearby table.

It's in the corner closest to the front door, and a man sits there, his attention buried in a phone call. Looking up from his watch, he pats his pockets before mouthing something, and I already know what it is. No cash.

"We'll need to schedule a tasting for the menu," Remi's voice chimes, bringing me back to the reality in front of me. Taking a deep breath, I turn back forward for a moment, where I notice her scribbling at the screen.

"And finalize the décor," she adds, and once again, I nod.

I'm not quite sure where my mind is right now, but I know it's anywhere but this conversation.

Looking back at the register, I watch as the girl rambles, the cashier shaking her head with each word said.

The cup sits in her hand, refusing to let go no matter what the girl says.

A jerk move, if you ask me.

Digging in my purse, I stumble with my wallet a bit before pulling out a couple of bills. "What are you doing?" Remi asks, and I shake my head.

"Give me a second," I mumble, and as she finally looks up from the screen, Remi gives me a look of confusion.

"Where are you—" she begins, but her question quickly fades out as I near the front counter.

I begin to tap the girl's shoulder, and she turns around briskly, a nervous expression painted across her face as she greets me.

She can't be older than ten.

"Here you go," I offer, smiling.

Something about her face, it's so…familiar.

She nibbles on her lip for a moment before hesitating, looking up at me one more time as I nod, a silent gesture letting her know that it's alright to grab the money.

As grasps it, her eyes linger on me for a couple seconds before she turns back toward the cashier and hands it to her.

The worker then lets go of the cup, opens the register, and hands the girl her drink. The girl beams, clutching her cup as she whispers a soft, "thank you."

"Have a nice day," the cashier mutters, and I narrow my eyes at her as the girl wanders back to her dad.

As I turn back to my table, a familiar voice pulls me back.

"Essence?"

I freeze.

That voice.

I turn, my heart lurching before my mind even catches up.

Aaron.

He's standing now, eyes wide with recognition. He leaves his phone forgotten on the table as he stares at me, just like the first time we met.

My breath catches in my throat.

It's been years, and yet it feels like no time has passed at all.

Our eyes meet, and neither of us says a word. But we both know what this is.

The beginning... or maybe the end.

For a moment, neither of us says anything. It's like time rewinds to that day, four years ago, when we first met in this same way. The memory comes rushing back—the shy smile, the dollar, the spark that started it all.

"Essence," he says again, his voice softer, as if testing the sound of my name on his lips.

I don't know what to say. My mind races, searching for words, but all I can think of is the way things ended, the promises we never made, the love we confessed—all just too late.

"What are you doing here?" he asks, but the question hangs heavy in the air.

Remi then clears her throat, pulling me back to the present.

I can hear her ruffling with our things, beginning to pack our bags to leave as she begins to speak.

"We should get going soon if we want to make that meeting."

I can't breathe for a moment. The weight of everything Aaron and I were—everything we lost—hangs in the air between us.

I swallow, but the lump in my throat <u>refuses</u> to go down.

I should say something, anything, but the words don't come. Instead, I stand here, staring at him, feeling the pieces of my rebuilt walls tremble.

His eyes search mine, and I can see the questions forming, but there's one thing I know for sure—the past few years haven't dulled what I felt for him. If anything, seeing him now, the weight of those feelings comes rushing back, sharper than ever.

Aaron takes another step, and I feel it again, that slow burn of something we never finished, something still waiting between us.

"Essence…" His voice lingers, like its something he's been holding onto for all this time.

And I wonder—can we pick up where we left off? Or is it too late?

Before I can answer, the door opens behind him, letting in the sharp bite of cold air. And in that moment, I know one thing:

nothing about this is over.

acknowledgments

As a young writer, there are many adults that underestimate me.

The things that I write, things that I say, how I think. Throughout the process of this book, I've been told time and time again that I can't do a few of these things because I started young. For example, marketing.

Marketing takes more than one foot to do. It needs your entire frame of attention, a decent amount of your energy, and a ton of patience. Be willing to put your best into it, or else it will result in quite literally nothing.

To accomplish anything isn't just about pushing your intention; it's about creating a connection. Whether you're writing a book or starting a business, the goal is to reach people on a deeper level.

That's where my passion comes in.

I started young, sure, but I've learnt that this is my *greatest* advantage. I grew up in the digital generation, meaning I've learned how to navigate social media, understand trends, and build a brand from scratch.

However, I couldn't accomplish this by myself.

Every successful person has a team behind them, just like anyone else.

Thank you to my family, friends, and everyone who's believed in my dreams since the beginning. Everything has been a journey, one long one.

My parents are the most empowering people in the world.

Thank you to my mom for giving me ideas, and always knowing how to help me get out of writer's block. The amount of those I encountered throughout the process of writing of this is unbelievable.

Thank you to my dad for always encouraging me, even though I often seem to overlook it. I want to express my gratitude to both of them for continuously motivating and inspiring me.

Thank you to my friends for always offering to help. I've made you guys read one too many drafts until it hit the spot, and I thank you guys so much for it. Even if you had no clue at all what was going on.

Again, I thank every single person who helped me. From my early readers to my editors, know that I appreciate every one of you.

It is impossible to do anything overnight.

It takes effort, just as everything does. And that's how I've been able to succeed, despite being told I couldn't. I made my voice heard, not by being the loudest, but by being real, and that's something that age or experience can't measure.

We're *young*, not stupid.

That's what my journey as an author is to prove.

I may be young, but I'm not stupid.

It may be a harder path, but it's not impossible.

There may be some sacrifices, but I'm more than willing to take them. Because with every step I take, I'm not just proving my potential—I'm rewriting what it means to dream at any age.

about the author

Zoë Harris is a young author residing within the state of Mississippi. She writes Contemporary Romance, Realistic Fiction, and Young Adult.

Follow her on Instagram @zharris_writes.

also by zoe aviya harris

The Bookposal